P9-ECK-673

Chaos Bites

The Phoenix Chronicles – Book Four

Lori Handeland

By payment of required fees, you have been granted the *non*-exclusive, *non*-transferable right to access and read the text of this book. No part of this text may be reproduced, transmitted, downloaded, decompiled, reverse engineered, or stored in or introduced into any information storage and retrieval system, in any form or by any means, whether electronic or mechanical, now known or hereinafter invented without the express written permission of copyright owner.

This is a work of fiction. Names, characters, places, and incidents either are the product of the author's imagination or are used fictitiously, and any resemblance to actual persons, living or dead, business establishments, events or locales is entirely coincidental.

The scanning, reverse engineering, uploading, and/or distributing of this book via the internet or via any other means without the permission of the copyright owner is illegal and punishable by law. Please purchase only authorized electronic or print editions, and do not participate in or encourage piracy of copyrighted materials. Your support of the author's rights is appreciated.

Copyright 2010, 2015 by Lori Handeland.
All rights reserved under International and Pan-American Copyright Conventions.

ISBN: 978-0-9863921-3-9

Print design by A Thirsty Mind Book Design
Cover design by Kim Killian thekilliongroupinc.com

Thank You

Chapter 1

Being the leader of the supernatural forces of good isn't as cool as it sounds. For one thing, I had to put the world first. So everything else was second, third, four hundred and fifty-ninth. And we're talking important things like love, friendship, family. Which is how I ended up killing the man I loved.

Again.

Oh, I didn't kill him twice. I killed two separate men. One didn't stay dead, the other... I'm not so sure.

Yes, I'm in love with two different guys. It was news to me, too. Add to that the beginning of the end of the world and you've got chaos. As anyone who's ever experienced it can tell you—chaos bites.

Since the night my foster mother died in my arms, leaving me in charge of the Apocalypse, chaos had been, for me, standard operating procedure.

Several weeks after I'd killed him, Sawyer invaded my dreams. He was a Navajo skinwalker—both witch and shape-shifter, a sorcerer of incredible power. Unfortunately his power hadn't kept him from dying. Considering that he'd wanted to, I doubted anything could have. I still felt guilty. Tearing out a guy's heart with your bare hand can do that.

The dream was a sex dream. With Sawyer they usually were. He was a catalyst telepath—he brought out the supernatural abilities of others through sex. Something about opening yourself to yourself, the universe, the magical possibilities within—yada-yada, blah, blah, blah.

I'd never understood what Sawyer did or how. Not that it didn't work. One night with him and I'd had more power than I knew what to do with.

In my dream I lay on my bed, in my apartment in Friedenberg, a northern suburb of Milwaukee. Sawyer lay behind me. His palm cupped my hip; he spooned himself around my body. Since we were nearly the same height his breath brushed my neck, his hair—long and black and sleek—cascaded over my skin. I covered his hand with mine and began to turn.

Our legs tangled; his tightened, along with those fingers at my hip. "Don't," he ordered, his voice forever deep and commanding.

He nipped lightly at the curve of my neck, and I gasped—both surprise and arousal. I knew this was a dream, but apparently my body did not.

With hard muscles rippling beneath smooth, hot skin, he felt so real. Living for centuries had given Sawyer plenty of time to work on every muscle group for several decades, honing each inch to a state designed to make women drool. He'd be perfect if not for the tattoos that wound all over him.

To shift, most skinwalkers used a robe adorned with the likeness of their spirit animal. For Sawyer, his skin was his robe, and upon it he'd inscribed the likenesses of many beasts of prey. Sometimes, in the firelight, those tattoos seemed to dance.

"Why are you here?" I asked.

"Why do you think?" He arched, pressing his erection against me.

I couldn't help it—I arched, too. Sure, it had only been a few weeks, but I missed him. I was going to miss him for the rest of my life.

Without Sawyer the forces of good—aka the federation—were in deep shit. Certainly I was powerful, and would no doubt get even more so, but I'd been thrown into this without any training. I was like a magical bull in a very full china shop, thrashing around breaking things, breaking people. So far I'd been able to keep those who followed me from getting completely wiped out, but only because I'd had help.

From Sawyer.

"It's a long trip from hell for a booty call."

His tongue tickled my neck in the same place he'd so recently nipped. "I'm not in hell."

"Where are you?"

He slid his hand from my hip to my breast. "Where does it feel like I am?"

He rubbed a thumb over my nipple, and the sensation made me tingle all over.

"I know you're not here," I said. "You'll never be here again."

Sawyer didn't speak, just kept sliding his thumb over and back, over and back, then he sighed and stopped. I bit my lip to keep myself from begging him to start again.

His lithe, clever fingers brushed across the chain that hung from my neck, then captured the turquoise strung onto it. "Why are you wearing this?"

Sawyer had given me the necklace years ago. I'd taken it off only recently. When he'd died, I'd put the turquoise back on. It was all I had left of him. I hoped.

"I—" I paused, uncertain. I didn't want him to know how badly I missed him. How I rubbed the smooth stone at least a dozen times a day and remembered.

"I'm glad," he said. "It brought me to you."

At first I'd believed the necklace was just jewelry. It had turned out to be magic, marking me as Sawyer's, saving my life on occasion, and allowing him to know where I was whenever he wanted to.

He let the turquoise fall back between my breasts. "What was the last thing I said to you?"

I stiffened so fast I conked the back of my head against his nose. The resultant *thunk* and his hiss sounded pretty real to me, as did the dull throbbing in my skull that followed.

"Phoenix, what was the—"

"Protect that gift of faith."

He ran his palm over my shoulder. "Yes."

"What does that *mean*?"

"You'll see."

I closed my eyes, drew in a deep breath. Right before he'd said those words, Sawyer had said a few others. Words that had kept me up nights almost as much as his death had.

I chose to leave a child behind.

I blocked out the horrible images of what had come after those statements with what had come not long before. He'd crept into the room where I was chained to a bed, a prisoner of my own mother, a woman I'd thought long dead. She'd been a winner. Five minutes in her company and I no longer regretted being an orphan.

The situation had been dire, yet he'd seduced me. I hadn't wondered why until he was gone. My hand moved to my still-flat stomach. Had he left a child behind in me?

I had so many questions. I didn't get to ask any of them.

"You need to wake up now."

"Wait, I—"

"Phoenix," he said, then more softly, "Elizabeth."

Most people called me Liz, but Sawyer never had.

"There's someone here."

In the next instant I scrambled toward consciousness, and as I did the sound of his voice, the weight of his hand, and the warmth of his body faded.

"Someone or *something?*" I asked.

"Both," he answered, and then he was gone.

My eyes snapped open, my hand already reaching for the silver knife beneath my pillow.

The world wasn't what it seemed. Beneath the facades of so many people lurked half demons bent on our destruction. They're known as the Nephilim, the offspring of the fallen angels, or Grigori, and the humans.

They've been here since the beginning, glimpsed more often in times past when wolf men and women of smoke were commonplace and gave rise to the legends we now see on the screen at the multiplex.

Unless you're me, and then they show up in your apartment.

My fingers wrapped around the hilt of the knife even as I stilled, waiting for the slight buzz that signaled *evil creepy thing* to wash over me. But it didn't.

I sat on the edge of the mattress, eyes narrowing, ears straining, then I took a deep breath, and my skin prickled. The bed smelled of Sawyer—snow on the mountain, leaves on the wind, fire and smoke and heat.

"Dream my ass."

Downstairs, outside, came a soft thud then the scrape of something hard against the pavement. A shoe? A toe? A claw?

As I crossed the room, I could have sworn fur brushed my thigh. I glanced down but saw only the flutter of the loose cotton shorts I'd worn to bed along with a worn and faded Milwaukee Brewers T-shirt.

An odd cry drew me to the window, where I kept to the side and out of sight. New moon and the sky was dark, the stars dim this close to the city. The single streetlight in Friedenberg revealed nothing but empty sidewalks and dark storefronts. Which didn't mean anything. Nephilim rarely used the front door. They didn't have to.

Uneasy, I glanced up—only shadows on the rooftops. Of course those shadows might become less shadowy at any moment.

"Psst. Kid." I kicked the cot shoved against the wall in the corner.

My apartment was an efficiency located above a knickknack shop. I owned the building, rented out the first floor, and was considering renting out the second. I rarely came to town these days. The only reason I was here now was that I'd promised my best friend I'd attend her daughter's ninth birthday party. I owed Megan so much, the least I could do was show up when she begged me to.

"Luther!" I nudged the makeshift bed again. I didn't want to touch him if I didn't have to.

I'd been psychometric since birth, I assumed, since I couldn't remember a time that I wasn't able to touch people and see where they'd been, what they'd done. In the case of the Nephilim, I could see what they truly were. Or at least I could until recently. Now I had Luther for that.

"Wha—? Huh?" Luther rubbed at his face. His kinky golden-brown hair stuck out from his smooth brown skin even more than usual.

"Getting any bad-guy vibes?" I gave the boy credit; he woke right up.

"No." His head tilted; his hazel eyes narrowed.

"You sleep pretty deep." From what I heard, most kids did, though Luther would say he was no longer a kid but a man.

He swore he was eighteen, but I had my doubts. Tall and gangly, Luther had huge feet and hands. Many Nephilim had believed Luther's awkward appearance meant he was slow and clumsy. However, Luther moved as quickly and gracefully as the lion he could become.

Luther was a breed—the offspring of a Nephilim and a human. Being part demon gave him supernatural powers. Being less demon than human meant he could choose to fight on the side of good. A lot of breeds did.

"I'd hear Ruthie if she had somethin' to say. Wouldn't matter if I was sleeping or not."

Ruthie Kane, my foster mother, had been the former leader of the light. Now I was. In the beginning, she'd spoken to me on the wind, in dreams, or in visions, to let me know what flavor of evil lay behind a Nephilim's human face. Now she spoke through Luther. I had demon issues.

"There's something out there," I said.

Luther's silver knife appeared in his hand as quickly as mine had. Silver kills most shifters, and if it doesn't, the metal at least slows them down.

"Ruthie talking to you again?" Luther was already making his way toward the door that led to the back stairs.

"No." I paused to retrieve both my gun and Luther's from the nightstand—if a silver knife works well, a silver bullet works even better—then I hurried to catch up.

We tossed our knives on the kitchen table. The kid reached for the door, but I shouldered in front of him. Luther was a rookie. Sure, I'd been on the job less than four months, but I was the leader, which meant I got to go through the door first.

In the past a seer—someone with the psychic ability to recognize a Nephilim in human form—worked with several DKs, or demon killers. However, that arrangement had gone to hell when the Nephilim infiltrated the federation and wiped out three-quarters of the group. Now the remaining members pretty much did whatever they could. Seers became DKs, DKs became seers, and everyone killed anything that got in their way.

"If Ruthie still isn't talking, then how do you know

something's out there?" Luther asked reasonably.

I wasn't going to tell him that I'd had a dream visit from the dead. Not that such news would be a shock. Luther got visits from the dead every damn day. I just didn't want to share right now. Right now I wanted to know what was out there, and then I wanted to kill it.

I crept down the stairs, silent on bare feet. Luther was even quieter. He'd been born part lion. He couldn't help it.

A door led into the parking lot behind the building. I opened it but didn't step out. Instead I listened; Luther sniffed the air, then our eyes met and together we nodded. Deserted as far as we could tell.

"Don't shoot anyone I'll have to dispose of later," I cautioned, a variation on *Don't shoot until you see the whites of their eyes* or, in federation-speak, *Don't kill a human by mistake.*

Most Nephilim disintegrated into ashes when executed correctly, eliminating impossible-to-answer questions and the annoying necessity of bloody body removal. People were another story.

Luther's only answer to my caution was a typical teenage sneer combined with an irritated eye roll. I didn't have to touch him to know his thoughts.

As if.

We stepped outside. No one shot us, not that a bullet would do much damage. Supernatural creatures, even those like Luther and me—more human than not—healed pretty much anything but the one thing common only to them. Which meant the killer had to know what that single thing was.

I indicated with a tilt of my chin that Luther should go around the building to the left, while I moved to the right. We'd meet back here then check out the dark gully at the far end of the lot where the Milwaukee River gurgled merrily.

My gaze shifted in that direction. There could be something hiding there—several somethings. Although the lack of a warning from Ruthie indicated that whatever I'd heard had probably been human.

Not that a human couldn't be a huge pain in the ass. They usually were. And anyone sneaking around in the dark just had to be.

As I slid along the side of the building, back to the wall, I caught movement near the river and spun in that direction, gun outstretched. For an instant I could have sworn something slunk there, low to the ground, a black, four-legged...

I blinked, and the shadow was just a shadow, perhaps a log with four branches, perhaps the reflection of a distant streetlight off the river. There were also foxes in Friedenberg, a few coyotes, and dogs galore. But that had looked like a wolf.

"Sawyer?"

My only answer was the high-pitched keening of the wind.

I lifted my face, waiting for the air to cool my skin. Instead humid heat pressed against me; there wasn't even a hint of a breeze. Not the wind then, but definitely a wail.

Luther.

I sprinted toward the front of the building. Every instinct I had shrieked for me to skid around the corner gun blazing, but charging into the open was a good way to get my head blown off. I didn't think even that would kill me, but it would take a long time to heal. By then Luther could be dead.

There was also the added concern of a possible pregnancy. I didn't *want* to be pregnant, could think of little I wanted less than that, except maybe slow, torturous death by Nephilim, but what was, was. If I carried Sawyer's child, he, she, or it was all that was left of his magic, beyond what he'd given to me. I had to protect his gift. I'd promised.

Fighting the adrenaline, I peeked around the edge of the building. Four AM on a Saturday and Main Street was deserted. Friedenberg boasted its share of taverns—this was Wisconsin, after all—but they'd closed on time, and everyone had skittered home.

Not a sign of Luther.

"Kid?" I didn't want to shout, but pretty soon I would have to.

I hurried along the front of the knickknack shop, so intent on the next corner I nearly missed what rested in the shrouded alcove of the doorway.

I'd already scooted past when what I'd seen registered. I stopped and took several steps in retreat.

On the landing sat a blanket-shrouded basket. Despite the lack of light in the alcove, and the lack of color to the blanket—either black or navy blue— I still detected movement beneath.

The back of my neck prickled, and I had to fight not to slap at an imaginary mosquito. I dared not touch that area unless I meant to. Sawyer wasn't the only one with tattoos, nor the ability to use them.

Had someone brought me a basket of poisonous snakes, tarantulas, or Gila monsters? Maybe something new like a land shark, a water-free jellyfish, a teenie-tiny vampire. Believe me, I'd seen stranger things.

The wail I'd heard before came again—from the basket. I leaned over, caught the end of the coverlet with the barrel of my Glock, and lifted. What I saw inside made my heart beat faster than any vampire ever had. I let the blanket fall into place and nearly tripped over my own feet in my haste to back away.

"Fan-damn-tastic."

Someone had left me a baby.

Chapter 2

The child started to cry in earnest; the sound could no longer be mistaken for the wind. Pretty soon someone was going to come outside and ask why I was creeping around with a gun. They'd also want to know why there was a baby in a basket on my front porch. I kind of wanted to know that myself.

I inched closer, yanked the blanket off with my hand this time. The kid blinked. Long dark lashes framed light eyes, the exact color indeterminate in the night. The round face darkened as the baby drew a deep breath and really let loose.

"Pick her up."

I started so violently, I almost dropped the gun. Luther carefully removed the weapon from my hand.

"Her?" I asked, and he shrugged.

"Looks like a her, doesn't it?"

The child wore only a disposable diaper, but it was pink. I guess that should have been my first clue.

"Pick her up, Liz, before my head explodes."

"Why don't you pick her up?" I tried to retrieve the guns, but Luther held them above his head. Though I was tall at five-ten, I still couldn't reach them. By the time he finished growing, Luther would rival LeBron in size.

"Not a chance," he said.

Leaning over the basket, I slid my hands under the baby. She was warm and wiggly, kind of like a puppy without the fur. Maybe ten pounds, a couple of feet long, I had no clue how old she might be, but she looked young—little, helpless, fragile. She scared the shit out of me.

As I lifted, she continued to cry. I couldn't blame her. I'd been dumped on a doorstep, too. If I'd known what was going to happen to me in the next decade, I'd have screamed my head off. Maybe I had.

"Any note?"

Luther peered into the depths of the basket. "Nope."

"Fabulous." I was having a hard time with the kid, who continued to squirm as if she *wanted* me to drop her.

"Sheesh," Luther said. "Watch her head."

He transferred both guns to a single huge paw before grabbing my hand and showing me how to cup her skull with my fingers while pressing my palm to her neck.

"Put her against your shoulder." He pantomimed the movement then reached over and patted her back. "Sometimes they like that."

The baby hiccuped—once, twice—took a deep breath, and I tensed, waiting for her to blow out my eardrum with the next wail. Instead she wiggled her butt and cuddled closer, then began to suck on my T-shirt.

"How do you know so much about babies?" I asked.

"I *have* held one before. What's your excuse?"

"She's my first."

"You've never held a baby? How'd you manage that?"

"Wasn't easy."

Sure I'd lived in a group home, but Ruthie hadn't taken in many babies. They required too much care, and her specialty was troubled preteens. Most people thought Ruthie preferred adolescents because she was good with them, and she was. But in truth, the supernatural talents of many breeds appeared or strengthened at puberty.

Ruthie ran that group home not so much for the benefit of those she took in as for the benefit of the federation. She was searching for recruits. That countless children were saved from life on the streets or in an unpleasant foster home because of her was a happy accident, nothing more.

"You don't have any friends with kids?"

I had one friend, Megan, and she had three kids. But I'd been so uncomfortable around them as babies that she hadn't allowed me to touch them—afraid, I was sure, that I'd drop them on their heads.

"We should go inside," I said, ignoring Luther's question. "Grab the basket."

After setting the guns at the bottom, he picked up the carrier, revealing a pink blanket on the step. Luther lifted the material, and it tumbled downward. Tiny kittens gamboled across the flannel.

"Maybe this is what she wanted." Gently Luther settled the blanket over the baby.

Light flashed so brightly the entire sky seemed to fill with it. In my arms the child shifted and wriggled. I tightened my grip, afraid she'd slip free.

"Shh," I murmured, hoping to keep her from crying again.

Meow, she said.

I looked down. I now held a fuzzy black kitten.

A police car turned left at the single flashing streetlight and rolled in our direction. With only three thousand people in our tiny suburb on the river, and most of those fairly wealthy two-career families and their kids, the cops had little to do in Friedenberg beyond harass the teenagers and chat with the populace. While a kitten would be a lot easier to explain than a baby, and our guns were safely out of sight in the basket, I still hurried toward the back door.

Though I'd been one once, cops now made me nervous, perhaps because I was breaking the law daily. And I wasn't jaywalking or parking in a red zone. I was committing murder, with a little fraud and sometimes a kidnapping on the side. Explaining that the "people" I'd killed weren't people would only get me locked up in a mental institution instead of the women's state prison.

Sure, I could get out. Wouldn't take much effort at all. If I became an escaped convict, however, I'd have not only the Nephilim after me but local law enforcement, too. Once I crossed state lines, the feds would get involved, and we'd have chaos on multiple fronts.

I needed to have unimpeded freedom to move across the country by any means necessary, including air travel. Which meant having my name and face on a "most wanted" list was not the way to go.

I clattered up the steps, then closed and locked the door. The kitten squirmed, and when I held her more tightly, she scratched me. I put her down. She promptly scooted under the bed.

"I guess we don't have to wonder whose kid that is." Luther seemed a little shook up. His eyes were huge, and he kept glancing at the place the kitten had disappeared as if he expected her to crawl back out—on human hands and knees. She might.

I found his nervousness strange considering he'd seen people turn into all sorts of things. Of course he'd never seen a baby turn into a kitten. Neither had I.

I tossed the blanket and the now empty pink diaper onto the table. "Guess not."

"What do you think her name is?"

As if he were speaking right next to me, I heard again Sawyer's words. *Protect that gift of*—

"Faith. Her name's Faith."

"You sure?"

I sighed. "Yeah."

"Who's her mama?"

"Got me." With Sawyer, could be damn near anyone.

"You think she brought Faith here?"

"Her mother? Why would she?"

Luther's bony, leonine shoulders shifted beneath his skin as he shrugged. "Maybe she's in trouble."

"Join the club." I contemplated the set of eyes shining beneath the bed. In the instant before she'd leaped from my arms I'd seen that those eyes were gray, like Sawyer's. "What am I going to do with a baby?"

"Protect her." I narrowed my gaze on Luther, who held up his hands in surrender. "Aren't you?"

"Of course. But—"

There were half demons all over the place that needed killing. I couldn't cart around a baby while doing that. I supposed I could wrap her in the blanket then put her in a cage.

Or not.

"Get Ruthie," I ordered.

Luther didn't argue. He merely closed his eyes and did whatever it was that he had to do to bring her forth. Seconds later, when Luther opened those eyes, Ruthie stared out.

It was the strangest thing. Luther's gaze was hazel, amber when his lion threatened, but when he channeled Ruthie his irises went deep brown. He moved differently, too—no longer the broad hand movements and rapid footsteps of a teenage boy, but the graceful gestures and measured gait of an old woman.

"I was just gonna come to you, child." Ruthie's voice flowed out of Luther's mouth.

"Why?"

"Found us another skinwalker. His name is Sani."

Sawyer's knowledge of magic had died with him. I might now possess his power, but I had no clue how to use it. Hence Ruthie's search for another of my kind. Sawyer had been able to talk to the dead, and right now... I really needed to.

"Man taught Sawyer everything he knew," she continued.

"The guy's still alive?" Since Sawyer was ancient, Sani had to be Mesozoic.

Ruthie gave me a long look out of Luther's face. A skinwalker only died if he chose to, therefore most of them were probably older than the hills— literally.

"How do I find him?"

"Take a right at the Badlands and don't stop until you hit the Black Hills. Place called Inyan

Kara. Sacred mountain of the Lakota."

"Skinwalkers are Navajo. What is one doing on Lakota land?"

"Sacred mountain is a sacred mountain, and skinwalkers need one of their own. Mount Taylor has belonged to Sawyer since—"

"The dawn of time," I muttered.

"Close enough."

"If this man taught Sawyer, why didn't he snatch Mount Taylor for himself?"

"He did."

"Yet he's in South Dakota."

"Wyoming," she corrected. "Inyan Kara is found in the portion of the Black Hills located in Wyoming. Creates a sacred triangle with Bear Butte and Devil's Tower. Powerful magic."

"*Lakota* magic."

Luther's bony shoulders rippled again. "Sani can draw magic from any mountain."

"I still don't see why he gave up Mount Taylor."

"He didn't give it up," Ruthie said, and something in her voice told me the truth.

"Sawyer took it from him."

Luther's chin dipped toward his chest in acknowledgment.

"Guy's going to be *so* happy to help me raise the man who stole his magic mountain." Indians are understandably touchy on the subject of land grabbing.

"Sani will help you. He'll have to."

"Why?"

"When your journey is complete, you'll know all you need to know."

I really hated it when Ruthie said shit like that.

I didn't bother to quiz her about *what* I'd learn from the journey. Even if she knew, she wouldn't tell me. The journey was part of the...journey.

"What does *Sani* mean?" I asked.

"Old One."

"What did they call him when he was young?"

"Sani was never young."

I opened my mouth then shut it again. I really didn't want to know.

"What's wrong?" Ruthie asked. "I figured you'd grab your bag and be out the door before the location left my mouth."

I'd thought I would be, too. But while I wouldn't pose questions about my journey, I did have questions about something else.

"I have a little problem." I lowered myself to my knees and dragged the hissing, spitting kitten from beneath the mattress.

Ruthie stared at it for a minute then lifted her gaze to mine. "Got no time for a pet."

"This was a baby ten minutes ago."

Luther's bushy brows lifted. "Don't say."

"Do."

Ruthie snorted. "Well. How'd that happen?"

I let the kitten skitter back beneath the bed and reached for the blanket, holding the soft material up so she could see the truth. "Get the picture?"

Luther's eyes widened. "No foolin'?"

"You didn't know?"

"No."

I wasn't sure I believed her. Ruthie existed these days in her own personal heaven. There the sun always shone and it never, ever rained. She watched over children who'd left this earth too soon, usually violently, giving them extra love and attention before sending them on their way into the light.

She also directed our side of the war from beyond. I might carry the title *leader of the light,* but the true leader was Ruthie and always would be.

However, sometimes she kept things from us. She had her reasons, or so she said. She also manipulated us, lied to us, and moved us around like living chess pieces. At times I'd hated her for it. Eventually I'd come to understand she'd do anything to save the world, because so would I.

"You'd have no clue who her mother might be?" That was bothering me more and more. The mother. Who was she? Where was she? Most importantly...

What was she?

"None," Ruthie answered.

I wasn't sure what I was going to do about that. As far as I knew, Sawyer didn't have a little black book.

"We're going to have to work something out for the child," Ruthie said. "You need to go *to* Sani. He no longer leaves Inyan Kara."

"Cursed?"

Until recently Sawyer had been unable to leave Navajo land as a man. His whack-job of an evil spirit bitch mother had cursed him. No sooner had the curse been broken, allowing him to walk on two feet instead of four anywhere that he wanted, than I'd had to kill him. Talk about bad luck.

"Yes." Ruthie shook her head, and Luther's curls bobbed. "No. Well, you'll see."

I *loved* it when I knew exactly what I was getting into.

"What am I going to do with—?" I jabbed my thumb toward the bed.

"Protect her."

Sheesh, I wished someone would sing a new tune.

"How?"

"You need a powerful ally who's been fighting Nephilim for a long time, who's very good at killing. Someone you trust. Someone who would do anything you asked just because *you* asked and would die before he let you down."

"Ah, hell. Not him."

Chapter 3

"Yes," Ruthie said. "Him. Take the child to Jimmy."

Jimmy Sanducci and I had history—a lot of it. We'd loved and lost each other and then—

I wasn't quite sure what to call what had happened lately. I still loved him, but I kind of thought he hated me. I couldn't blame him, but it still hurt. Declaring to the universe that I also loved Sawyer had not helped the situation.

Jimmy and Sawyer did *not* care for each other. Asking Sanducci to watch over Sawyer's child was going to be as much fun as asking your boss for a raise right after you wrecked the company car.

"There's gotta be an easier way."

"In your experience, Lizbeth, is there ever an easier way?"

"No."

"You can't send another to Inyan Kara. *You* have to be the one to go."

As far as I knew, only skinwalkers could raise ghosts. I'd become one the first time I slept with

Sawyer. Besides being psychometric, with latent channeling abilities, I was also a sexual empath—I absorbed supernatural powers through sex. Talk about a mood killer.

While I supposedly had the power to raise ghosts, I hadn't been able to raise Sawyer—another check mark on our "why we need a skinwalker" list. I hoped Sani could reveal what I was doing wrong.

"I'll take Faith with me," I said.

"Not a good idea." Luther's great big hand went up, forestalling my inevitable *why?* "Sawyer stole his mountain, child. You think Sani's gonna forgive that? You think he's gonna let the opportunity for revenge pass him by?"

"I can protect her."

"Maybe you can; maybe you can't. You don't know what kind of magic the Old One has found on top of that Lakota mountain. You wanna take the chance he's strong enough to go through you and get to her?"

"Fine. I'll leave her with Luther."

"He's a child himself."

"Don't tell him that."

Ruthie's lips curved. "I've brought up plenty of kids. Along the way I did learn a thing or two about teenage boys and their egos."

"*You* could watch her. Just stay..." I waved vaguely at Luther's body. "In there."

But Ruthie was already shaking Luther's head. "I got children back home that need me. Can't just leave 'em on their own when they died the way they did."

"Jimmy isn't going to like this," I said.

"He don't like much lately. What's one more thing for his list?"

Ruthie was right. I couldn't leave a baby with a teenager—no matter how responsible Luther was, no matter how vicious he could become—and the only other person left alive with whom I'd trust a shape-shifting infant was Sanducci.

"Where is he?" I asked.

"The Badlands."

I narrowed my eyes. "Convenient."

"Coincidence or fate?" Luther's shoulders lifted then lowered. "You be the judge."

"Why's he there?"

"Nest of Iyas."

"Some type of vamp?"

Jimmy was a dhampir—the son of a vampire and a woman. His father had been an asshole—I mean a strega—translation, "Italian vampire witch." No one knew what his mother had been. Probably lunch.

Dhampirs can sense vampires, and they're very good at ending them. Jimmy was ultra-fast, super-strong, and damn hard to kill. Once again, due to sexual empathy, so was I.

"Lakota storm monster," Ruthie explained. "Possesses a hunger food can't satisfy. Only blood."

Sounded like a vamp to me. "What else?"

"Wherever they walk, winter follows. They wear the heads of their victims as trophies."

"How exactly do these things blend in?"

"They're human when they choose to be. Only in battle do they become Iyas, faceless monsters of the storm."

"How do you kill them?" I asked.

"Sunlight."

For a vampire storm monster, I guess that made sense.

"We'll leave this afternoon." I was going to have to bring Luther along. I couldn't handle Faith by myself.

"Why not now?"

"I promised Megan I'd be here for her daughter's birthday party."

"Tell her you can't make it."

"No."

"Lizbeth—"

"No," I repeated. "I won't stay for the whole party but I *am* going."

I'd broken one promise to Megan. I hadn't taken care of her husband. Instead I'd gotten him killed. I'd sworn not to break another promise to her again if I could help it.

Max Murphy had been my partner. He'd trusted my "instincts." He'd wound up dying because of them, because of me. I hadn't been able to stomach remaining a cop after that so I'd taken a job as a bartender in the tavern owned by the widow. It was the least I could do.

"All right," Ruthie agreed. "How long until you reach Inyan Kara?"

"A day or so. I'll have to drive."

Certainly I could shape-shift, and so could Luther, but I didn't relish carrying a kitten in my mouth all the way to South Dakota. Besides, a lion loping down the road might cause quite a commotion.

We could fly, but I wasn't sure about the rules for taking a baby on an airplane. I had no paperwork, and I'd need some. Then we'd get to the nearest airport, which I bet wasn't exactly close to where we wanted to be, and we'd have to rent a car anyway. Better to take one already loaded with the weapons I liked to keep near.

"Can we use the Impala?"

The voice was Luther's again. His hazel eyes were avid. He loved that car nearly as much as I did. Too bad the powder-blue '57 Chevy wasn't really mine.

"Sure." I grabbed my still-packed duffel off the floor next to my bed.

"Can I drive?"

"No."

"But—"

"No license. No way."

"If I can kill a prehistoric werebat—"

"Camazotz," I corrected. "Mayan shape-shifter."

Last week Luther and I had hopped a flight to

Mexico, and I'd let him take the lead when we went after the bat-headed beast. He'd bagged it with his first shot.

"If I can kill a *camazotz*"—he rolled his eyes—"with a bronze-tipped arrow from a wooden bow, I think I can drive a stick shift."

I knew letting him kill that thing was going to come back and bite me on the ass. Now he thought he could do anything.

"You get to hold the baby."

"It's not a baby," he muttered.

"Kitten. Kid. Whatever."

An hour later we were showered and packed. I'd tried to get Faith to eat something more solid than a bowl of milk but she just turned her nose up at the Chicken of the Sea I scrounged from a cabinet.

"You can't feed tuna to a baby!" Luther objected as he scrubbed the water from his corkscrew hair with a towel.

"You said she wasn't a baby."

"Har-har." He tossed the towel into the bathroom. It hit the floor with a wet *thunk.*

"Seriously?" I asked, and with a put-upon sigh he shuffled into the steamy room and hung the towel on a rack.

"How does she become a baby again? The blanket turns her into a kitten but—" Luther waved at Faith as she chased dust through a spray of sunshine on the floor. "How does she turn back?"

I frowned.

"*We* have to imagine ourselves ourselves," Luther continued. "But she's so little. I don't think she knows how. And it's kind of hard to tell her when her vocabulary consists of *wah* and *meow*."

"Fuck." See why I had no business taking care of a baby shape-shifter? I had no idea what made them work.

"You're going to want to clean up your language or the first word out of her mouth is going to be—"

I lifted my hand. "I get the picture."

I didn't plan on being around Faith that long. I was going to Inyan Kara, learning what I could from Sani, raising Sawyer's ghost, and finding out the answers to a few important questions.

For instance: Who was his next of kin? There was no way I was raising a kitten-kid.

Megan lived on the east side of Milwaukee, about twenty minutes from Friedenberg on a block of older, closely spaced houses broken up by the occasional corner pub. Back in the day, every neighborhood boasted a tavern—at least in Wisconsin. Murphy's had been one of them.

Now it was mostly a cop bar, though a lot of locals often hung out. Besides booze, Megan served sandwiches and heart-attack-producing appetizers such as deep-fried cheese curds. For the health-conscious she provided a wide selection of deep-fried vegetables. If you still weren't dead, the dessert menu offered deep-fried Oreos, Twinkies, and cheesecake.

They were really quite good.

However, for her daughter Anna's party Megan had promised pizza, lemonade, and birthday cake—*not* deep-fried. The celebration started at eleven AM since Megan would have to be at work by three. Saturday night was a big night at Murphy's, and any tavern owner knew that the only way to make sure everything ran smoothly, and no one dipped into the till, was to be there.

Megan opened the door at our knock, took one look at the kitten in my arms, and slammed it in my face. I blinked, glanced at Luther, shrugged, and rang the bell.

"Go away!"

"You ordered me to be here."

The door flew open with such force, the displaced air blew Megan's curly red hair back from her cute little face. And if she ever learned I thought of her as cute, she'd slug me. One thing Megan Murphy didn't appreciate was the depth of her adorableness. She wanted to be tall and voluptuous, dark and exotic—like me.

"Did you get a brain amputation?" Megan's bright blue eyes narrowed in her Irish-pale face. "We have rules here." She held up one finger. "No rodents." Then a second. "No reptiles." A third. "No animals that say *rarhh*."

I glanced down at the kitten in my arms. "Oh."

"Yeah. Take that right back where you got it."

"I—um. Well, you see—uh. I can't."

"You will. You cannot give my daughter a—"

The sudden bright light was followed by an audible whoosh as the kitten in my arms became human. Megan's eyes went as wide as pie plates as she finished her sentence with, "baby."

Said baby waved her arms joyfully and giggled.

"You did that on purpose," I accused.

Megan recovered from her shock quickly, laughing, although it sounded a little strained. Who could blame her?

"That's a baby, Liz, or at least I think it is. They don't do much on purpose. Although it does seem, at times, like they're in league with Satan."

I winced.

"Oh! Sorry."

Megan had known about the Nephilim even before I'd told her. Meg's explanation? She was Irish. They believed in all sorts of spooky shit.

"Is she—?"

"No." Or at least I didn't *think* she was in league with Satan. Yet.

I nearly bungled the baby when she attempted a swan dive toward Luther, who stood at my side. I uttered a curse that earned me a frown from both Luther and Megan then gathered Faith close and tried to hold her down. She continued to reach in Luther's direction. I turned just as he held out her kitty blanket.

"Whoa!" I snatched it away an instant before she touched it. "Oh, no you don't. Bad kitty. I mean, bad girl." I tossed the thing to Luther. "Put that in the car."

He did as I ordered. Faith began to cry.

"Give her the binkie, Liz." Megan put her hands over her ears. "Are you nuts?"

I stepped inside. "Are you? You want her turning from kitty to kid and back again in front of all your friends and relatives? She isn't a party favor."

"What is she?"

Since I'd never told Megan about Sawyer, and didn't want to now, I decided to stick to the basics. "Shape-shifter."

"No kidding. Is she—"

"Is she what?" I repeated absently, still doing my best not to drop a squirming, slippery skinwalker. "Yours?"

"Huh?"

Faith took advantage of my distraction to jerk backward and nearly flipped end-over-end out of my arms.

Megan snatched the baby then turned her so that Faith's back was against Megan's side, the child's butt on Megan's hip, with Megan's forearm across Faith's chest, hand clasping the baby's opposite leg. The kid had nowhere to go. She stopped squirming and gave me a smirky, toothless grin.

"Well?" Megan demanded.

"You think I could pop out an infant in the few

weeks since I saw you last?"

"I think you can do just about anything."

"Slight exaggeration." Megan lifted a brow, and I hissed in exasperation. "I certainly can't cook a bun in my oven at the speed of sound." Or at least I didn't think I could.

I'd been so focused on Faith since she'd dropped onto my porch that I hadn't had much time to do the happy dance over not being pregnant myself. I still didn't have time, so I did a quick one in my head.

"What are you grinning about?" Megan asked. "Whose kid is this if it isn't yours?"

Luther opened the door and stepped inside. Megan's gaze narrowed. "His?"

"Nuh-uh!" Luther held up his big hands in surrender. "No, ma'am."

"Better not be. You're not old enough to shave."

"Am too."

I pointed my index finger at him. "Stop," I ordered. I was not having the *I'm a man* discussion with Luther again. "Meg, this is Luther Vincent. Luther, my best friend Megan Murphy."

Megan nodded. She had her hands full of baby. Luther nodded back.

"There's soda in the kitchen," Megan said. "Snacks on the table." Before she finished the last word, Luther was gone. "Where'd you get him?"

"Indiana."

"Parents?"

"Dead."

"Human?"

"A little."

Megan made a *keep going* gesture with the index finger of her free hand. Faith was gumming the heck out of the other one.

"Luther is a Marbas. His mother was a descendant of the demon Barbas—a lion that could become human. His father was a conjurer with the magical ability to keep her that way."

"What can Luther do?"

"Shift into a lion, fight demons, heal his wounds." I bit my lip then decided to come clean. "He can also channel Ruthie."

"I thought you did that?"

"I did until…"

My voice faded. I didn't want to admit this, either.

"Come on," she said, striding through the house, stopping in the kitchen to snatch two Miller Lites out of a cooler by the door before stepping onto the concrete slab that served as a deck in the backyard.

Luther was occupied with a plate of cheese, summer sausage, and olives. I hoped there was some left when the other guests arrived.

I sat in the lawn chair next to Megan's. "Where are the kids?"

"A friend took them for the morning so I could get things ready for the party."

Megan had another friend besides me? That was new. Her hours at the bar weren't conducive to a social life, not that she'd wanted one. In the years since Max died I could count on one hand the times Megan had hired a sitter to do anything other than work.

"Enough about me," she said. "Why is the prince of the jungle hearing Ruthie and you're not?"

"I've got—" I couldn't finish.

"A cold?" Megan asked. "The flu?"

"A demon."

Chapter 4

Megan, who'd been leaning closer, reared back. Faith gave a *ho* of surprise. I waited for her to start screaming; instead she peered up at Megan then went back to chowing on my friend's hand. Lucky the kid didn't have any teeth yet.

"Let me—"

Megan scrambled to her feet, putting the chair between us.

"—explain," I finished.

"D-don't touch me. I'll... Luther!" she shouted. The kid came to the door, mouth greasy with chips. "Mmm?"

"You know how to kill her?"

His eyes widened and met mine. "Liz?"

"Megan, calm down," I said.

"Oh, you'd like that wouldn't you? Calm down so you can...whatever it is you do to people before you kill them."

"I'm not evil." Or at least I wasn't right this minute. I lifted my hand to the jeweled dog collar around my neck. "Didn't you notice this?"

"Of course. I figured you'd gone Goth."

Considering the collar looked like something you'd find on a poodle, that made no sense at all.

"She went vamp." Luther let the door bang behind him as he came outside.

I shot him a glare. "*Don't* help me."

"You're a vampire?" Megan shouted.

The baby started to mew. She sounded more like a kitten now than when she'd been one.

"Keep it down. You're going to freak out the kitty-cat, and believe me, you don't want to. The lungs on that kid will puncture your eardrums."

"I don't care," Megan snapped, although she did lower her voice. "Just tell me what happened before I cut off your head and stuff your mouth with garlic."

She'd been studying ways to kill a vampire. Good for her.

"It's a lot harder than you think to cut off someone's head." Without the proper tools it was damn near impossible. Right now the only thing nearby was a butter knife.

Megan scowled at Luther. "Why haven't you killed her?"

He popped half a cupcake into his mouth, chewed three times, and swallowed. "Because she isn't evil, as long as she's wearing the collar."

"And if she isn't wearing the collar?"

"Hide," Luther said.

Megan gnawed on her lip, contemplating first me, then Luther, then me again. The baby began to fuss in earnest, and Megan automatically bounced her, which for some unknown reason seemed to work. If I were cranky, bouncing would really piss me off.

"How did you become a vampire?" she asked.

"I told you how I absorb powers."

She wrinkled her nose. "You slept with a vampire?"

"Yes and no."

"That's a yes *or* no question. Pick one."

"It's not that simple."

"Never is with you." She sat in the lawn chair, glanced at Luther. "Go play on the Internet. Computer's in the living room."

"Sweet." Luther headed for the house.

"No porn!" Megan called. "I have munchkins."

"Yeah, yeah." The door banged behind him.

Megan faced me again. "Spill."

"It all started with the woman of smoke."

Megan paled. She'd met the Naye'i, or woman of smoke, a Navajo evil spirit witch and former leader of the darkness. She was also Sawyer's mother, which had explained a lot about Sawyer.

The Naye'i had been jockeying for the position of Antichrist. She would have gotten it, too, if I hadn't killed her. As it was, she opened the gates of hell and all the fallen angels that had become demons flew free. They'd had a field day repopulating the earth with Nephilim before I'd managed to put them back again. Now we were seriously outnumbered.

"I thought you killed that bitch," Megan said.

"I did. But in order to be strong enough, I had to—" I took a breath. "—become as evil as she was."

"Hence the banging of the vampire."

"Yes and no," I repeated. I *had* slept with a vampire, but that wasn't how I'd gained an inner demon. "Jimmy is a dhampir."

"Part vampire, part human," Megan said.

I couldn't remember if I'd told her that or if she'd found it out for herself. It didn't really matter.

"Stronger. Faster. Better."

Sounded like she was advertising *The Six Million Dollar Man.*

"Why couldn't he kill the Naye'i?" She frowned. "For that matter, why couldn't you? Considering what you've told me about you and Jimmy, you've gotta be a dhampir, too, by now."

"I am." Megan knew me so well. "But dhampirs, as powerful as they are, aren't quite powerful enough. They're only *part* demon."

"Ticky-tac," she muttered. "You should have just nuked her."

"Wouldn't have worked. There's usually one way to kill these things and one way only. For the Naye'i, I had to toss evil to the four winds."

"How did you manage that?"

"Tore her into four pieces and sent them express air" —I flung my arms to the sky, releasing my fingers as if I were throwing something away— "to the farthest corners of the world."

Silence settled between us. Finally Megan broke

it. "I wish I could have seen that."

"No, you don't."

I'd been a vampire at the time—mad with fury, lusting for the kill, bathed in the blood.

"If you didn't sleep with a vampire then how did you become one?"

"Dhampirs can become vampires by sharing blood with other vampires."

Jimmy's daddy had made him a chip off the old block just a few months back.

"Ew." Megan wrinkled her nose.

"Yeah." I peered up at the blazingly blue sky, remembering when it had been dark, with a full moon shining down, as I became a monster for the sake of the world.

"Sanducci was okay with this?"

"Not really. He refused to cooperate. So I... seduced him." He still hadn't forgiven me. I wasn't sure he ever would, could, or even should.

Jimmy had begged me not to become like him. He'd said it was damnation—for both of us. But that was a risk I'd been willing to take.

"Liz," Megan said quietly, and I looked up. Her gaze was sympathetic. She'd always been able to hear what I was unable to say.

I'd been forced to choose between Jimmy's "soul" and the lives of millions of people, which wasn't really a choice at all. Jimmy had wound up broken inside. He could barely stand to look at me. I had to live with what I'd done, as well as the knowledge that if given a second chance, I'd do it all over again.

"You still love him," she said. It wasn't a question, so I didn't bother to answer.

I hadn't talked about Jimmy much, but Megan knew the truth. No matter what he did, no matter what I did, no matter how many others we might love, too, I'd feel the same way about Jimmy Sanducci until the day I died as I'd felt about him when I was seventeen. I couldn't help myself.

Jimmy and I had shared similar childhoods, even before I'd come to Ruthie's at twelve, straight from another foster home that didn't want me. I'd also spent time on the streets, preferred it in fact to the parade of homes I'd been through. The streets might be rough, but they were honest.

Jimmy was the boss at Ruthie's, and he didn't much like having to move in with some of the other boys so I could have his bedroom. To welcome me, he'd left a grass snake between the sheets. I'd put the snake in a cage, named him James, then loosened a few of Sanducci's teeth.

What followed was five years of living in the same house, pretending to loathe each other, while what we felt in truth was developing into something much different. Not long after the lust erupted, we fell in love. Jimmy would have done anything for me. It wasn't until years later that I'd found out he had.

"Doesn't matter." I spread my hands. "Every

time he sees me he remembers things he'd rather forget."

"Which explains why you're working with Luther instead of Sanducci these days."

That actually wasn't the reason. Jimmy and I had worked together after the Naye'i. What had separated us had been something else entirely.

"Someone's gotta train the kid," I said, and with Sawyer dead, that someone was me.

"Explain why you haven't bloodsucked your way through Milwaukee and started on Chicago."

Faith's eyes had gotten heavy. She was nearly asleep in Megan's lap.

"I have a control." I tapped the dog collar. "Bespelled. When this is in place, I'm me. The demon is contained."

Megan nodded as if she heard tales of magical necklaces every day. "And the tattoo?"

I really wished my hair was longer. I was going to have to stop hacking at it with any sharp implement I could grab whenever it grew half an inch. At least let it spill past my shoulders and cover up the image of a phoenix inked onto the back of my neck.

"That's a long story," I said.

Megan checked her watch. "We've got fifteen minutes. Talk fast."

"My mother—"

"Whoa! Thought she was dead."

"She rose." Then she'd gone around lifting others

out of the grave, too. They'd been called revenants, and they'd all been eager to do her bidding.

"From your expression, that wasn't a good thing."

"It rarely is." Really, how many times had the raising of the dead been good beyond the *one* time? "To make this long story short, she was evil, had to kill her." Along with her zombie-like friends.

"That seems to happen to you a lot."

"And it's probably going to keep happening. Right now I'm a dhampir, a vampire, and a skinwalker." I tapped my tattoo with one finger. "I can shape-shift."

Understanding flashed in Megan's blue eyes. "Like the baby?"

I nodded.

"But she isn't yours?"

I shook my head.

"Yet you slept with her father."

I spread my hands and didn't answer.

"The tattoo allows you to become a bird," Megan said. "Handy."

"So far."

In the distance, a doorbell rang. Megan stood and handed me a sleeping Faith. "Showtime," she said.

"I have to leave early and head west, talk to Faith's dad."

"Why don't you just call him?"

"He's dead."

Megan rubbed a thumb between her eyes. "That doesn't even surprise me."

Chapter 5

Megan left to answer the front door. Faith curled into me like the kitten she could become. Her soft breath brushed my arm; the dark sweep of her lashes and the sharp slope of her cheek reminded me so much of her father, my heart contracted. No one would ever hurt her while I was around.

Minutes later Anna, Aaron, and Ben spilled into the backyard. Eight, six, and five respectively—or maybe I should say nine, six, and five, as it was Anna's birthday.

"Aunt Liz." Anna gently stroked Faith's knee. "Where'd you get a baby?"

Her voice was soft, her expression rapt. Did all little girls stare at babies as if they were the best dolls on the shelf? Not me, but then I hadn't been much of a little girl.

"What's her name?" Ben shouted. Shouting was Ben's normal volume.

"Shut up, dummy!" That was Aaron, who hadn't spoken any more quietly than Ben. "You'll wake her."

Anna smacked both of them in the back of the head. Right hand. Left hand. Whack. Whack. They turned on her, mutiny in their eyes, and Megan came out the back door.

"Stop," she ordered, then pointed at the football in the grass. "Go."

The boys shuffled off, though they threw glares at their sister over their shoulder. She didn't seem worried.

"What *is* her name?" Anna asked.

"Faith."

"Pretty."

I wasn't sure if she was talking about the name or the baby.

"Where'd you get her?" Anna repeated, as if I might have ordered Faith off the Internet and she wanted to know how.

At least Anna wasn't looking at me as if she thought Faith were mine. Megan's daughter might only be nine, but she knew how the whole baby thing worked and that it took humans a bit longer than a month to have one. What she didn't know was that Aunt Liz wasn't quite human. I planned to keep it that way.

"I'm babysitting for a friend," I said.

She continued to stroke Faith's knee. The baby sighed and smiled in her sleep. I barely stopped myself from saying, *Aw.*

"Why don't you take her upstairs?" Megan came up behind my chair. "Put her down for her nap."

I wasn't sure if the kid should take a nap or not. Wouldn't she then stay awake all night? I would. I also wasn't sure if I should let her out of my sight. Who knew what Faith could do besides shape-shift.

"Come on." Megan took my elbow and drew me into the house. "I've got a playpen left from when the kids were small. She can sleep in there. She won't get out."

I snorted.

"Oh." Megan paused. "I also have a baby monitor. You'll be able to hear her as soon as she wakes up."

"I don't know—"

"She has to sleep. Then she'll need to eat." Megan eyed Faith. "She's probably still on formula. What have you fed her?"

"Tuna." Megan's face took on such an expression of horror, I muttered, "She didn't eat it."

"What on earth possessed you—?"

"She was a kitten!" I glanced furtively over my shoulder at the kids. The boys were playing, but Anna stared at me with curiosity, so I lowered my voice. "What was I supposed to feed her? Mice?"

"Hell if I know." Megan opened the back door and stepped into the kitchen, where she pulled a can out of a cabinet. "Powdered formula. My cousin left this behind when she visited with her new baby. You can take it, along with some bottles." Megan eyed the diaper-clad Faith. "I've also got a bag of diapers, and I'll find some of Anna's old clothes."

"You kept all that crap?"

Megan shrugged, but she wouldn't meet my eyes. In a burst of clarity, I understood that she couldn't bear to part with anything that reminded her of the life she'd shared with Max.

I didn't think that was healthy, but I also wasn't the one to say so. As far as I was concerned, Megan could do whatever she needed to do to survive without him. I did.

Megan yanked the playpen out of a closet in the boys' room, and I placed Faith on the padded bottom, taking the blanket Megan provided. I leaned over to cover the baby, but jerked back at the last second.

"Whoa!" Blue elephants marched right to left across the cotton. I threw the thing far, far away.

"What the heck?"

I grabbed Megan's arm before she could retrieve it. "You can't cover her with anything but plain material." At Megan's continued blank expression, I said, "Kitten blanket, kitten Faith."

"Oh." Megan smacked herself in the forehead with the heel of her hand. "Duh."

"Even a baby elephant would have put a crimp in your playpen."

"And a hole in my ceiling."

I hadn't thought of that. I was going to have to watch this kid and everything around her.

"Maybe you should leave Faith here."

"What? No!"

"You don't think I can take care of her?"

"No. I mean yes. No." I ran my hand through my shaggy dark brown hair. "She's not a regular baby, Meg."

"I want to help. You've got enough on your plate, and face it, Liz, you aren't Mary Poppins."

"You think?" I jerked my head toward the hall. This conversation might get heated, and I did *not* want to wake Faith. Megan and I stepped out of the room and closed the door.

"Luther is good with her," I began.

"What if something attacks you? One of you gonna hold Faith while the other fights?"

"If we have to." I didn't plan on getting attacked. I planned on hauling ass all the way to the Badlands. "Listen, I appreciate the offer, but who knows what she might turn into. Who knows what she can do. Her dad was a skinwalker, but her mom…not a clue."

Megan frowned. "I can handle it."

"I'm sure you can, but you'll have to work."

"Not much more cost for four kids with the sitter than three."

"How you gonna explain a baby that turns into a giraffe?" Megan's frown deepened. "What if she wakes up ravenous and gets her hands on a tiger T-shirt? I couldn't live with myself if your kids were hurt."

Her shoulders slumped. "Neither could I."

"I appreciate the offer, but she's my

responsibility." The doorbell rang again. "Go on. I'll be there in a minute."

Megan left; I stepped into the bedroom, glanced into the playpen—still asleep—then snatched the receiver for the monitor and made sure the base was on. Back in the hall, I sensed I wasn't alone.

Since I couldn't very well wear my knife in a sheath at my waist during a kid's birthday party, I'd strapped it to my calf beneath my jeans. I went down on one knee as if to tie my shoe, my fingers creeping beneath the cuff toward the weapon.

"You're wearin' sandals, love."

The instant I heard the voice, I blew out a relieved breath and stood.

A man stepped free of the shadows at the far end of the hall. "Mistress."

Quinn Fitzpatrick was tall and sleek with shiny black hair and eerie yellow-green eyes. He was also a gargoyle, though you couldn't tell it by looking at him. He was handsome to the point of stunning, warm and solid and alive. Yet not long after bar time he would be curled up in Megan's garden as still as a statue, literally.

When God tossed the Grigori into the pit, he slammed shut the pearly gates. However, while some had broken the rules, others had not. Those angels too good to go to hell, but too corrupt for heaven, became fairies.

Left behind on the earth, they were lost. Suddenly human with no idea how to be, they would never have survived without help. They got it from the beasts. As a reward, those animals that offered aid were given the gifts of flight and shape-shifting. They could sprout wings; they could turn to stone.

Once the fairies could manage on their own, the gargoyles began to protect the weak and unwary from demon attack. The more humans they saved, the more human they became.

With the grace of the black panther he could become, Quinn moved forward.

"I told you to call me Liz," I reminded him.

I was the leader of the light but I didn't much care to be called *mistress* or any other form of similar address. Many of my people were ancient, however, and such titles came naturally to them.

Quinn's gaze had strayed to the stairs Megan had so recently trotted down. I heard the low murmur of her voice as she welcomed her guests.

"She would like a baby in the house again." His voice held the slight cant of the Irish. He'd been on this side of the Atlantic long enough—centuries perhaps—to lose most of his accent.

"Oh, no you don't."

"Don't what?" He continued to stare toward the sound of Megan's voice.

"You're here to protect her, not impregnate her."

A soft growl rumbled from his chest. "I would never hurt her."

"If it hurts," I said, "you aren't doing it right."

"Mistress—" At my glare he began again. "Liz. I know my place. I know my job."

I'd had him sent to watch over Megan after a seer was murdered on my doorstep. Who knew when another Nephilim might show up looking for me. Who knew what they might decide to do if they couldn't find me, but found Megan instead. I wasn't going to take that chance—hence the arrival of Quinn.

That he appeared to have fallen in love with Megan was a bonus. He would die to keep her safe. If I couldn't be here, the next best thing was Quinn Fitzpatrick.

"She still thinks you're nothing more than the slightly lame day-shift bartender?" I asked. In an attempt to seem more human, Quinn dropped things a lot.

His shoulders slumped. "Yes."

Megan hadn't a clue who or what Quinn was, or that he loved her. With three kids and a thriving business, Megan was lucky she could figure out her own name most days.

"Have you caught any more Nephilim slithering around?" I asked.

"Half a dozen since the last time you were here, Mis—Liz." He puffed out his chest. "They are ashes."

The more Nephilim Quinn dusted, the more human he became. As it was, he had to spend a certain number of hours in every twenty-four as a panther— statue or flesh and blood, didn't matter.

But those hours dwindled every time he protected the innocent. Soon he'd be completely human. Or so he said.

"You could leave the child with Megan. Nothing would hurt her while I'm here."

"I'm sure nothing would. And you'd get double points, right?"

"I don't understand."

"Protect a baby, big-time innocent, wouldn't you get more tickets in the soon-to-be-human sweepstakes."

Quinn stiffened. "I wouldn't protect her for my own gain."

"No?"

"No." He seemed truly insulted. "She's an infant. What kind of man would I be if I required payment in order to help her?"

"You aren't a man yet."

"And I wouldn't deserve to be one if I were a man like that."

I liked Quinn more and more every time I saw him. "Thanks for the offer, but I can't leave her behind."

I rattled off the same reasons I'd given Megan, and Quinn nodded. "The child could be of any mother. Even Sawyer's own."

Hadn't thought of that. But wouldn't Sawyer have— What? Drowned Faith in a burlap sack? I didn't think so.

Still, his mother had been the evilest of evil, the

vilest of the vile. Witness that she could have given birth to her own son's child.

At the least, Sawyer would have told me. Unless his mind shied away from the idea as completely as mine had, and really, why wouldn't it?

"He wanted her protected." I didn't think he'd have bothered if Faith were the daughter of psycho hell bitch.

But maybe I was wrong.

Chapter 6

"Dude. Who are you?"

Luther stood at the top of the steps. His eyes shone amber. His hair began to rustle in a nonexistent wind.

"Who are *you?*" Quinn's gaze flared more yellow than green. "Dude."

"Down, boys," I ordered. "We're all friends here."

Luther tilted his head, listening to a voice only he could hear. Understanding washed over his face. "Gargoyle."

"Shh," both Quinn and I hissed at the same time.

"Why?"

"Megan doesn't know," I whispered. "She'd kick my ass if she found out I'd planted a guard in her bar."

The boy's eyes faded to hazel. "Okay."

"New sidekick?" Quinn asked.

"No," Luther answered.

"Yes," I said at the same time.

Then we both glared at each other.

"I'm your seer," Luther insisted. "You're *my* sidekick."

"I'm the leader of the whole federation, kid. I'm no one's sidekick."

"You keep on believing that."

Quinn laughed; I fumed. I didn't take orders well, but lately I didn't have much choice. If Luther said come, I went. If Luther said kill, I killed. If Luther said jump off a cliff, I learned how to free-fall.

"What's going on?" Megan trotted up the steps, her flip-flops smacking against the carpet with muted thuds. When she got to the landing, she frowned at the three of us. "Something wrong?"

"Just making introductions. Quinn and Luther hadn't met."

Megan had heard enough lies in her lifetime—she was a mom and a tavern owner—to spot one from a space shuttle. Though I'd learned to construct falsehoods so much more convincingly since becoming the leader of the light, I still couldn't fool Megan Murphy.

"And then what happened?" she asked.

"They shook hands."

Megan lifted a brow.

"Bumped chests, talked sports, Quinn brought out a *Playboy,* and they admired the centerfold. They were just going to get a beer then practice spitting. They've really bonded."

Megan's eyebrows lowered. Shit. Why couldn't I shut up? Elaboration did not help a lie. Less was more when it came to bullshit.

"We should get downstairs." Quinn stepped forward. "I promised I'd take care of the drinks. People are going to be thirsty in this heat."

Megan opened her mouth to argue. If she kept at me very long, I'd spill everything. I wouldn't be able to help myself. But just as Quinn reached the top of the steps, the toe of his shoe caught in the carpet, and he lurched forward.

Both Luther and I leaped, but Megan was closer and she managed to snatch him back from the edge before he took a swan dive.

"Wow." He leaned on her a little. He appeared to be shaking. "Thanks."

Interesting how different Quinn behaved in Megan's presence. His language became more modern, his diction less formal, and his accent, as well as his grace, nonexistent.

"Sheesh, Fitzpatrick." Megan smacked him between the shoulder blades. "Spit out that gum so you can walk."

"Yeah." He laughed faintly. "Good idea."

Together they started down the steps. Megan seemed to have forgotten all about her suspicions, whatever they might have been.

They reached the foot, and Megan disappeared around the corner toward the kitchen. Quinn glanced back at me and winked.

By any nine-year-old girl's standards, the party was a success. Lots of pink loot. Madness-inducing music that pumped from two speakers shoved into the back windows. Pizza until someone puked. Lemonade to take the pizza taste away, followed by enough pink-frosted cake to give everyone a bellyache.

Faith remained asleep despite the noise. I shoveled in as much food as I could and not burst. Who knew when I'd get the chance to eat again.

Around one, murmurs drifted from the monitor, which I'd kept pressed to one ear most of the time. I caught Luther's eye. He had so much frosting on his upper lip, he looked like part of the "Got Milk" campaign.

Times like these brought home how young Luther really was—not that I knew for sure, but he wasn't a man no matter how much he might want to be. Certainly he was more mature than most boys his age—living in foster care or on your own tended to do that—but he was still an infant in the ways of my world.

It bothered me to send a child out to fight. It bothered me that I'd no doubt have to send a lot more of them out to do the same thing. That kids were usually the ones who bore the brunt of every war did not make me feel any better. More wrongs never made one thing right.

I waggled the monitor then tilted my head toward the house. Luther nodded. I'd told him we would leave as soon as Faith woke.

We slipped away. No one seemed to notice. The children were playing games, led by Quinn who was amazingly good with them, while Megan cleaned up in between serving second and third helpings of cake.

As we hurried upstairs, Faith's soft cries headed toward a wail. The instant she saw us she stopped. Her solemn gray gaze rested on my face. For a moment I could have sworn Sawyer was staring out of them, and I shivered.

"She's soaked," Luther said.

I shook off the remnants of the spooky feeling. "How?" I reached over and touched her arm, her belly.

Faith giggled and kicked. Was she *trying* to be cute? Just the sound of her joy made me happy, too.

"The diaper." Luther handed me a fresh one from the pack on the bed.

I pushed it back in his direction. "Go nuts."

"Not happening." He tossed the thing into the air, and I had the choice of catching it or fishing it off the floor. I caught it.

"I'm not sure how—"

"It isn't rocket science."

It wasn't. Off with old, on with the new. Bigger half to the rear, sticky tabs locked in place. Wham, bam, clean dry baby.

"I didn't think you had it in you." Megan spoke from the doorway.

"It isn't rocket science," I said, and Luther snorted.

"Ha-ha-ha!" Faith's face began to turn red. I

picked her up in a great big hurry. She plucked at the gauzy yellow camisole I'd donned for the special occasion.

"Here." Megan held out a bottle of formula. "She's not going to find anything where she's looking."

Sure enough, the kid was doing her best to yank my breast out of my shirt. Like father like daughter in more ways than one. "How does she know that?"

"You'd be surprised what they know."

"But wouldn't she have had to have nursed at one time?"

"With a human child I'd say yes, with her…" Megan lifted one shoulder then lowered it.

Faith caught sight of the bottle and dived for it. I nearly fumbled her again.

Luther took Faith and the bottle. Curling the baby into his arm and popping the nipple into her mouth, he sat on the Green Bay Packers bedspread that covered the nearest twin bed. Faith seemed so tiny in his big hands.

"Were you going to sneak out without saying goodbye?" Megan asked.

The idea had crossed my mind. Good-byes gave me hives. However—

"You had the formula."

"I'm not stupid."

Megan knew me better than anyone.

"Here." Megan held out a huge denim purse.

"Ug-ly." I waved her off. "Besides, I'm not much

for purses." They tended to get in the way when I was kicking demon ass.

The corner of Megan's mouth lifted. "This is a diaper bag."

"Oh." I took it. "Thanks."

"I put everything I had in there. Formula, bottles, bottle brush, diaper wipes, cloth diapers, bibs, towels, a few washcloths."

I held up my hand. "Does she really need all that?"

"And more." Megan pulled forward a rolling suitcase.

When had she packed all this stuff? For the past two hours she'd been entertaining close to thirty people. The woman never ceased to amaze me.

"What's in there?" I asked. "Tiny tiaras, teenie-weenie high heels, itty-bitty mini skirts?" This kid was shaping up to be a diva of epic proportions.

"Clothes. She can't run around in a diaper."

"She can't *run* around at all."

"You know what I mean."

Actually, I didn't.

"Faith's a baby," I said. "She couldn't care less if she's naked. She'd probably prefer it."

"People don't drag infants around wearing only diapers. Especially little girls."

"Why not?"

"Because little girls are clothes magnets. Everyone buys them every beautiful thing they see. Their closets look like Clothes 'R' Us exploded."

"Just because a kid owns eight thousand shirts doesn't mean she has to wear them."

"No, but she needs to wear something. If she doesn't, you'll stand out. Running around with a kid who obviously has nothing to her name but what can be bought at the nearest grocery store makes it seem like you snatched her."

I hadn't thought of that.

"Fine. Grab whatever and put it on her."

Megan reached into the suitcase then tossed something pink—was *everything* Anna had ever owned pink?—in my direction. "You need to get used to taking care of her."

I examined what appeared to be a fancy T-shirt. Snaps at the bottom, short sleeves, lace around the neck. Not a single animal insignia that I could see.

I threw the garment at Luther, but he was still feeding the baby. The piece of clothing hit him in the face. "What the hell?"

"Language," I said. "Put that on her when she's done eating."

"Nope." He set the bottle on nightstand and laid Faith on the bed. "I'm a guy. She's not."

"She's a baby."

"That doesn't matter to a lot of people." He walked out.

Luther had been the victim of an even more unpleasant experience in foster care than I had. He'd torn one of his foster fathers into pieces and strewn him around the backyard. From what I'd seen of Luther's past when I'd touched him, the guy had gotten off easy.

"The world is sick," Megan murmured.

"You have no idea."

"Let's keep it that way," Megan said. "You'd better burp her before she starts to cry again." At my expression Megan appeared both amused and exasperated. "Pick her up, put her on your shoulder, pat her back until she burps."

Suddenly Megan's eyes widened, and she took two fast steps toward the bed. I spun, but Faith was still in the center; she'd just flipped from her back to her belly then pushed up on her hands so she could watch us.

"She's okay," I said, as much for my own comfort as Megan's.

"Yeah," Megan said slowly. "Except…"

"Except what?" I sat on the bed, checking for pins, staples, something that might explain Megan's concern.

"She shouldn't be able to do that."

"Do what?" As far as I could tell the kid was great at crying and drooling, but not much else.

"Turn over, push up, lift her head like that. She's what? Two? Three months old?"

"I have no clue how old she is." But now that Megan mentioned it, this morning Faith's head had been kind of floppy. I'd had to support it when I held her. She appeared to be gaining abilities at the speed of light.

"Maybe she's just small for her age," Megan said, though she didn't sound convinced.

Neither was I. Faith was a skinwalker. For all I knew she might be a teenager by next week, and wouldn't that be swell?

Or maybe it wouldn't be so bad. Teenagers I could manage, bad attitudes and all. I had a nasty bad attitude of my own.

"Burp her," Megan ordered again. "Make sure you do it every time she eats or you'll be sorry."

Since I was already sorry, I did as I was told and was rewarded with a belch that would make an NFL lineman proud.

Megan packed the bottle and the diapers into the bag. "You're going to call me more often, right?"

"Sure."

"No, you aren't."

"I might." I juggled the baby and the diaper bag. Faith showed her displeasure by spitting white goo onto my neck. "I'm no good at this. I'm gonna need advice."

"First tip, wipe the gack off your neck." She handed me a tissue.

"I could have figured that out for myself." I swiped the spittle into the tissue and handed it back.

Megan put her hand on my arm. "I'll be right here. Anytime you need me. Twenty-four seven."

"I know." I headed for the stairs before she hugged me or something. I was no damn good at PDAs. They made me twitchy.

Luther had put the baby's suitcase in the trunk. He stood on the small strip of grass between the sidewalk and the curb, leaning on the open door of the Impala.

"Where'd you get that car?" Megan asked.

"Confiscated from a traitorous fairy."

Megan wisely said nothing.

While we'd been inside, an infant seat had miraculously appeared as well.

"I never even thought of that."

"Considering she was a kitten when you came here, understandable, but it would be illegal, dangerous, and uncomfortable for Luther to hold her all the way to..." Megan spread her hands waiting for me to answer, but I didn't.

"Well, thanks." I slid awkwardly inside, one leg in the car, one leg out as I did my best to strangle the baby with the various straps and buckles necessary to keep her in the seat.

By the time I was done, Faith was glaring at me exactly as her father would have. Except her father would have impatiently flicked his hand and sent me flying five feet without ever touching me at all. I certainly hoped Faith didn't grow that talent anytime soon.

As I inched out of the car and began to straighten, Faith lunged to the side, straining to reach something that had captured her attention. Figuring it was a flicker of sunlight or a dust mote, maybe even the shiny buckle on the other seat belt,

I nearly kept going. Then I caught a flash of pink flannel.

"Frick!" I exclaimed, and managed to snatch the kitty binkie right before she did.

Faith wailed. I felt like an ogre. Even more so when I straightened out of the backseat, blanket in hand, to discover a middle-aged couple taking a stroll on the sidewalk. Their gazes went from the pink material to my face and they frowned.

"She—uh—puked on it." I rolled the thing into a ball and tossed it at Luther. "Put that in the trunk."

He narrowed his eyes at the order but did as I asked. The couple moved on but not before they gave first me, then Luther, an oddly disgusted look.

Megan watched them then turned back with a grin. "They thought she was yours."

"I get that a lot."

She lowered her voice to just above a whisper. "And his."

"Yuck! He's like fourteen."

"He isn't." Megan sobered. "Remember that."

"And again I say 'yuck.' "

"I didn't mean remember it because I thought you'd touch him."

I made a gagging sound, and she punched me in the arm. "I meant other people will think so, too, and you might get hassled. Not just because of his age but because…well, you know."

I frowned. "I don't. Know. What are you talking about?"

"He's, um—"

"Black." Luther slammed shut the trunk. Nothing wrong with his super-duper hearing. "I'm black. You're not."

"I'm not white, either." I was part Egyptian and part who the hell knew.

"Your eyes," he said. "They're pretty white."

My eyes were blue, and they did appear darn strange in my darker-than-Caucasian face. But so did Luther's.

"We're both something other than white. So's the baby."

"My point exactly," Megan said. "In some areas of the country, you're asking for trouble."

"Still?" I asked.

"Still," Luther answered.

Chapter 7

The drive from Milwaukee to South Dakota was fairly uneventful. We passed by Madison, then La Crosse, drove over the Mississippi River and into the West, stopping for the night in Sioux Falls.

Faith had been extraordinarily good, but she was done, and so was I. Just me and Luther, I'd have continued driving across the inky black unknown roads toward the Badlands. But fiddling with Faith, even if I wasn't the one doing the fiddling, had worn me out. The constant tension in my neck that came from waiting for her to wake up, to whimper, to whine, to cry had developed into a full-blown pain that shot from my shoulders and into my brain.

We found a cheap but clean motel that boasted free Wi-Fi. Sure enough, when I asked for one room, the same dirty look I was beginning to expect passed over the clerk's face as he glanced from me, to Luther, to Faith, and back again.

"Second marriage," I whispered conspiratorially.

You'd have thought I rammed a poker up the clerk's butt. I guess I was lucky he deigned to rent us a room at all.

"I'll get some food while you give her a bath." Luther scooped up the room key.

"What? No. Hey!" The last was shouted as he opened the door to our room. "Why can't I get the food?"

Luther just rolled his eyes. Right. No naked girl babies around the kid.

"Does she really need a bath?" I asked. "It's not like she's been jogging or mud wrestling."

"May have been a while since she's had one. She smells a little funky."

"Fine." I waved my hand. "Go."

He started to, then paused and glanced back. "You know you can't leave her alone in the tub."

"Duh."

"You have to hold on to her every second. You only need an inch of water. Not too hot. But she can still drown in an inch."

"You sure you don't want to—"

He stepped outside and shut the door.

"Guess not."

Faith was having a very important conversation with her toes. I took the reprieve to hunt through the diaper bag for anything that seemed like bath stuff. Finally I gave up, grabbed both the bag and the baby, and went into the bathroom.

Five minutes later I was as ready as I was going to get. I had an inch of water in the tub—not too hot. I'd dumped the diaper bag and found a washcloth and towel, along with some baby shampoo. I'd managed to remove Faith's pink sun suit, as well as her diaper, without making her cry.

I lifted her and set her in the water. Faith's eyes went wide and she caught her breath. If she screamed, this was going to be the world's shortest bath. Instead she gurgled, kicked, splashed, cooed, and—

Grrrr.

Growled?

I peered at the washcloth I was running over her chubby, slippery body. Not a dog in sight. Nothing on the shampoo bottle but an unbelievably cherubic child with a head full of suds. No dancing bear anti-slip stickers on the bottom of the tub.

Maybe she was imitating Luther. Although I couldn't recall him growling in her presence, that didn't mean he hadn't when I wasn't around. Could babies this young imitate sounds? Only one way to find out.

"Can you say *Liz?*" I asked in a chirpy voice that made Faith stop kicking and stare at me wide-eyed. I couldn't blame her.

"*Liz,*" I tried again.

Faith blinked. Maybe *Liz* was too difficult. There had to be a reason children said *Da-Da* or *Ma-Ma* first.

"Luther? Say Luther. Lu-Lu-Lu?"

"Glurg," Faith said.

I felt like an idiot.

Quickly I finished washing then drying her. I slapped on a diaper and found a one-piece deal with feet that snapped from the ankle to the neck. It was soft and yellow and looked like pajamas to me.

Faith began to tug at my shirt again so I grabbed a clean bottle and the can of formula, read the directions, and managed to get her fed before Luther returned.

She was falling asleep on my lap when he came in. "Wake her and die a thousand deaths."

He grinned before setting the bags of takeout— hamburgers and fries from the smell of them—on the dresser. "You did fine."

"Piece of cake."

"I'll put her down." He leaned over to take her but I tightened my hold.

"She's okay. Go ahead and eat."

"You're not hungry?"

"I'll wait."

I couldn't explain it but I didn't want to let the baby go right now. She was warm and soft. She was quiet. Her mouth continued to suckle even though the bottle was nowhere near. When she rubbed her cheek against my breast, the scent of water and trees wafted upward.

My eyes stung. How could she smell just like Sawyer?

I held her for an hour. The steady pace of her breathing lulled me. I hadn't felt such peace since—

I'd *never* felt such peace. My life had been one long, unholy jumble of chaos.

While I held Faith I opened my mind, tried to see anything that I could. But she was a baby. She lived in the now. All I saw in her head was a swirling array of faces—mine, Luther's, Megan's, Anna's, Quinn's—then a bottle and the binkie. Not a hint of *Mommy,* not a trace of *Daddy.* Must be nice to have such simple dreams.

Luther took a shower and crawled into bed. He flicked on the television, kept the sound turned low. Before I fell asleep in the chair, I set Faith in the middle of my mattress, quickly ate a cold hamburger while I researched a few things on the Internet, then yanked off my jeans and climbed in. I lined the far side of the bed with pillows and curled my body around hers.

"Sawyer," I whispered. "Why did you think this was a good idea?"

I awoke to a darkness so complete, I immediately understood the power had gone out. The only thing that glittered was a thin slice of the moon. Every security light in the parking lot was black, the neon of the sign cold and bleak, the glow from the complimentary night-light long gone.

"Liz?" Luther breathed, not even a whisper.

"Shh."

I listened for the whip of the wind, the slash of rain, distant thunder. A storm having gone through would explain the power outage—although I couldn't believe I would have slept through it.

I hadn't. Someone was in the room. I could feel

them. I could almost smell them.

I tilted my head, searching for the telltale buzz that would indicate Nephilim, and got nothing. That should be a good indication of a human; however, the Nephilim had found ways in the past to cloak their nature.

Still, be they human or be they demon, the lack of light and the sneaking around rather than knocking on the door gave me a pretty good clue that they weren't here to help.

For the first time since I'd received it, my knife was not under my pillow. I hadn't been able to bring myself to take a knife to bed with a baby. Go figure.

My gun was on the nightstand, but instead of reaching for it, I snatched the kitten blanket off the floor, then lifted the bedspread, tossed the blanket over Faith, and yanked the spread back down to muffle the flash as she changed. An instant later, someone shone a light into my eyes, nearly blinding me.

Luther snarled and went for his weapon. One of the dark shadows punched him. His nose snapped like uncooked spaghetti.

As I came off the bed, something looped around my neck and wrenched me back down. I fell so hard I bounced several inches off the mattress. My neck burned as if the rope had been dipped in acid. Before I could try to pull it off, my wrists were captured, as were my ankles. Wherever the bindings touched, agony erupted.

These intruders knew more about me than I liked. They'd come prepared with golden chains to bind a dhampir.

Luther's lion rumbled just below the surface. I glanced in his direction, hissing when the movement rubbed the chain where I was already raw. The boy lay so still I would have feared him unconscious if he hadn't been growling. He had to be bound as well.

"Shift," I ordered.

"Can't." The word came out choked, full of pain. Whatever they'd done, it had not only incapacitated Luther but kept him from changing.

I counted four shadows. Big and hulking. Maybe men, maybe not.

"I'm going to kill you for this," I said. Although not right now. Right now I was going to lie here and ache.

Someone laughed. A man. "All we want is the kid, and then we'll leave y'all alone."

Smooth and southern, nearly genteel, the voice was at odds with the size of the shadow and the behavior of its owner.

I took a deep breath, trying to catch a whiff of lion. The shifters who'd killed Luther's parents were still searching for him. He'd killed a few, but I was sure there were more, and I figured these were them. How else would they know the secret that would keep this boy from sprouting claws?

"You should have thought of that before you

broke his nose," I said.

"Not him. Her."

"Her, who?" I asked.

Another shadow backhanded me. My teeth sliced my lip, and I tasted blood. My stomach rumbled. My collar might contain the demon, but it still crouched inside me, and blood called to it like a siren on the deep blue sea.

I wished I knew enough magic to take off my collar without benefit of hands. There wouldn't be anything left of these guys but toenails. Unfortunately, once my demon was loose there wouldn't be much left of Faith or Luther, either.

"We came for the baby."

"Do I look like someone who'd drag a baby around?"

"Then what's that?" He jabbed a gun at the lump on the bed. A third shadow grabbed the comforter and yanked it from the mattress. The lump beneath the kitty-cat blanket wiggled. The sound of a gun being cocked echoed in the sudden heavy silence of the room.

"Are you insane?" I must have surprised whoever was holding my leash because I managed to throw myself over the lump just as the gun went off.

Agony stabbed my shoulder. I had no time to dwell on the pain since the chain around my neck tightened, effectively cutting off my air, scalding my skin, and dragging me off the bed.

I twisted and kicked and wound up slamming

face-first into the carpet. My nose went crunch, too, and blood flowed like rain.

The room went silent. My shoulder stung, but whatever had been in the gun had not been gold, so the pain was bearable. I scrambled to my knees— not easy when bound hand, foot, and neck—and discovered that when they'd dragged me off the mattress, I'd dragged the blanket off the baby. Now everyone could see that she wasn't a baby at all.

The adorable black kitten yawned, blinked into the bright light, then began to wash a paw with her pretty pink tongue.

"It's a...cat. Where's the baby?"

"I don't know who gives you your info, pal, but that" —I lifted my chin toward the kitten, and a few droplets of blood arced through the air— "is the closest thing to a baby I've seen in years."

Luckily I'd repacked the diaper bag, which now sat on the dresser looking like just another ugly purse. Of course, if they checked the garbage they'd find a used diaper. I'd try to BS my way out of that somehow, but I didn't think they'd buy it.

"Why would you believe I had a baby?" I asked. If I kept them talking, they weren't searching the place. "And why do you want one?"

"I do what I'm told, sweetheart. I don't ask questions. That's how I've lived this long."

"How long?"

The man laughed again. I could make out nothing but the shape of his face, his height. The spotlight in my eyes kept me from seeing specifics like hair color or nose size. But I'd remember that voice and that laugh for a very long time.

"Let's go, boys."

"Shouldn't we—" one of the others began, but he cut them off.

"I wasn't paid to do anything but take that baby."

I twitched my shoulder—the one with the bullet still inside. "You weren't paid to take her. You were paid to kill her."

"They told me you were smart," he said, and then he was gone.

As soon as the door shut behind them, I was up and hurrying toward Luther, who lay on the bed, still as death but snarling. Faith stretched, yawned, tucked her nose beneath her tail, and went back to sleep.

"Why didn't you see them coming?" I asked. "Didn't Ruthie warn you?"

My hands and ankles were bound with golden cuffs. I wasn't sure how I'd ever get them off, but first things first. I needed to free Luther.

I had to use both my fingers and my teeth on the ropes—and thank God they were ropes, not chains. Still, they tasted like mud soup seasoned with pepper. The blood from my broken nose dried on my skin and began to flake off, casting onto the white sheets like rust-colored dust. As soon as Luther was loose, he unwound the golden chain from my neck.

"You need to go after them," I said. "I'll" —I lifted my cuffed hands— "call a locksmith."

Luther grabbed his knife and began to pick the locks. I pulled away. "Luther! Go."

He shook his head, curls bobbing. Since he still hadn't answered any of my questions, I asked one again. "What did Ruthie say they were?"

"She didn't."

Panic made my heart race. "What did they do to you?" Something that had made him unable to change into a lion, but what if— "Did they take all your powers?"

"No. Just put the kava-kava on the ropes to keep me from shifting."

"What's kava-kava?"

"Herb from the South Pacific. Mostly used for stress relief. With shifters, it makes the muscles too lax to change."

How did he know this stuff when I didn't? It was infuriating.

"If you've still got all your powers, why don't you know what they were?"

"Oh, I know what they were." *Click.* The handcuffs fell to the floor, and Luther lifted his blazing amber eyes to mine. "They were human. Not Nephilim at all."

Chapter 8

"Human?"

Luther nodded, lips tight as he picked at the lock on my ankle cuffs.

"You're sure?"

"Did you feel any vibe? Because I didn't."

When evil's near there's a buzz. Nothing too flashy, just a vibration, both tactile and auditory, like a thousand bees around your head or a very large lawn mower idling right next to you. But I hadn't felt it and neither had Luther.

My ankle cuffs fell to the carpet with a muted *clank.*

"Not bad." The kid obviously had experience.

I rushed to the door, glanced outside. The power was still out, but the sliver of a moon reflected off the concrete lot, as well as the hoods of all the cars—just enough to reveal that no one was there.

"You're bleeding." Luther stood behind me, looking over my shoulder. His eyes shone dark topaz, and his nostrils flared as he scented the night. He shook his head. He didn't think anyone was there, either.

"So are you." His nose was crooked. I was going to have to fix that. It was going to hurt.

"I've got a flashlight." He turned away from the door, which I shut and locked. However they'd gotten in, it hadn't been by breaking anything.

I was tempted to tell Luther to forget about first aid until morning. With only a flashlight, I doubted he'd be able to dig the bullet out of my shoulder anyway. Then the power went on with a *thunk*. The TV flashed blue flame at the center of the screen before an infomercial detailing the one hundred greatest hard-rock love songs—were there a hundred?— began.

Luther's fist shot out and crunched the OFF button as he went past. I had a feeling that TV was never going to go on again.

I glanced outside once more. The parking lot was now lit like a carnival. On the road, a MUNICIPAL LIGHT AND POWER truck idled.

In the bathroom, Luther and I stood side by side in front of the mirror. Both our noses were crooked and swollen, our faces flecked with blood. If we were human we'd have black eyes tomorrow. Because we weren't, the swelling had already stopped.

To heal even faster, we'd need to shape-shift, and I planned to once we were put back together. By morning no one would ever suspect Luther and I had passed anything other than an uneventful night.

Before I could think about it too much, I jerked

my nose into place. Shards of pain pierced my brain, and I bent over, breathing through my mouth as my eyes streamed. "Damn, that smarts." But when I straightened, my face was back the way it should be.

I'd been told often enough that I was exotically beautiful. Probably because of the contrast between my bright blue eyes and darker-than-Caucasian skin. My cheekbones were high, my nose— usually—a straight blade. I was tall and slim, with a decent-sized rack. Guys liked me even though, more often than not, I had little use for them.

I'd known since I was old enough to know such things that appearances deceive. A pretty outside often covers a very ugly inside. People who took one look at me and decided they wanted to get to know me because of my appearance never got to.

"Here." I reached for Luther's mashed nose.

He lifted his upper lip in a silent snarl and twitched his nose into place himself. The bone made an audible *crack,* and his snarl became decidedly un-silent.

I pulled off my ruined gauze top and turned so I could see my shoulder. The skin was already knitting back together over the hole. "The bullet has to come out."

I wouldn't die from an infection, but I wouldn't feel too great while my body fought one, either.

"I don't think I can do it myself."

I carried a heavy-duty first-aid kit in my duffel. Luther sterilized the scalpel with alcohol then pressed a soaked piece of gauze to the hole. I clenched my teeth until the fiery sting faded.

"Better sit." Luther indicated the toilet seat. "You might want to take off the bra or it'll be ruined."

"Nice try, big boy. The bra stays on."

Luther snorted then hissed in a sharp breath. His nose might look fine, but it obviously wasn't. Not yet.

The kid still hesitated, and I glanced up. "Just do it. Quicker the better, okay?"

He nodded, and then he did it. If I'd thought putting my nose back in place hurt, I'd been mistaken. That had been a bug bite in comparison.

At least the boy was fast. Less than a minute later the bullet pinged into the sink, and he pressed another alcohol-laced gauze pad to my shoulder. I muttered curses until the bright shiny lights at the edge of my vision went away.

Luther grabbed a roll of gauze, but I held up my hand. There was a better way.

My mother's initial death had given me life—only one phoenix at a time, born from the ashes of the last. But a combination of black and white magic had kept my mother in limbo—dead enough to give birth, with the promise of resurrection as Doomsday moved toward Armageddon. Because of that magic, her powers had remained with her, leaving me clueless as to my heritage.

But now I was *the* Phoenix, among other things.

While I should be able to become a firebird without benefit of the tattoo, old habits died hard, and though I was like my mother in many ways, I didn't *want* to be like her at all.

So I placed my palm against the tattoo at the back of my neck, and the change rolled over me like a winter wind, stealing my breath. Lightning flashed, so intense I closed my eyes. My body went cold and then hot. Bones realigned, feet became talons, arms spread into wings, and brightly colored feathers sprang from my skin. They tickled.

When I opened my eyes, I was a phoenix. In this form I could fly. I could command fire, but I would not burn. I was sure I could do a lot more, but I'd only become one a few weeks ago. Right now I didn't care about any of my talents beyond healing, and the shift itself took care of that. So only moments after I'd become a phoenix, I centered an image of myself in my mind and changed back.

I was alone in the bathroom, naked since becoming a bird had allowed the clothes I'd still worn to fall to the floor. I snatched a towel then took a quick glance in the mirror at my bullet wound. If not for the blood, I'd never know it had been there at all.

A flash from the other room had me sticking my head out just in time to see Luther snatch the sheet off his bed and cover himself. I pulled my head back in. "Nose okay?"

"It is now."

I shut the door and took a shower, letting the water sluice over me until it ran clear. When I was done, Luther and I switched places.

Faith-the-kitten was still crashed. I put on my idea of pajamas—shorts and a T-shirt. When Luther came out of the bathroom, he held the bullet in his hand.

"Silver?" I asked.

He nodded. "I can't decide if they knew a lot or a little."

"What does that mean?"

"They knew what we were," Luther said slowly. "So they brought a silver bullet and kava-kava for me, golden chains for you. But they didn't know what Faith could do."

"Which means," I continued, following his train of thought, "that they aren't after her because of Sawyer."

Silence settled between us as we continued to work things out.

"Maybe," Luther murmured, "they're after her because of her mother."

"Whoever that is. But why send humans? That's like sending a guppy after a shark."

"They kicked our ass."

"Your idea of an ass kicking and mine are radically different," I said.

"We're broken, bloody, and shot. They're not."

"We're alive."

"So are they." Luther set the bullet on the

dresser. "They could have killed us if they wanted to."

"Not me."

Luther cast a quick, wary glance into the mirror on the wall. The only people on this earth who knew how to kill a skinwalker were skinwalkers, and they were understandably closemouthed on the subject.

"They knew how to put us down quick and easy without killing us." Luther's forehead creased.

"I wonder who told them."

"I wonder how long it'll take me to find them and kill them."

I frowned, and Luther's hands tightened into fists.

"We can't leave those guys out there. They know too much."

Behind his bravado lay fear. Breeds were hard to kill, but they weren't indestructible. This was the first time Luther'd had that truth shoved in his face. Poor kid.

"We have other things to do first," I said, trying to distract him.

"You don't need me."

I made the sound of a game-show buzzer as I pushed an imaginary button in the air. "Wrong answer. Would you like to try again, Mr. Vincent?"

"Liz, it makes sense for me to follow, beat the name of their contact out of them, and—"

"What?" I interrupted. "Kill four men? That smells like murder to me."

"But they're—"

"People."

"Assholes," he muttered.

"If we killed every asshole in the world we'd have no time left for the Nephilim."

His lips twitched, but he sobered almost instantly. "They're killers. You can't tell me we were their first job. They were too good at it."

"We aren't the police." I held up a hand to forestall any argument. "We aren't vigilantes, either. We were given our powers to kill Nephilim, plain and simple."

Luther hung his head. His hair fell across his face, and his shoulder bones stuck through his T-shirt, making him appear impossibly young. Guilt flickered again. He did not belong here.

"What if they come back?"

He'd really been scared. Tied down with no way to access what made him stronger, he'd been helpless, which had no doubt brought back memories of other times he'd been helpless and those stronger than him had taken horrible advantage.

Many breeds did not come into their magic until later in life, and Luther had been one of them. Because of this, his childhood had been a lot like Jimmy's and mine, two others who'd been late bloomers.

"Hey." I touched Luther's arm, got a quick flash of things I didn't want to see, and drew away.

Besides the fear, Luther had been embarrassed. Taken by surprise, he hadn't protected the baby or me. That embarrassment was fueling him now, making him angry and vengeful. If those guys came back anytime soon, they were toast.

While the thought of their deaths was appealing—they'd planned on shooting a baby, for crying out loud—death was too easy, and I didn't want Luther involved.

"If they come back, I'll deal with it," I said. "They'll wish they hadn't."

He studied my face. "But I—"

"Will stay out of it. I mean that. Humans are not in your job description."

"But they're in yours?"

My gaze rested on Faith. "They are now."

We decided to catch a few more hours of sleep. Being captured, threatened, wounded, then shape-shifting and healing took a lot of energy.

We'd also keep watch. I didn't think the hired killers would come back, but who knew what might.

Luther insisted on taking the first shift since I'd been hurt worse than he, and therefore I'd had to expend more energy to heal. Since he was right, I let him.

I fell into bed, into sleep, into the dream.

I'm on Mount Taylor, one of the four sacred mountains that mark the boundaries of Navajo land. They refer to it as their *sacred mountain of the south* or the *turquoise mountain.* There Sawyer found the stone I wear around my neck. The mountain is magic, and it is his.

He had a secret place on the banks of a clear, cool mountain lake where he went to perform rituals he dared not practice anywhere else. Perhaps that is what has drawn me here—a ritual, a spell, magic.

I stand next to the lake in the night and listen to the mountain rumble. A few million years ago Mount Taylor was an active volcano, and sometimes, when Sawyer walks across its surface, the mountain still shakes. I wait for him to step out of the trees as he has done so many times before, but he doesn't.

"Sawyer?"

The wind cants across my face, bringing the scent of water, evergreens, the earth. Sawyer's scent but the mountain's, too. Is he here or isn't he?

Then I catch a hint of smoke. My eyes search the darkness, but no telltale glow appears. I breathe in. Not a forest fire, not even a campfire, but cigarette smoke.

"I know you're there."

A match is struck; the flare of a flame draws my eyes. For only an instant before the tiny fire goes out I see the shadow.

Of a wolf.

Though Sawyer can turn into many beasts, the wolf is his spirit animal. Perhaps, now that he is a spirit, a wolf is the only form he has.

The scent of cigarette smoke continues to waft my way. I breathe it in like a lifetime smoker on her second year of abstinence.

I assumed Sawyer had been smoking since the Mayans discovered tobacco. He probably showed them where to find it. I'm not surprised that even in death, he's got a cigarette.

A tiny orange glow draws my eyes to the forest. I don't think, I run, but before I get there it's gone. So is Sawyer, if he was ever there at all.

In the distance the low buzz of a motor begins. My chest suddenly feels heavy, as if something is weighing it down, perhaps despair. Every time Sawyer disappears, it reminds me of the day he died. Because right after I killed him he went poof.

He'd been dead and then he'd been gone. No body. No ashes. No Sawyer.

I turn back to the lake. Reflected on the surface are clouds in the shape of a wolf, yet when I look up the clouds are as nonexistent as Sawyer appears to be.

"Where are you?" I shout.

"Everywhere."

The voice comes from right behind me. I spin. Again there is nothing but smoke.

"Am I dreamwalking?"

"The dead don't dream, Phoenix."

"Don't call me that."

He always had, and I never minded. Until I met my mother, heard him call her the same thing, discovered they'd once been lovers and then he'd had to kill her.

His sigh is the wind with just a hint of rain. "What should I call you? Lizzy?"

"You really want to call me Lizzy?" Jimmy was the only one who'd ever called me that.

The mountain rumbles beneath my feet. Guess not.

"If this isn't dreamwalking, what is it?"

"Just a dream… Elizabeth."

The name stirs my hair as if Sawyer himself is touching it. Teachers, librarians, social workers, lawyers, cops—people who don't know me and don't want to—call me Elizabeth. But Sawyer knows me. I think, sometimes, better than anyone. When he murmurs *Elizabeth* I like it.

"So" —I trail my fingertips over my hair where I imagine he has— "you're only in my head?"

"Where else would you like me to be?"

I can feel his heat against my back, as if he's right here with me. I lean into him and the heat, the pressure, intensify. He feels so *there.* But if I turn, if I try to see him, he'll be gone. Instead I close my eyes and wish that he'd hold me.

I haven't realized how alone I've felt with Sawyer gone from this earth. It isn't as if we were lovers in the true sense of the word. I don't think Sawyer can love—at least not anymore—and I only discovered my love for him when his death brought me his magic.

Skinwalkers are both witch and shape-shifter. The shifting comes at birth; the magic comes later—when the skinwalker murders someone he loves. Sawyer obtained his by killing my mother. I, in turn, received more power than I knew what to do with by killing him.

I can bring up a storm, control the lightning, toss people across the room with a flick of one hand, and more. But what that more is... I have no idea. Just because I've taken the magic doesn't mean I know how to use it, or even what powers I have. With Sawyer dead, I needed to talk to another skinwalker for more reasons than one.

His arms come around me, and his lips brush my neck. Sawyer has always told me he can't read minds, just faces, and mine is easy. Does he understand from my expression what I crave? Perhaps he just craves it, too.

My head lolls against his shoulder. If he isn't really here, then this isn't really happening. I don't care. If this is a dream, I'll make it a good one.

I imagine myself naked, and I am. Then I lower my hands and rest them on top of his at my waist. I feel the warmth of his skin, the spike of his bones, the movements of the muscles when I raise his hands and show him what I want him to do with them.

Together we cup my breasts, lift them to the moon like an offering. He needs no encouragement to stroke the nipples, to tease the tips with just a slight hint of nail.

I shiver despite the heat of the night, the heat of him, shuddering when his hair tumbles over my collarbone, cascading across my skin, smooth and fragrant as summer showers. The lake laps against the shore, the soothing sound a startling contrast to the turmoil within.

His erection pulses in the hollow of my spine. When he pumps his hips—once, twice, again— sliding along the crevice of my backside, the pleasure is just short of pain.

I lift my arms, wrap them around his neck. He feels so solid and real, but I know better than to open my eyes. If he disappears right now, I'll want to die myself.

His hair spills over my wrists, the muscles of his shoulders rippling against my knuckles. The position is odd—me with my back to him, arms twisted ballerina-style up and behind his head. But it also presses us together in a lot of great places. I shift my shoulders, rubbing my tingling skin against the sleek, sturdy length of his chest.

The movement also creates friction between his hands and my breasts, his penis and my ass. His mouth at my neck goes from soft to sharp, a caress to a cut, lips to teeth, gentle to rough, and I crave it.

One hand slides across the slope of my breast, down the curve of my waist, a thumb outlining each spike of rib before his fingers trace my belly, swirl around my navel, then dip into the curls beneath.

Unerringly he finds my center, first teasing

with a brush so light I gasp then testing my control by pressing and rolling the swollen flesh between his thumb and the bone beneath.

One long finger probes lower still, imitating the act of completion as I rock my hips forward and back, taking that finger all the way in, then all the way out, as his erection rides me from behind.

I need him inside me so I reach back as I bend over, fumbling, grasping, finding, then guiding him. Draped over his arm, he supports me, even as his finger continues to worry me, keeping the tension at a near-explosive pitch as he plunges within. His movements are slow, almost tender. I nearly sob. I'm so damn close.

"Sawyer," I say, and in my voice lies everything I feel.

At the sound of his name, he swells, stretching, filling, completing me. One final stroke between my legs and I come, too, the pulse of his orgasm fueling, fueling, fueling my own.

Limp with satisfaction, I can barely stay on my feet, but I force myself to straighten. Then I turn my head, eyes still closed.

"Elizabeth," he whispers, and his breath caresses my cheek.

"Yes." I rub my face against his. He never has stubble. His skin is as smooth and silky as his hair.

"You found my gift?"

The distant motor suddenly becomes louder; the weight on my chest shifts; tiny needles of pain shoot through me, and I begin to wake up.

I fight it. I can't go yet. There are things I need to know. Even if this is a dream, my dreams are seldom meaningless.

I take a quick glance at the surface of Sawyer's lake, but the wolf, the clouds, even the moon is gone. However, that single look is all I need to center myself again in this world. But I need to hurry. The other is calling me home.

"I found your gift," I answer. "Someone tried to kill her."

"That's bound to happen."

"Because of her mother?"

He stills. "Why would you think that?"

"They didn't know she could shape-shift. They thought a kitten was just a kitten, which means they didn't come after her because she's like you."

Sawyer takes a deep breath, his chest pressing against my back, so warm and real, I clench my hands to keep from turning and touching him.

"You're right," he says. "They didn't come after her because of who she is. They came after her because of who she will become."

Chapter 9

My eyes snapped open. Another set stared directly into mine. Faith sat on my chest, kneading her paws, pricking me periodically with her kitty claws and purring loud enough to wake, if not the dead, at least me.

The gray light of dawn peeked around the curtains. Luther sat in the chair by the window, staring at the parking lot.

"You never slept."

"I wasn't tired." He continued to peer outside.

"You will be."

"I can sleep in the car."

Since I still wasn't going to let him drive, he could. Use a gun, wield a knife, face a dragon, go nuts, kid. But drive? I had to set some limits.

"You were really tossing and turning." Luther faced me. "Mumbling. Sighing."

I hoped I hadn't been moaning, too.

"Dreams."

"Anything useful?"

I sat up, and Faith tumbled off, emitting a surprised and slightly annoyed *brrr* as she did. Then she gave me a dirty look and stalked away with her tail in the air. The kitten had 'tude. She'd need it.

"According to Sawyer—"

Luther's eyebrows shot up. "Sawyer?"

I shrugged. Dead people giving us advice wasn't anything new. "He said they aren't after Faith because of who she is but because of who she'll become."

"What does that mean?"

"I'm not sure." But there was one way to find out. "I need to raise Sawyer and have a little chat."

Luther's gaze went to Faith as she began to shred the curtains just for fun. "Who do you think she'll become? Someone good, or someone bad?"

I hadn't thought about that. I guess it depended on who her mother was. I wished I knew. But wishing had always done me about as much good as crying—which meant no damn good at all.

"What if she's—?" Luther stopped, pressing his lips together as if to keep a secret from tumbling out. Then he got quickly to his feet, startling the kitten so badly she scrambled backward, hissing.

However, when she recognized Luther, she quieted, and she didn't shred him when he picked her up and sheltered her in his long, gangly arms.

"The Antichrist?" I finished.

Luther's grip tightened. "You're not killing her. I won't let you."

If I could save the world from annihilation by drowning a baby, would I? I wasn't sure, and that I wasn't freaked me out so much I started grasping at any straw I could find.

"Sawyer wanted me to protect her. He wouldn't protect evil."

"Sawyer's… Sawyer," Luther countered. "I don't know what he'd do, and I don't think you do, either. His mother was one of the psycho-est psychos ever. Who knows how badly she fucked him up."

"Language," I murmured, hating to admit that Luther was right. "The Nephilim sent those guys to kill her. Why would they pay for someone to off their future leader?"

"Are you sure the Nephilim sent them?"

I rubbed my forehead. The kid was starting to get on my nerves.

"I refuse to accept that anyone on the side of light would send assassins after a baby." Not that I didn't think they might; I just refused to accept it.

"The only way to know who wants her dead is to find out who she'll become, and the only one who knows that is—"

"Sawyer," I finished. "Which brings me back to the original plan—find Sanducci, dump the baby with him for safekeeping, then head for the hills."

Luther stood. "Let's do it."

Since we'd showered the night before, we were dressed and gone in ten. Would have been five if Luther hadn't thought to take Faith for a walk in the tall grass.

I had no worry that she'd dart off and we'd never see her again. She followed Luther around like an adoring little sister. Did her kitten sense his cub?

Once Faith was finished, we found the nearest McDonald's drive-through, then hit the road. In this form Faith was easier to deal with—no crying, no bottle, no begging for her binkie, no fighting against the car seat.

She turned her nose up at the pancakes but devoured her sausage patties as well as mine, then lapped water out of a cup and settled into Luther's lap to play with the sunbeams that traced across his jeans. When she got bored she trailed into the backseat, and the next time I looked her way she was asleep.

Being a kitten had to be easier than being a baby as well. She could move. She could eat food. She could pretty much do whatever she wanted. I didn't blame her for crying while in human form. It had to suck to find herself in the body of a frail child after she'd experienced the freedom that came from becoming a quick and clever little cat.

Six hours later we pulled off the highway and stared at a whole lot of empty. Called *maco sica* by the Lakota, or "land bad"—very original—the region was the epitome of desolation. Buttes and spires, canyons and gullies stretched in a seemingly unending stream toward the horizon.

"How, exactly, are we going to find Sanducci in the middle of that?" Luther asked.

From what I'd read on the Internet last night, the Badlands consisted of 244,000 square miles of constantly eroding sediment. So massive, so silent, so intimidating they went beyond creepy. Considering what I'd seen in the last several months, that was saying a lot.

The Badlands were also quite pretty. The erosion had revealed every color of the earth and sky. Purple and yellow, tan and gray, red, orange, and white—when the sun hit the land just right, the place called *maco sica* was nothing short of exquisite.

"I'm not sure how to find him," I admitted.

"We just drove for two days," Luther said, "and you're not sure?"

"Any word from Ruthie?"

Closing his eyes, Luther tilted his head. I caught my breath, but when Luther opened his eyes, they remained hazel instead of brown.

"I called, she didn't answer." Luther shrugged. "Sometimes she does that. Usually when she's already told me what I need to know."

I'm only gonna say somethin' once; you'd best listen.

A Ruthie-ism she rarely, if ever, broke. Which meant she'd told me where Jimmy was; I'd just been too preoccupied to hear it.

"Take the cat for a walk and let me think."

Luther and Faith disappeared into the dry grass; I sat on the hood of the Impala and racked my brain.

Jimmy had been sent to the Badlands to deal with a nest of Iyas.

"Badlands. Check."

Iyas were Lakota storm monsters that drank blood, a vampire in any language. When not in faceless, storm monster mode, they blended in.

I glanced at a nearby sign. "Pine Ridge Reservation. Check."

According to my quick Internet jaunt last night, the Pine Ridge Reservation covered more area than Rhode Island and Delaware combined. Though an exact tally of inhabitants was impossible due to the terrain of the land and the nature of the Lakota, estimates placed the population at around forty thousand.

With unemployment hovering near eighty percent and an alcoholism issue that defied sanity, it was easy to understand how the Iyas could blend in. The people of Pine Ridge had enough problems of their own without worrying about vampire storm monsters hiding among them.

In fact, maybe those vampire storm monsters were partially responsible for one of the shortest life expectancies of any group in the western hemisphere. Adult males of Pine Ridge only lived to be around forty-seven, with females lasting into their early fifties. While I was at it, I might as well go ahead and blame a four-times-the-normal rate of adolescent suicide on the Iyas, too.

"What else?"

Iyas brought winter wherever they walked.

My gaze wandered over the hills and valleys,

the spires, gulches, and gullies, drawn inexorably to one flat-topped precipice that appeared capped with white. Behind it cobalt-colored clouds roiled.

"Bingo."

I turned to call for the kid, but he was already barreling out of the tall grass with the kitten in his arms. My hand went immediately to the knife at my waist, and my gaze searched the peacefully swaying foliage for an enemy. None appeared.

"Lizbeth!" Ruthie's voice flowed from Luther's mouth.

"Now she talks."

"Jimmy's in trouble, and you're the only one who can help."

Chapter 10

Luther hopped into the car; I did the same. Faith was wired, and at first bounced off the windows screeching. When Luther tried to grab her she scratched him.

"What if we bought a blanket with a baby on it? Would that make her change back?" Luther asked around the bleeding finger he'd shoved into his mouth.

Ruthie was gone; the kid had returned, which was fine by me. If Jimmy was in trouble, I needed Luther's talent for fighting creatures of the damned, not Ruthie's talent for talking about them.

"Good idea." I spun gravel as I put us back on the road. "I'll get right on that once everything calms down."

"As if."

Right again. For me, for him, nothing ever calmed down.

As we approached the flat-topped mountain, signs proclaimed it SHEEP MOUNTAIN TABLE— summit 3,143 feet above sea level. I wasn't sure how high that was, but it appeared pretty high from where I sat.

Continuing upward, the road became less traveled, more a trail, better for bikes, but the Impala was no more a quitter than I was, and she made the climb, gravel pinging against the undercarriage, weeds tangling in her bumper, dust spraying over the glistening powder-blue paint job.

I was driving faster than I should, but the sense of urgency that had sprung to life with Ruthie's voice only increased the closer I got to the top. I could smell a storm—sweet rain and ozone. Thunder rumbled and lightning crackled overhead. The wind began to whip up dust devils, twirling the red, brown, and gray particles of earth into a thousand mini cyclones.

We came over the rise too fast, and the bottom of the car crunched nauseatingly. But the sight that met my wide-eyed gaze made my stomach lurch even worse.

"Looks like a scene from *The Mummy Returns All Over Again*," Luther said.

I'd have laughed if anything about this— beyond Luther beginning to talk like me—were funny.

Jimmy *was* here, and damn but he needed me. Sure, he had help. Summer Bartholomew—his current seer—and Sanducci fought, back-to-back, in the center of a spotty grass-covered plain atop the mountain. Patches of snow melted here and there, and what trees there were shuddered beneath the weight of far too many icicles.

The Iyas were something to see. The bodies of warriors, honed strong, their skin glistening as snowflakes swirled about them, melting wherever they touched. They wore traditional Lakota leggings made from hides, probably buffalo, and from their waists hung the skulls of those they'd killed. The clack of the bones whenever the Iyas moved was louder and more terrible than thunder.

Even worse were their faces. They had none. Just a swirling miasma of gray, as if the storm overhead gained power from the evil within them.

And they *were* evil. The telltale humming in my head was so loud, I wanted to put my hands over my ears and wail.

Jimmy and Summer used spears against the Iyas. Whenever they pierced one, sunlight seemed to pour from the wound, incinerating the monster-man in seconds. But there were hundreds, and all too soon Jimmy and Summer would be overrun.

Even without discernible eyes within the swirling fog of their faces, the Iyas had no problem seeing. They headed straight for the demon killers in their midst, and when Jimmy and Summer attacked, every Iya countered.

I'd known that upon their release the Grigori had immediately begun to have sex with humans and repopulate the world with their half-demon seed. As a result, the Nephilim had increased—a lot.

But I hadn't really understood what *a lot* meant until I saw the Iyas pouring over the opposite ridge, running across the tabletop mesa toward Jimmy and Summer, trailing snow and ice in their wake. There were so many of them, they nearly blotted out the horizon. The more that appeared, the darker the sky became, and the more furious the coming of the storm.

"Sheesh, talk about a last stand." We were in the right place for one.

Luther leaped out of his seat, popping the trunk on the Impala to reveal an impressive cache of weapons, including spears. I had a feeling they weren't going to be enough.

"Hold on," I called.

Faith was upset, mewing at the glass, pawing at it, trying to get to Luther.

"Sorry, honey, but you can't go." I opened each window a fraction of an inch, then got out and quickly shut the door. Her face slammed against it as she tried to escape, and she sneezed, shook her head, then glared at me.

I ignored her. What else could I do? She couldn't wander around out here. I didn't want to see *her* head swinging from a belt.

Luther tossed me a spear, which I caught with one hand. He took a step toward the melee, and I lowered the weapon in front of him like a gate. "Wait."

"Liz, they're going to die out there."

"Ruthie sent us here for a reason."

"To dump the kid on Sanducci and talk to a skinwalker in the Black Hills."

I shook my head. "It's more than that. I could have taken the baby to New Mexico, or had Jimmy come to me. That would have made more sense, been safer for everyone."

Luther bounced on his toes, so pumped with adrenaline, so ready for the battle he could scarcely contain himself. "Are you going to fight or aren't you?"

"They have to have done something to their weapons." I watched Jimmy and Summer work.

"What?" Luther had one hand around my spear, probably in preparation for wresting it from my grip.

"Either coated them in... I don't know. What mimics sunlight?"

Luther's answer was a blink.

"Or maybe a spell, a blessing on the weapons?"

Luther glanced at the roiling thunderclouds. Not a single ray of sun pressed through them.

"So if I stick them with this—" He tugged on my spear, and this time I let him have it. He seemed to be catching a clue as to our dilemma.

"You'll probably do nothing more than piss them off."

"Let's see," he said, and launched the weapon at the nearest half demon.

I was quick, but not quick enough to grab the spear before it sailed out of reach. The nearest Iya stood a good hundred yards away, but Luther managed to hit him. The boy had skills.

The monster-man roared. The sky above him opened and poured down rain. He turned, and the gray swirl of his face had deepened to black. A slash of lightning cut across the oval. An instant later lightning struck the ground two feet away from us. My toenails sizzled.

"Uh-oh," Luther said.

I cast him an annoyed glance as the Iya yanked the spear free, tossing it aside as if it were nothing more than a toothpick, and ran toward us.

"Luther."

The kid had tensed, prepared for a fight, gaze on the approaching threat. The clack of the skulls at the Iya's waist was so loud I had to raise my voice.

"Luther!"

His eyes flicked to mine. They'd gone amber.

"I need you to do something." I lifted my hands to my collar.

"Liz, you shouldn't—"

"Ruthie sent me because I could help in a way no one else could."

"If that was the way, Sanducci *wouldn't* need you."

Jimmy had a demon, too. His was just a bit harder to release than mine.

"He would," I corrected. "Better if only one of us releases the beast, so the other can..." I took a deep breath. "You know."

Once I became a vampire, I was evil incarnate. Because we'd contained the demon, when we released it... Well, hell hath no fury like a vampire in a box. I'd decimate every Iya, and then I'd start in on whoever was left. The only one who'd be strong enough to contain me again would be another just like me.

"Get out of the way, kid." I fumbled with the catch on my collar, fingers thick and unruly. They did not want to follow the dictates of my brain. Becoming an evil thing always left me with a bad taste in my mouth. Usually blood.

I lifted my gaze and scowled at the heavy, dark clouds, imagining just one single beam of light. "I wish there was sun."

The lead Iya was only a few feet away when a small ray of gold pierced the storm and shone across his face. He went up in flames like a Buddhist monk. The heat forced me back a step, then two. I bumped into Luther.

"What did you *do*?" he whispered.

I wasn't sure. I could command a storm, bring the lightning and the thunder and the rain. I could even create a magic tattoo for shape-shifting by wielding that lightning like a mystical needle complete with supernatural ink—hence the phoenix on my neck.

But get *rid* of a storm? *Bring* the sun? Hadn't seen that coming.

I tilted my face to the sky, imagining a giant split in the charcoal twilight. I envisioned the bright yellow daylight bursting through. I thought about it so hard, I broke a sweat. Reaching upward with both hands, I smacked my palms together then pushed them apart.

And the sun came out exactly as I'd wanted it to.

Chapter 11

Within minutes every last Iya was gone.

Luther appeared as shocked as I was. "Lucky you didn't take off the collar," he said.

"Lucky."

There'd have been a lot of blood before the ashes that way. Been there, done that, didn't like it. Ashes and blood created a paste reminiscent of tar-and-feathering. I much preferred this method. The wind stirred, and the remains of the Iyas simply fluttered away.

"Why didn't Ruthie tell me I could bring the sun?"

"Got me."

"Well—" I waved my hand. "Get her ass out here."

Luther lifted a brow. "You really want to go with that statement?"

"No."

Ruthie had raised us with love and an iron fist, and she saw no reason to change what worked even when the kids became adults. Since Ruthie's fist came in the shape of Luther's hand these days, any disrespect and I might wind up snacking on my teeth.

"Just let me talk to her."

Luther did his thing, and this time Ruthie appeared.

"Lizbeth, you can't be callin' me all the time. I got things to do. Children to manage."

"The world to save."

"Darn right."

"Why didn't you tell me I could bring the sun and exterminate the Iyas?"

Luther's body, usually in constant, teenage motion, stilled. His head tilted. "Say what?"

"I thought I had to go vamp, and I almost did. Then—" I wasn't sure how to explain what I *had* done, or how. "I brought the sun and chased away the storm and they all—"

I made a gesture that indicated fire, explosion, kaboom. She got the picture.

"I nearly took off my collar." I shuddered at the thought of what would have happened then. "You should have just told me to bring the sun."

"I would have been happy to." Luther's eyes narrowed and his mouth tightened. "If I'd known you could."

I'd been rubbing the grit of a hundred Iyas out of my eyes, but at her words I dropped my hand. "Say what?" I repeated.

"I sent you because I knew your vampire could deal with several hundred Iyas, and Jimmy could deal with your vampire. I had no idea that you could bring the sun."

"And why can she?"

Sweat had drawn squiggly lines in the dust on Jimmy's face. Streaks of blood—his? theirs?—marred his hands and forearms. Tiny burn holes randomly dotted a T-shirt that proclaimed TEAM EDWARD. Sanducci was a real comedian.

Jimmy's cover for his globe-trotting-demon-killing was portrait photographer to the stars. He was a genius with a camera. Almost as good as he was with a silver knife. His photos had graced magazines, books, posters, CD cases, once even Times Square. Everyone who was anyone understood that if Sanducci took their photograph, they had arrived, or they very soon would.

However, there was one final test of glory—Sanducci and his T-shirts. He wore them all the time—with jeans or a jacket, for breakfast or bed. But no matter how many were stuffed into his post box every month—and there were a lot—he only wore the shirts of those he had photographed. It became a stamp of stardom if Sanducci himself was photographed in your shirt.

Sanducci gave great photograph. Beneath the mess, he was just short of beautiful. Olive skin, black eyes, hair so dark it appeared blue in certain lights, and a face that had been known to stop traffic in small to midsized towns. For just a few seconds, I enjoyed staring at him. Then Summer Bartholomew appeared, and all my warm, fuzzy feelings evaporated.

"Who'd you bang lately?" she asked.

My fingers curled into my palms. Why was it that every time we met, I wanted to slug her?

Oh, yeah. Hated her guts.

Even after a dusty, bloody battle with storm monsters, she appeared the same as always—blond and petite, with wide blue eyes and perfect pink lips that matched her perfect pink nails. Her usual outfit—skintight jeans, size zero, a fringed halter top, boots, and a white cowboy hat—was in place and there wasn't a speck on it.

"Rodeo fairy."

"You say that like it's a bad thing." Summer put her arm through Jimmy's.

Jimmy jerked away. Summer's face fell. She blinked as if she might cry. I'd feel sorry for her if she hadn't sold her soul to Satan. Literally.

"Any word from your boss?" I asked.

Her gaze narrowed. Behind the pretty blond facade, something slithered.

Summer was a fairy. She could practice glamour, a type of shape-shifting that made her more attractive to humans. However, since her magic didn't work on anyone on an errand of mercy—and that was pretty much my schedule 24/7 these days—I figured she was as annoyingly cute as she appeared. I'd always thought there was more to her than we knew about.

I'd been proven right when we discovered she was moonlighting for the other side. Her excuse: She'd had to save Jimmy. The price? Her soul. Lucky for Summer I'd sent the soul snatcher back to hell before he could collect. She hadn't been all that grateful.

"Kiss my ass," she said sweetly.

Ruthie had ordered Jimmy and Summer to work together so Jimmy could keep an eye on her. I kind of thought that was rewarding Summer for bad behavior. All she'd ever wanted was Sanducci. Too bad he loved me.

"What are you doing here, Lizzy?"

Or he had. Now I wasn't so sure.

"You don't look happy to see me."

Summer snorted. I flicked my hand, and she flew backward a few feet, landing on her perfect little butt with a thud and a grunt. Dust cascaded over her pristine boots. A deep growl rumbled from inside that did not match her outside. She lifted her arms and shot sparkling dust from the tips of her fingers.

The sprinkles hit me in the face, cool and a little sticky. I'd closed my eyes, and when I opened them diamonds seemed to twinkle on my eyelashes. But I remained on my feet, and I felt no compulsion to cluck like a duck. Instead, I stuck out my tongue.

Jimmy sighed. "It's hardly fair to zap Summer when she can't zap you back."

"There's fair" —I let my gaze wander over the fairy as she got up, trying to dust the dirt from her jeans but somehow managing to grind it in farther— "and then there's fun."

Jimmy's lips twitched. So did mine. Sometimes it seemed as if nothing had changed.

Then his mouth tightened, his eyes hardened, and he turned away.

Other times I knew that everything had.

There were so many things about Jimmy I no longer understood, so many years we'd been apart, years when I thought he'd been gallivanting around the world boinking his way through the *Sports Illustrated* Supermodel Club. He probably had been. But in between boink-a-thons he'd been killing demons. A lot of them.

"You weren't aware she had the power of the sun?" Jimmy's voice contained not even the slightest tingle of warmth.

"No," Ruthie said softly. "Could be a power she inherited from her mother."

"A phoenix was a symbol of the sun god in Egypt," Jimmy continued. "So I'd say that was possible. Ever see her mom do what she just did?"

"She's right here," I said.

Everyone ignored me.

"No," Ruthie repeated. "Though that doesn't mean she couldn't."

"Sawyer?"

"No."

"You're sure?"

Ruthie's dark, bland gaze met Jimmy's. Ruthie was always sure.

"What about her father?"

"Not a clue who he is."

"Is that not a clue, *not* a clue?" I put in. "Or not a clue but you secretly *have* a clue?"

"What are you talking about?" Jimmy asked.

"She said she didn't know who my mother was, either, but surprise! She did."

"I still think you slept with something else and absorbed another power," Summer muttered.

"I still think I should ram a steel rod down your throat and bury you with rowan so you never rise." I shrugged. "But we can't always get what we want."

"Girls," Ruthie said. "Enough."

Summer and I shut up, satisfying our craving for physical violence by glaring at each other.

"Why are you here?" Jimmy asked again.

"Ruthie said you needed help."

Jimmy scowled at Luther. "I could have handled this."

"Yeah, you were doing a great job." For that I earned a glare from Sanducci that matched the equally vicious one I was still getting from the fairy.

A bright flash of light drew his gaze past me, and he paled despite the olive tone of his skin. "What the fuck?"

I spun. Lord only knew what could make Sanducci pale like that.

Faith—once again a chubby baby—had her face pressed to the window. Her gray eyes shone luminescent with unshed tears as she pounded against the glass. Her naked chest hitched as she drew in a breath that would no doubt break every eardrum in the vicinity.

Once again she'd developed human skills in far too short a time to *be* human. A few days ago I'd had to support her neck like a just-born infant. Now she stood on her own two feet, albeit leaning against the car door, and pounded the glass hard enough to make it rattle. If this kept up, she'd be sneaking joints and dating inappropriate young men by next Tuesday.

Something shot past me—a flare of motion too fast to distinguish an identity. I figured it was Luther, with Ruthie manning the controls. Instead, Summer materialized next to the car.

She tugged once on the door, then zapped it with make-me dust, which, from what I'd seen of it so far, worked just as well on things as people. Next time she touched the handle, the door swung open, and she swept Faith into her arms.

The baby hugged her as if they were long-lost relatives. I wanted to stalk over there and yank the child away, but I refrained.

Summer rounded on me, lips pulled back from her teeth, face furious. "You can't leave a baby in the car like a dog! You shouldn't even leave a dog in the car if it's over seventy degrees, let alone ninety in the sun like it is now."

"The sun wasn't out until I brought it out," I said. "And she wasn't a baby when I left."

That put a stop to Summer's tirade.

She leaned back, stared into the child's face, then glanced at me, Jimmy, and Ruthie-Luther in turn. "You'd better explain."

Luther took a breath to answer, and I shook my head then crossed to the car. Summer inched out of my way as I passed. Smart move, though I wouldn't have shoved her when she had the baby in her arms.

Faith gurgled and cooed. I glanced at her with a smile—believing for an instant that she was gurgling and cooing at me—but instead she patted Summer's face and babbled to her like they were BFFs.

"I thought fairies *stole* babies." I leaned inside and grabbed Faith's blanket.

"That's goblins."

Backing out, I nearly bumped my head when I straightened too quickly. "Goblins?"

"Little people. Mischievous to the point of evil. Their laugh curdles milk. They hide small objects from humans."

"Like babies?"

Summer lifted one shoulder and went back to playing *goo-goo* with Faith.

"If goblins were stealing babies, wouldn't there be a lot more talk about missing tots?"

"Who says there isn't?" Summer asked.

True.

"Except goblins only take babies when they have one to give." Summer crossed her eyes and scrunched up her face. Faith giggled, the sound pure joy, and I couldn't help but smile before glancing at Jimmy.

He wasn't even looking at me. Instead he stared at Faith as if she'd just sprung from the ozone, which she kind of had.

"No one notices they've got a goblin instead of a baby?" I found this hard to believe. But so many things were.

"Goblins leave changelings behind," Summer said.

"Which are?"

"Ugly goblin babies."

"Still not getting why no one notices this."

"Because an ugly goblin baby is an adorable human one."

Shades of *The Munsters.* The ugly cousin was really quite a swan.

I met Ruthie's eyes. "What are we doing about this?"

"It's rare, Lizbeth. When it happens, we do our best to track down the goblin and take back the baby."

There was so much I didn't know about this world, my job, hell, everything.

"Why are we talking about goblins?" Jimmy demanded.

"I needed to know."

"Not right this second. The last changeling I heard about was a good three years ago. The Nephilim have bigger fish to fry. Like you."

"And you," I countered.

Jimmy shrugged, unconcerned as always with the legion of half demons that wanted us dead. "What was she when you left her?"

I figured show was always better than tell, so I tossed Faith's binkie over her head. The pink flannel muted the bright flash. Summer's eyes widened, and she nearly fumbled the baby as the child's bones shifted, and her soft bronze skin sprouted fuzzy black hair. At least I wasn't the only one with butter fingers.

"Voila!" I yanked the blanket off. The black kitten's tail twitched back and forth as she contemplated each of us in turn with her pale gray gaze.

"Is she yours?" Jimmy asked.

I threw up the hand that wasn't holding the blanket. "Why does everyone ask me that?"

"She's a shape-shifter."

"So are half the people I meet these days."

"You're denying she's yours?"

"Hell, yeah."

"She's quite obviously Sawyer's." Summer smoothed her hand over Faith's dark head, and the kitten began to purr. "Why wouldn't we think she's yours, too?"

I glanced at Jimmy, but his eyes revealed nothing. How could he believe I'd bring a child into this world with anyone but—

I cut that thought off before it showed all over

my face. What Jimmy and I had once had—a love so deep I thought it would never die—had been wounded so often and so badly, I wasn't sure it could survive. The dream of a future for us—especially one that included the white-picket-fence hopes I hid in my heart—was no longer possible.

I pulled my gaze from Jimmy's stoic face. "I have power, but not enough to cook a kid in less than a month."

"So you say," Summer murmured, "but you lie."

"You are so lucky you're holding the baby."

Summer shoved the kitten at Jimmy, but he refused to take her, behaving as if Faith were still an infant, backing away, shaking his head. "Nuh-uh. Not me."

The fairy turned to Luther, who shook his head.

When she glanced again at me, I allowed my lips to curve just a little. "I may lie, but at least I didn't sell my soul to Satan."

"Yet." Summer tilted her pretty, pointed chin. "Just because you aren't capable of loving someone—"

"I can love!"

"Loving someone *enough*," she continued, "to choose a fate *worse* than death. Oh, we know you're perfectly capable of dying for someone. You throw yourself headlong into danger every chance you get." Her tone sneered *overachiever* even louder than her expression. "But try picking the worst thing you can imagine. Try pledging eternity in the flames to save him." She glanced at Jimmy. "Even though you know he might hate you for it."

"That's enough," Jimmy said quietly.

But Summer wasn't finished. "She wouldn't have done it for you."

"I know."

Summer smiled, a thin, nasty smile that did not fit on her sweet, heart-shaped face. "You think she might do it for him?"

Chapter 12

"Do what for who?" I asked.

"What do you think?" Summer didn't even glance at me, just continued to hold Jimmy's gaze. "Sell your soul for Sawyer."

I laughed. "Right."

"You're on your way to the Black Hills to see a skinwalker about raising his ghost."

"How do you know that?" I glanced at Luther, but he shook his head.

Summer tapped an index finger against her temple. She was psychic, too. I took ridiculous satisfaction in observing that her manicure was chipped.

"Someone's gotta do it." I avoided Jimmy's gaze. "And as usual that someone's me."

"Let him rest, Lizzy."

I couldn't help it. I met Jimmy's eyes, and then I couldn't look away. "He isn't resting. He's wandering." I swallowed. "Through my dreams."

"You've got to let him go," Jimmy continued. "He's dead. You of all people should know that."

"Low blow."

"It had to be done."

"Just like raising him has to be."

"You sure about that?"

"He disappeared with the key."

What I referred to was the original text of the *Key of Solomon*. A grimoire, or book of spells, supposedly composed by the biblical King Solomon. Inside were incantations used to summon, release, and command demons—for starters.

My mother, the Phoenix, had had the key in her possession. Then I'd killed her, turned my back—I'd had a few things to clear off my plate at the time—and when I went to retrieve the thing, it was as gone as Sawyer.

"Did you ever consider that someone took both the body and the book?" Jimmy asked.

"They would have had to be awful fast and awful quiet. Awful invisible, too."

Jimmy, Summer, and I had all been within a few hundred feet of the key and Sawyer. We hadn't been paying attention, but we were also a little above average in the hearing, seeing, and sensing departments.

"Maybe they were," Jimmy said.

Conversations like this always gave me a headache. "Whatever."

I flapped my hand, and Jimmy stepped back. So did Summer and Luther. I guess I couldn't blame them. When I used that tone and flipped my fingers, people usually flew.

"If someone or something took Sawyer as well

as the book, his ghost should know who. We need the key. If the Nephilim have it, they'll just let all the Grigori out again."

If they were going to, don't you think they would have?"

"They *did*."

"I mean again. It's been weeks."

"You know as well as I do that the first step to starting Doomsday is killing the leader of the light."

The Nephilim had begun this whole mess by killing Ruthie. But I'd managed to stop the Doomsday clock by ending their leader then sending the demon horde back to hell.

However, they'd be back for round two. No matter how many battles the federation won, the final war was inevitable.

"They're going to have a pretty hard time killing you," Jimmy said.

"Bummer for them, huh?"

Jimmy grinned, and for just an instant I caught a glimpse of the boy I'd adored. I didn't want to lose that memory, not right away. Sometimes the memories of good times were all that kept us from giving in to the bad.

As if he'd read my mind, Jimmy's smile faded. "We need to stop screwing around searching for the key when we have better things to do."

"Like?"

"Kill Nephilim. If we manage to obliterate them all, don't we win?"

"I don't think we can."

"Why not?"

Jimmy was the best DK in the federation, had been since he was eighteen. He'd been Ruthie's right-hand man. He'd be mine now if he could stand to be near me for more than a minute.

"There'd always be one that we missed," I said. "Or a breed would take it into his head that he wanted to rule the world, then run through the sequence that opens Tartarus" —the lowest level of hell reserved for the worst of the worst— "release the Grigori, repopulate the earth with Nephilim, and so on and so forth."

"I think we could take care of a breed before he managed all that."

"What if he had the *Book of Samyaza*?"

"That's a myth."

"So are we."

It was an old argument. One we'd never resolved. The *Book of Samyaza* was a legend. No one had ever seen it, but according to the stories it had been written by a minion of Satan whose ear was filled with revelatory prophecies for the dark side.

The Bible said good would triumph, and I believed that. I had to. Unfortunately, the *Book of Samyaza* said just the opposite. And the Nephilim believed that, too.

I didn't hear Jimmy approach until he spoke right next to me. "You need to let sleeping wolves die."

"Very funny."

"I liked it." He remained silent until I met his eyes. "Sawyer's gone. He isn't coming back. Even if you raised his ghost, then what?"

"I ask him the questions I need answered."

"And then?"

"He goes into the light?"

"Sure he does."

Sawyer had told me himself he was too damned to be innocent, although that had turned out not to be true. Still, I wasn't sure the light was in his future. But I didn't think the darkness should be, either.

"I don't know what happens then," I snapped. "All I know is that I have to talk to him one more time."

"You think he'll forgive you?"

"I don't think he blames me."

"No." Jimmy turned away. "That's all you."

Jimmy and Summer had left Jimmy's black Hummer at the base of Sheep Mountain. I couldn't believe we hadn't seen the thing on our way up. It was visible from outer space.

"We can ride there in the Impala," I offered.

"My Impala?" Summer asked.

"Not anymore. Forfeit your soul, forfeit your very cool car. It's in the manual."

"There's a manual?"

I wasn't actually going to keep the Impala. But I *was* going to use the vehicle for as long as she'd let me get away with it.

"Can I drive?" Luther had returned.

I didn't even bother to answer.

We piled inside. Summer sat in the front seat and held Faith. The kitten's eyes were heavy. She'd had an upsetting day.

The men were in back, spears across their laps. Which reminded me. I glanced in the rearview mirror.

"What did you put on the tips?" At Jimmy's confused frown, I elaborated. "To kill the Iyas."

Understanding dawned. "Vitamin D."

"Huh?"

"Lack of sunlight causes vitamin D deficiency. Increase of vitamin D cures that, so to reproduce the effects of the sun we coated the tips of the spears with vitamin D."

Sometimes the methods of ending these creatures were almost as bizarre as the creatures themselves.

We neared the foot of the mountain and, sure enough, there on a dusty side track sat Jimmy's Hummer. He'd done a decent job camouflaging it with brush. The storm clouds had done the rest. Now the hood of the SUV reflected the sun, drawing the attention of every passerby—if there'd been any—to what appeared to be a behemoth alien land cruiser.

I'd said it before, so I said it again. "Whoever thought selling US Army tactical vehicles to the public was a good idea?"

Jimmy lifted his hand. He loved that thing. As we climbed out of the Impala I realized that I'd neglected to mention the reason we'd come to the Badlands in the first place.

"I need a favor."

"I'm not coming with you to the Black Hills to raise Sawyer." Jimmy opened the rear door on the Hummer and tossed the spears inside.

"I didn't ask you to."

That surprised him. He'd been headed toward the driver's seat, but now stopped and turned. "Then what do you want?"

"For you to watch the baby while I search the Black Hills for Sani, the skinwalker."

"Watch the baby," he repeated. "Where's her mom?"

"That's almost as good a question as *Who's her mom?*"

"You don't know?"

"Why would I?"

"You didn't ask?"

"A kitten?"

Jimmy made a sound of annoyance. "Sawyer."

"Dead, remember?"

"You said he was in your dreams."

"He is, but it's strange. You know how dreamwalking feels?"

Jimmy nodded.

"It's not like that."

"Because the dead don't dream."

"Is that on a T-shirt or something?" I asked.

Jimmy just lifted a brow and waited for me to go on.

"I can't control the dream. I can't get Sawyer to answer questions. He tells me things, but not everything. And I don't know if it's really him in there" —I rapped my knuckles lightly against my temple— "or if it's just me wishing he were."

"What about Ruthie? Doesn't she have any info about the kid?"

"She was as surprised to see Faith as I was. Claims she knows nothing about her."

"You believe that?"

"I'm not sure."

Ruthie had lied to us both when it suited her—always for the good of the world. That didn't make her lies any easier to stomach, and it didn't make her any easier to trust now that we knew about them. But it was also difficult *not* to trust her since we had for most of our lives, and in the end we all wanted the same thing. To save the world.

"I guess you have more than a few questions for Sawyer."

"More than a few," I agreed.

"Why drag the kid all the way here?" Jimmy asked.

"Ruthie—"

"Said," Jimmy finished. "But why? What's wrong with Luther?"

I glanced over my shoulder. Luther and Summer were playing with Faith. They'd each grabbed a pussywillow, and the kitten was trying to catch one, but she couldn't decide which one to grab. She glanced back and forth, back and forth. Then she'd snatch at a fuzzy toy, only to have it rise higher than she could jump. She'd lose interest and focus on the other one, only to repeat the same process. The scene could make Norman Rockwell sit up in his grave just to paint it.

"What happened?" Jimmy always knew when something had.

Quickly I told him about the men in the motel room—what they'd known, what they hadn't, and what Sawyer—be he dream or vision—had said.

"They're after her because of who she will become," Jimmy repeated.

I spread my hands. "I promised to protect her."

"Then do it."

"I am!"

Summer, Luther, and Faith turned their heads toward us as my voice carried. Summer began to get up. Luther murmured something and pulled her back down. That she let him was quite a surprise. I wasn't sure what there was between the boy and the fairy, but they had connected the first time they'd met. Kind of like the baby and the fairy. Was Summer using magic?

I lowered my voice. "I have to find that skinwalker. Ruthie said Faith would be safe with you. You think I'd ask this of you if I had any other choice?"

His dark eyes stared into mine. He was so

beautiful. My gaze lowered to his mouth. He could do amazing things with that mouth. Once Sanducci and I had spent hours just kissing. I missed that.

Our breath became shallow. His gaze lowered as well. He took a step forward, and I stopped breathing altogether.

He caught himself before we could touch, backed up, and lifted his face to the sun. "I wish things could be the way they were. I want to forget, but I can't. Every time I look at you I see what hides beneath that collar."

My demon. He hated it. And since that demon resided in me...well, you do the math.

"I don't know what you want from me. You're pissed because I love Sawyer, but you don't want me to love you, either."

"I didn't say that." His lips twisted. "I want you to love me; I just don't know if I can love you back."

"Bite me."

He turned away, but not before I saw his haunted expression. "Already did."

There wasn't much I could say to that. He'd bitten me; I'd bitten him. We'd both become vampires, and there was no going back.

"Hold on." I grabbed his arm, got a jolt as soon as I did.

Images washed over me—of us as kids, teens, young adults, in bed, out of bed, under the bed. I caught a hint of our dreams—the home, the family—those things we'd never had and now, never would.

Those thoughts were replaced by the memory of me as a vampire—lying to Jimmy, seducing him, and worse. I yanked my hand free and rubbed it on my jeans.

He was right. I didn't know if we could ever get past that. Our love was all tangled up with the guilt, the lust with the blood, the hope with the hatred, the dreams with the fear.

I stuck my hands in my pockets so I wouldn't be tempted to touch him again. "Will you keep Faith safe?"

"Sounds like the title of a Sunday sermon."

"Jimmy." He was avoiding an answer as well as my gaze.

"I'm no good with kids, Lizzy."

"She's not a kid."

"I'm no good with baby shape-shifters, either."

"I've asked you for worse things than watching over a kitten-kid."

"And I gave you every one."

Something in his voice made me swallow against a sudden thickness in my throat. When I had myself under control, I asked, "What's one more?"

Chapter 13

"Hasn't he done enough?"

Summer had left Luther and Faith behind and fluttered over to horn in on our conversation.

"Yes," I said.

She'd opened her mouth to argue, but when I agreed, she shut it again. Summer had no more idea how to handle me when I was being pleasant than I'd know how to handle her if she were.

"But I still need his help and I have to leave, preferably today."

"He wants to keep you from leaving" —she shot Jimmy a disgusted glare— "by giving you a hard time about babysitting. Try to keep up."

Well, duh. That made sense.

"Have a nice trip," Summer said. "Try not to die."

"I never knew you cared."

"I don't. Problem is, you die and we've got Doomsday—new leader of the darkness, death, destruction, crack in hell's doorway, and so on. I'm bored."

"It does get old. I'll try not to get killed and ruin

your life. Getting back to the baby…"

"I'll watch her."

Actually, that worked. Summer might look like a petite, blond rodeo groupie, but she was dangerous. She also had a virtual fortress in New Mexico.

"You'll bring her to your cottage?" I asked.

"Of course."

"And Luther?"

"Wouldn't leave without him."

"What about—?"

We both turned to Jimmy. He stared back at us with no expression.

"I could knock him over the head and take him, too."

Yeah, that oughta work.

"Got any gold chains?" I asked.

"Not on me."

"I have some in the trunk of the car that you can borrow."

"Good ones?"

"Worked on me."

"That'll do."

Jimmy lifted his eyebrows. "You through?"

"You going back to New Mexico with Summer the easy way or the hard way?"

Now his eyebrows shot downward, and his fingers curled into his palms. "I'd like to see you try it."

"I'd like to see me try it, too." I took a step

forward, spoiling for a fight. Sometimes that was the only way to feel human these days.

But Jimmy shook out the tension in his hands and held one up. "There are a lot of people—or unpeople," he conceded when I took a breath to correct him, "that are after this child and we don't know why."

"Do we know who?" Summer cast a glance at Luther and the kitten, but they lay on a small patch of grass watching the clouds drift by and paying no attention to us, or at least pretending not to.

"Not really," I answered, then explained all that had happened at the motel.

"Why send humans?" Summer asked.

"That appears to be the sixty-four-thousand-dollar question."

"No," Summer said slowly. "It's pretty clever. You didn't get a read on them. No whisper from Ruthie. No buzz. Because they're human." Her perfect pink lips tightened. "Brilliant."

"Except most humans would be hamburger if they tried it."

"If they were unprepared, as most humans are. But these weren't," Summer said. "We're going to have to stay on our toes. This could be the new norm."

"Hiring human hit men?"

"I bet they do it again."

"Frick."

Summer laughed. "Frick? Since when do you watch your language?"

"Since—" I jerked a thumb at the kids.

"Oh."

"I better go." All of a sudden I didn't want to, and I wasn't sure why. Summer drove me insane; Jimmy wasn't much better. The baby, cute as she was, made me nervous. The only one I could stomach lately was Luther, and I had to leave him behind.

I headed for the Impala. Luther hailed me before I got there, and I made a detour over the crunchy August grass toward him and Faith.

Luther stood. "They gonna watch her?"

"Summer is."

Luther nodded, as if he'd expected nothing else, then headed for the Impala.

"Whoa, big guy." I put a hand on his arm, got a flash of lions roaring, teeth and claws flailing, blood flying, before I yanked away.

I needed to do a better job of shielding myself or I was going to blow a blood vessel one of these days. I used to be much better at it, but my mind was so full of everything else, sometimes I lost my focus.

"You can't go," I said.

"Like hell." Luther started for the car again.

"I'm serious."

He didn't stop. "Me too."

Faith began to bound after him, and I snatched her right out of the air with both hands. She hissed, but when I snapped, "Knock that off," she did.

I tucked the kitten under my arm like a football and went after Luther. I caught him as he opened the passenger door and slapped my palm against it to keep it closed. "I have to go alone."

"Every Nephilim on earth is gunning for you."

"They have been for a while now."

"I can't let you leave without me." His kinky long hair fell over his face. "We're partners. How will you know what's coming at you and when?"

I took a breath, glanced up at the bright blue sky, then let it out. "I'll manage." Although I wasn't sure how. "Besides, the new SOP appears to be sending well-informed humans. You won't feel them coming, either."

"Two is always better than one," he insisted, then more quietly, "You wouldn't let me go off alone."

"I'm not sixteen."

That brought his head up. His hair flew back. His eyes flared amber. "Neither am I."

My head gave a low, painful thump. I was *so* not having this argument again. A distraction was in order.

I glanced over my shoulder conspiratorially. Jimmy was watching us, no expression on his face. Summer was occupied digging through the rear end of the Hummer, probably searching for something that might kill me.

I turned back, lowered my voice. "I need someone I can trust, Luther."

As his eyes widened, they slowly returned to hazel. "For what?"

"You know I can't take Faith with me."

His head tilted as he studied my face. "What are you planning on doing up there?"

I couldn't help it. I glanced again at Jimmy, who lifted his eyebrows as if he'd heard. Though Luther and I had been speaking in a whisper, maybe he had. Sanducci's ears were as supersonic as his eyes.

"Whatever I have to."

Jimmy knew what I'd done to raise the last ghost. Or should I say who? He also knew I might have to do the same thing again. No doubt another reason he'd been trying to stop me.

Thus far I'd only slept with two men for power. But sooner or later I'd need something that only a stranger could give. I wasn't looking forward to it.

I forced myself to turn away from Sanducci and face Luther again. From the way the kid's cheeks had reddened, he knew exactly what I'd meant. Good. I didn't want to elaborate. Especially not to him.

Ruthie thinks Faith would be safer with Jimmy," I continued, "but he's being…" I lifted one shoulder then lowered it. "Jimmy. And Summer—"

"Doesn't like you."

"Can't say I blame her." The feeling was oh, so mutual. "I doubt she'd hurt a baby, but—"

"You didn't expect her to sell her soul to Satan in exchange for Sanducci's life, either."

"Right. If you're there, I can do what I need to without worrying, and the quicker I go, the quicker I'll get back. If we're lucky I'll find out from Sawyer not only who's after Faith and why, but also who took the *Key of Solomon.*"

Luther stepped away from the car. "You can count on me."

I could. I trusted this kid as much as I'd once trusted Jimmy. As much as I'd still trust Jimmy—if he hadn't gone soft on soul-selling fairies.

Luther held out his arms for Faith, and as I began to hand her over, there was a bright flash, and she was a baby again. I nearly dropped her at the unexpected increase in weight and wiggliness.

Luther snatched the child, and Faith giggled.

"She's messing with you," he said.

I couldn't help but smile. If I'd been a shape-shifting infant, I'd probably have messed with everyone, too. I wouldn't have been able to help myself. Faith was growing on me—in both forms.

I headed around the rear of the Impala—a long trip, the car was a real beast—but I was distracted by outrageous kissy noises. Turning, I discovered Faith smooching out her lips and holding out her arms.

"Where did she get that?" I asked.

"Beats me."

I studied the child for several seconds. "Have you noticed she's maturing at the speed of…

"What?" Luther asked.

"Not human, that's for sure."

"She isn't."

"I think you need to write down what she does differently every day. Weigh her, measure her. See how fast she's growing."

"What for?"

"I don't know." It wasn't as if I was going to be able to do anything to stop Faith from becoming whatever she was.

"You better give her a kiss before she flips out."

Faith had continued to make smoochy sounds, and the longer I ignored them, the louder and more insistent they'd become.

I wasn't wild about kissing the kid. Her entire chin shone with spittle, and there was something that looked like dog-do on her knees. Her chubby hands were gray with dust; she had grass in her teeth. But really, what choice did I have?

I went back and let her drool on me.

It wasn't so bad.

Chapter 14

How had Faith wormed her way into my life so fast? Was it because she was Sawyer's, and Sawyer was gone?

What would happen when she was old enough to ask where her father was? What happened when she asked how he'd died?

I wasn't going to think about that.

Instead I drove northwest for nearly an hour then stopped at a cafe with a parking lot full of semis. Truck drivers knew the restaurants with good food and even better coffee. They had to.

I was tired and hungry, and I needed to study the map. I wasn't quite sure how to get to Inyan Kara from here.

I ordered coffee, orange juice, eggs, sausage, and wheat toast, then I poured over the map. I preferred actual maps to my phone. I liked to get the whole picture and it was pretty hard to on a screen the size of my palm.

From what I saw, I should reach the mountain in two or three hours, depending on how decent the roads were and how good the map was. I could shape-shift and fly there. But that would leave me naked when I returned to human form. And returning was a given. No matter how special I might be, I wasn't a talking phoenix.

While naked might be a good way to convince a man, regardless how old, of anything, I'd rather try cool, calm, rational logic first.

I experienced a few seconds of concern at the size of Inyan Kara. How would I find this guy?

Truth was, I'd been in this situation before and the *how* always worked itself out. Take my trip to the Badlands to find Jimmy. They were huge but within minutes of seeing them, I'd known exactly where Sanducci was. I had no doubt the location of Sani would make itself known when I needed it to be.

Worst-case scenario, once I got to the top of the mountain I would use my speed or my shape-shifting or even my psychometric talent, if I came across something the old man had touched, to find him.

I finished my food, paid the bill, made use of the large, clean facilities—there was even a shower available for customer use; the number of female truck drivers on the road had increased in the past few years—then took the "go" cup of coffee I'd ordered and got back into the Impala.

The road went on and on, seeming to disappear into the flat land surrounding me, but every once in a while I could have sworn I saw the dark brush of mountains against the horizon.

I'd just slowed to take a nearly hairpin turn around a small grove of trees and what appeared to be a cemetery in the middle of nowhere when something shot into the road.

I slammed on the brakes; my coffee went flying, soaking me, the seat, the floor. I barely noticed. All my attention was riveted on the white face and terrified eyes of the young woman just inches from my bumper.

She slammed her scraped and bloodied hands onto the hood. "Help me!" she screamed, then glanced over her shoulder. Blood trickled from the fang marks in her neck.

I closed my eyes for just an instant and caught the telltale buzz. When I opened them I knew even before I followed her gaze what I'd see.

Vampires. A lot of them.

However, the dozen or so figures moving in our direction resembled no vampires I'd ever seen. Covered in dirt, their clothes were torn, disintegrating into dust as I watched.

The girl scrambled to the passenger door, yanked on the handle, began to beat on it, sobbing, when it wouldn't open. I reached over, lifted the lock, and she tumbled inside. The scent of blood filled the enclosed space, and my demon murmured.

I got out of the car, breathing deeply, and

caught the distinct odor of rot. Were they zombies? I didn't think so. I'd never felt the vampire buzz for a zombie. Of course I'd never seen a *true* zombie, either. Revenants were something else.

Maybe these were zombie-vampires. And wouldn't that just be special?

"Hey! Come on!" The girl's volume control seemed stuck on shriek. Understandable, but my ears. "Let's get out of here!"

"Tell me what happened."

"Fuck that!" She started to slide into the driver's seat, and I flicked her back with a jerk of one wrist.

"Tell me what happened," I repeated.

My magic hand twitch shocked the desire to scream right out of her, although now she looked at me with the same expression she'd looked at them.

"I-I took flowers to my grandma's grave. Then smoke b-b-began to rise."

"From where?"

"The *graves*," she said in the same tone she might have said *freaking moron.* "The smoke got thicker and—"

She bit her lip, frowning, already doubting the truth of what her eyes had plainly seen.

"Say it," I ordered. "I'll believe you."

"The smoke became them. One of them grabbed me and—" She shuddered. "He bit me, and I could feel his lips, his tongue, his teeth. Sucking. He got a—" She swallowed. "Hard-on."

Definitely vampires, not that I'd had much doubt.

I cast a quick glimpse at the approaching horde. They weren't moving very fast. I wasn't sure why. But I was glad.

"Stay here."

After grabbing my keys to make sure she did, I hurried to the trunk where I eyed the biggest knives I had. I possessed one sword, and I wished momentarily for two. I was going to have to do some beheading.

I took the sword in my right hand and a bowie knife in my left then shut the trunk. The girl was gone. A quick glance across the road revealed her running across a recently shorn field of unidentifiable crops. She was making excellent time.

Good. I wouldn't need to worry about one or more of them flanking me and getting to her. I didn't need to think up a plausible excuse for what she'd seen—not that there was one.

I returned my attention to the problem far too close at hand. Beheading usually discouraged the most determined vampire, but I'd met things in the past that were capable of picking up their head and putting it back on. I hated when that happened.

The vampires closed in, and the smell of death intensified.

"What are you?" I asked.

They were either smart enough not to answer me, or incapable of speech. I counted fourteen—all men, all blond, blue-eyed, offensive lineman-types—

six-seven or more, no necks, huge biceps and legs like oak trees. They looked like Vikings.

"I hate Vikings," I muttered—both the NFL team and the ruthless invaders from the north—then swung my sword at the nearest one.

He grabbed the blade before I chopped off his head. I managed to slice several fingers, but that was nothing more than a shaving cut to a vampire. He reached for me with his uninjured hand; I ducked then rolled.

I was back on my feet in an instant—a state champion gymnastics medal had turned out to be the most useful part of high school. Add to that supernatural speed and strength and I could hold my own.

Sensing a vampire creep close, I spun; sweeping out with my sword, I managed to slice his neck. Blood sprayed, but he didn't die. His head hung half on and half off.

Three others were near enough that I could smell their rancid breath. I flicked a hand, and they bowled over two more who hovered behind, all five going down like pins on a lane. I finished off the wounded one just as he began to heal. The instant his head separated completely from his body, both halves burst into ashes.

"Yes!"

Whirling, I kicked another in the chest. He flew several feet and landed on the hood of the Impala. I winced at the resulting crunch. Summer was going to make me pay for that in ways that had nothing to do with money.

I kept flicking, kicking, and beheading, but I didn't seem to be making much progress. They were like the proverbial fishes. The more I killed, the more seemed to appear. I thought of the Iyas spilling over the horizon in a never-ending stream. Was this going to be the way every battle went from now on?

I was beginning to tire, to wonder what I was going to do when I ran out of gas. Then I felt a ripple in the air around me. Not the wind. There wasn't even a trace of a breeze.

In that instant of distraction, a vampire slunk close enough to bear-hug me from behind. He tried to sink his teeth into my neck and got a mouthful of dog collar instead. The necklace was good for more than just demon containment.

Howling—I think he lost a fang—he dropped me. I landed on my feet swinging and nearly took off the head of a man with a distinctly different appearance from all the others.

Though blond, he was sun-burnished instead of winter-pale. His eyes, while blue, were more indigo than sky, and though he seemed short compared with the others, he was still several inches taller than me, which put him over six feet. Wiry and quick, he brandished a sword in each hand, and he knew exactly what to do with them.

As I continued to gape at his sudden appearance,

the man hacked off the heads of two vampires at once before moving on to two more.

I couldn't stop staring. Blood trailed over his bare chest and back. Copper armbands engraved with fleurs-de-lis cupped his biceps. He wore a necklace of silver charms, and something shiny hung from one ear, tangling with the golden length of his hair.

Strands of white threaded the gold and fine lines of age creased his eyes, but his body was honed and hard. He might be anywhere from thirty to fifty.

One of the half demons managed to grab him by the throat. The Nephilim's hand got tangled in the necklace, and he screamed as first fire then smoke flared from his fingertips. I really wanted to know what that guy wore around his neck, and then I'd get me some.

"Duck," the man shouted, so I did. A vampire's arms slapped together above my head. "If you can't help, you're hurting. Run and hide."

"Never."

Embarrassed to be caught losing a fight, I hacked my way through more than my share of what remained. Ten minutes later the only things still moving on the road were Blondie and me.

Breathing heavily, covered in blood and ashes, I headed for the Impala, where I kept bottles of water in the trunk. We could both use a drink and a wash.

As I came around the rear of the car, a vampire

shot out of the backseat and buried my favorite silver knife in my kidney. Blood spurted, and the vampire got distracted, falling to his knees so he could place his mouth beneath the flow. I hacked off his head with a backhanded swat, not even taking a very good look where I was swinging. Practice makes perfect.

I wiped off my bloody sword with an old towel before tossing it into the trunk along with the barely used bowie, then snatched up some water and shut the door. A flash of movement in the glass had me dropping to a crouch. A silver sword sliced off a big sheet of the Impala's sky-blue paint.

I reacted instinctively, ramming my elbow into the guy's crotch, then snatching the sword that had nearly cleaved my head and yanking it from his now lax grip. "What are you doing?"

Recovering with admirable speed, he brought his remaining sword across in a smooth arc toward my neck. I tightened my grip and slammed the weapon in my hands against it. The shock reverberated all the way to my teeth.

"No human could stay on their feet after a knife wound like that, let alone keep fighting."

"Damn straight." I gave my sword a shove.

He fell, hitting the ground hard and nearly doing a reverse somersault before nimbly flipping to a crouch, eyes narrowed. I'd not only admitted my lack of humanity but proved it by sending him flying. He lifted his weapon again.

"I was killing them before you showed up. Don't I get points for that?"

"Just because you were killing them doesn't mean you aren't a different type of 'them.' You hate one another. You fight among yourselves." He frowned. "Though not so much lately."

Because lately we—I mean *they*—were too busy killing us.

"Don't you know who I am?" I asked.

"No, but I'll figure it out."

He came at me swinging; I lost patience and snatched the sword out of his hand with my super-speed then threw both weapons far, far away.

The guy grabbed his necklace and held it up. The sun glanced off a crucifix. Now that I was closer I could see that all the charms around his neck were some form of a cross, as was the earring dangling from one ear. Which explained the fire and the smoke when the vampire had touched it. Not that any old cross would do. The piece had to be blessed.

Reaching out, I pressed the tiny items flat against his chest. He flinched, obviously expecting to be burned by the flames that would soon incinerate me. Instead—

Nothing happened.

Chapter 15

"I'm not a vampire," I said.

Liar.

Okay, I wasn't a vampire right *now*. But he didn't need to know that.

The man stepped away, leaving my hand hanging in the air between us, but not before I saw a few flashes in his head.

A church. Candles. Crosses. Blood.

"What *were* those?" I asked.

"Vampires."

"That much I know."

His eyebrows lifted. "You believe me?"

"You think it's normal to carry a sword around in your trunk?"

"Normal for me."

"Me too."

His gaze held mine. "You've seen things like them before."

"More than you can imagine."

"I've never met anyone else who had."

He wasn't one of us, didn't have a clue about the federation, perhaps not even a clue as to exactly what he was fighting. He just knew they needed killing.

In times past Sawyer had "recruited" new federation members, though as he told it no recruitment was required. Most, if not all, of those who fought for the light possessed a little something extra, and they'd been "seeing" monsters for years.

That they were still alive was usually thanks to a paranormal ability they didn't know they had—or pretended not to because they couldn't explain it. Sawyer had been able to sense those abilities in others. He'd told me once he could feel a vibration from seers and DKs along his skin.

I remembered the odd shimmy in the air when this man approached. Was that what Sawyer had meant?

Sawyer had also been able to bring forth supernatural powers and teach the refinement and control necessary to use them as a weapon. Obviously I had those talents now, too.

Just what I needed, more to do.

"What's your name?"

"What's yours?"

He was starting to get on my nerves.

"Elizabeth Phoenix." I held out my hand.

He put his behind his back. "Bram."

"Bram," I repeated. "You expect me to believe that a guy I find dusting vampires is really named Bram? Like Stoker?"

He lifted his chin, and the golden cross in his ear caught the sun, nearly blinding me. "My name's Abraham."

"First name or last?"

He just smiled. Guys with one name. Man, I hated that.

"Well, Abraham, there's gonna be trouble if you don't tell me what those things were." I held up a hand. "I know they were vampires. Be specific."

"Why would you cut off their heads if you didn't know what they were?"

"Beheading has worked pretty well in the past."

"But—" Confusion spread over his face. "Not just anyone can behead a draugar and kill them."

Now we were getting somewhere.

"What's a draugar?"

"Norse vampire." Bram continued to stare into my face, searching my eyes, for what I wasn't sure. "They rest in the graves of Vikings and inhabit the bodies of the dead."

Vikings. Right again. Sometimes I was so good at this I scared myself.

Although I'd prefer to hear Ruthie's voice instead of making psychic-boosted guesses, however spot-on they were. One of these days I was going to guess wrong, and then someone would die.

Not me. But someone.

"They rise as wisps of smoke," Bram continued, "and prey on the blood of the living. To die they must be beheaded."

I nodded.

"By a hero."

I stopped nodding. "Huh?"

"Only the strength of a true hero will kill them."

"How, exactly, is a hero defined?"

"If the draugers die when you behead them, you're a hero."

"And if they don't, you're a dead loser."

He shrugged. "That's a chance I was willing to take."

"Why?"

Bram cocked his head, and that earring twinkled. "I'm sorry?"

"Why would you take that chance?"

"Why would you?"

"It's my job."

"You get paid for..." He motioned at the ashes swirling around our feet.

"Not exactly."

"What exactly?"

"We need to have a talk."

I didn't like wasting time; I had to get to the top of Inyan Kara. But I couldn't just leave this guy to run around chopping off heads because he thought he was a hero. The federation had several purposes, and this was one of them—bringing like-talented individuals into the fold.

I moved the Impala off the road, then we sat on the dented hood sipping water.

"What do you know about the—" I paused,

uncertain what to call them in case Bram was more clueless than I thought.

"Nephilim?"

I lifted my eyebrows, and his lips curved, though he didn't quite crack a smile. "The descendants of the fallen angels. Half demons masquerading as humans."

"How do you know this?"

"I was a priest."

Hadn't seen that coming.

"You aren't anymore?"

"Do I look like a priest?"

"Appearances deceive."

"Touché." He took a sip of water.

"What happened?"

"They didn't believe me."

"What, exactly, did you say?"

His lips quirked again. "I went into the priesthood in the first place because my dreams often came true."

I didn't comment. That happened to me all the time.

"I thought God was talking to me," he said.

"Maybe he was." *Probably* he was.

"But I also had nightmares of horrible creatures hiding behind the faces of humans."

"Join the club."

He appeared intrigued, but he continued with his story. "My family was very religious. Psychics, magic, soothsayers—bad idea."

"Because?"

"*Thou shall not suffer a witch to live.*"

"Sounds like something you'd get in Salem. Over three hundred years ago."

"I've heard it more recently than that."

I'd *done* it more recently, but now wasn't the time to confess.

"I was given a choice—priesthood or…" His voice faded; his gaze drifted into the past.

"Death?" I might not suffer his parents to live if they'd threatened that. I had memories of my own "witch hunters" that I'd like to erase. People like us always did.

"No." Bram cleared his throat. "Psych ward."

"How old were you?"

"Fourteen."

My eyes narrowed. I'd been an orphan—or at least I'd thought I was—and spent a lot of time in places and with people I did not want to remember. But the older I got, the more I discovered that having parents wasn't always so great, either.

"You went into the priesthood at fourteen?"

"Seminary high school, then the seminary, then—" He rolled his hand to indicate *and so on.* "I thought the dreams would stop when I gave my life to the church. Obviously I was being possessed by a demon."

"But they didn't stop, because you weren't possessed by anything. You have a gift."

"Or a curse."

I'd often thought the same.

"You dreamed of the Nephilim, and they came."

"I'd dream about a person, then I'd see the terrible things they'd done, that they would do, and the horrific *beast* that lived inside them."

"And then?"

"A day, a week, a month later, there they'd be. They'd look just like everyone else, but as soon as I saw them I remembered and for just an instant I could see the demon they tried to hide."

Interesting. Most seers heard a voice or had a dream. But I'd yet to meet one who could peer past the mask and see the truth. And most seers just saw. DKs fought. Until the recent heavy losses of federation life had changed everything, I'd been the first one who was both.

"What are you?" I asked.

"I'm *Bram.*"

"Not who. What?"

"I don't understand."

"Your parents. Could they do anything... freaky?"

"No! I'm not one of *them!*" His mouth curled in horror.

I kind of thought he was; he just didn't know it yet. Though after the initial ripple at his approach, I hadn't felt anything else. No buzz of a Nephilim, no hum of a breed. Which was downright strange.

I reached out, brushed his arm with my fingertips. "Never mind."

Once I'd have been able to touch him and hear a whisper revealing what he was. Now I touched him and felt his fear, his loneliness, his hatred of the Nephilim. I caught flashes of battles, glimpses of near misses, glances of victories, but I heard nothing beyond the harsh rasp of his breath.

I was going to get rid of this demon inside me even if I had to rip the thing out myself.

Bram withdrew his arm. "What are *you*?"

"What do you think I am?"

His gaze wandered over me, from my increasingly shaggy dark brown hair, to the jeweled collar around my neck, touching on the tip of the phoenix wing that curled over my shoulder just a bit. There was nothing odd about a girl my age having a tat at the nape of her neck. However, Bram's expression made me think he had an inkling of what it might be for.

He peered at the turquoise that rested between my very nice breasts. The flush that crept over his cheeks as he moved on made me wonder how long he'd been out of the priesthood.

"Bram?" I asked. "What do you think I am?"

His pupils were dilated so large they blotted out the dark blue shade of his eyes. I reared back before I could stop myself. He looked so demony, I half expected him to reach over and yank out my throat.

"I don't know," he said slowly. "I think you could be anything."

How right he was.

Chapter 16

"There are others like you," I said.

A tiny white lie. I didn't know of anyone quite like Bram. But that didn't make him any less one of us. There was no one like me, either, but that just made me the leader of this whole mess.

"Do you see the demons?" he asked.

"I—uhh—" Did. But if I told him why I didn't anymore, he'd only try to kill me. "I'm what we call a DK, or demon killer."

I was. That just wasn't *all* I was.

Quickly I explained the federation and how we worked. "I think you should join us."

"I'm not much of a joiner anymore."

"Since you left the priesthood?"

Bram's gaze shifted away. "I didn't exactly leave."

"Thrown out?"

"No."

"You're AWOL?"

He gave his almost-smile. "I left, and I didn't go back, but I don't think they care. I'm sure they excommunicated me as soon as they realized I was gone."

"Excommunicated? Why?"

"I—well—you see…there was this dream, and in it there was a man, but he wasn't a man."

"Sounds familiar."

"He was a priest. A monsignor to be exact."

"What did he do?"

Bram's eyes met mine. "Terrible things."

"What did *you* do?"

"Went to the bishop, but I couldn't explain why I knew what I knew."

I'd gotten myself into all sorts of trouble as a kid by telling people what I'd "seen" when I'd touched them. Eventually, I'd stopped sharing—until Ruthie had convinced me that my curse was in fact a gift from God.

"Because you couldn't explain, they didn't believe."

"But I kept dreaming, and the more time that passed, the worse the dreams became. So I—" He took a deep breath, then blurted, "—stabbed him."

I liked his initiative.

"Let me guess," I said. "He didn't die."

"Stabbing wasn't the way to kill him."

"How did you find out what was?" I couldn't believe that his dreams weren't clueing him in. Seemed a little half-assed to me. But so much did.

"He was in pain, a little out of it. Said he'd done nothing but what an incubus had to do to survive."

"Moron."

"He thought I was powerless. That I wouldn't have the guts to try again."

"But you weren't powerless, and you did have the guts."

"I had his eventually."

An incubus was a sex demon. They came in the night; they seemed like a dream. They had sex with their victims, sucking energy from them during the act like a vampire sucked blood, leaving the sufferers pale and dazed. Eventually the victim would die, and no one would ever know why.

Historically, an incubus was a man who preyed on women, while a succubus was a woman who preyed on men, but they could also be bisexual if they chose. I was pretty certain most chose. When dealing with a demon that ingested sex like canapes, I had a hard time believing they'd be bound by anything as minor as sexuality.

"What did the trick?" I asked.

"Evisceration."

"Messy."

Bram smiled for the first time I'd ever seen. "Very."

"How'd you figure out the best way to kill one?"

"I didn't spend half my life in a seminary without learning a thing or two about demons, and what I didn't know off the top of my head, I knew how to find out."

"In a copy of *Incubi for Dummies*?"

He gave a half laugh, which made me like him all the more. Some people found me...not funny.

"You'd be surprised what you can discover in

the dusty corners of a seminary library."

"You were excommunicated for rearranging the insides of your monsignor on the outside?"

"No."

"What else did you do?"

"Nothing." He lifted one shoulder then lowered it. "There."

"You better explain."

"There wasn't a body." He clapped his hands, then his fingers made the gesture of rain while he whispered, "Whoosh."

"Ashes. Which means they had nothing on you."

"Except I'd accused the man of horrible things, then I'd stabbed him, and then he disappeared."

"And then?"

"I ran."

"Good choice."

"They aren't looking for me. I'd be an embarrassment. The priest who thought he saw a demon."

"You *did* see a demon. How could the church refuse to believe that? Aren't they in the anti-demon business?"

"They were. But hellish fiends are something from the Middle Ages. Certainly there's evil. We can't not concede that when it's in our face all the time, but demons?" He shook his head. "Quite a stretch. Besides, what were they going to do? Pray the Nephilim away?"

"I don't think that works."

"It doesn't. The priests I knew were gentle men of charity and hope. They couldn't kill things."

"So what happened to you?"

"I witnessed the truth. Over and over and over again until I couldn't *not* kill them."

The more I talked to this guy, the more I wondered just how random his showing up to save my ass had been. I'd come to understand in the last few months that random just wasn't what it used to be.

"You saw the draugars in a dream?"

He nodded.

"Did you see me?"

"No. I saw the cemetery and the Vikings. They were attacking a really big, colorful bird that shot fire from its wings. You see anything like that?"

I forced myself not to scratch the very itchy tattoo at my nape. "Not me."

"First I thought it was an actual nightmare. I have those sometimes. But the same dream kept returning, and when that happens, I have to act or never find a moment's peace." He tilted his head. "I wonder what that weird bird was."

"Maybe the girl's name was Robin."

"This bird wasn't a robin. More like a—" He glanced at the sun. "Thunderbird. That would make sense around here."

"Because?"

"The Sioux say the thunderbird is huge and many-colored with the power of the storm and command of the rain. The flap of their wings is the thunder; the breeze created by the beat brings together the clouds, and when the thunderbird blinks the flash of its eyes is the lightning."

Sounded pretty phoenix-y to me, but most cultures had their own version of every legend.

"In the old days the thunderbirds killed monsters," Bram continued.

"Which means they weren't one."

"Anything can become a monster if it chooses to be."

Bram reminded me of Xander Whitelaw, who'd been a prophecy professor at an Indiana Bible college. Intelligent, knowledgeable, yet innocent in so many ways, nevertheless I'd sent him looking for clues about both the *Key of Solomon* and the *Book of Samyaza.* Big mistake.

He'd found the location of the key. Unfortunately, the Nephilim had found him. I still had nightmares.

The loss of Xander had been a big one. He'd known a lot and what he hadn't known, he'd been able to discover.

My gaze took in Bram's hard hands, bulging biceps, and collection of crosses. I didn't think he'd be killed as easily as Xander.

"You're sure you don't want to join the federation?" I asked.

"I'm sure."

I wasn't willing to give up that easily. "How'd you like to freelance?"

He lifted a brow. "I'm listening."

"Ever heard of the *Key of Solomon*?"

"I was a priest," he said.

Which I took to mean yes.

"I need it."

"There are copies all over the place."

"The original."

"*That*, there's only one of."

"And the *Book of Samyaza*."

Now his brows tilted downward as he frowned. "It's real?"

"Wanna find out?"

"Actually, yeah. I still have connections."

"One more thing."

I reached for his arm, but he pulled back. Instead of being hurt, I was glad. The less he trusted, the better. I didn't want to walk into a room someday and find pieces of him all over the place.

"If the Nephilim know you're searching for it—"

"They'll kill me. They try that all the time."

"I was going to say 'they'll follow you.' If you find it, they'll kill you."

"Then they'll take it and march all over the earth in glory," he finished.

"I'd hate to see either of those things happen."

"You and me both."

I gave him my cell phone number and e-mail address. He did the same.

"Where you headed?" I asked.

"Where are you?"

I decided not to share. Bram might try to burn me for a witch if he heard I was raising ghosts.

"I'm not sure," I said.

"Me either."

We were both lying, and we both knew it. Welcome to my world—trust no one who hasn't proved trustworthy, and sometimes not even them. It was a sad, bad, lonely way to live.

I glanced at the sky. The sun was falling rapidly. There was no way I'd be able to find the Old One today. "You know of any motels nearby?"

"I don't stay in motels."

"Ever?"

"Sometimes I wake myself screaming. Had the cops called a few times. Better to sleep in the van."

Talk about sad, bad, and lonely. Poor guy. His life had not been easy. A weaker man would have gone stark, raving loony. But Bram had the confidence to believe in his dreams and the strength to do something about them. We needed more like him. The problem was finding them.

I might now possess Sawyer's talent for detecting candidates. What I didn't have was the time to troll the population waiting for a ripple.

Ruthie had used the social services system to discover kids turned out of foster homes again and again, often for very strange reasons. Weird stuff happened around breeds all the time—usually deadly, bloody, scary stuff.

But Ruthie was gone and the federation didn't have the manpower to spare a member to run the group home that had been the salvation of so many. At Ruthie's everyone was loved no matter what. Hers was the first place I'd ever felt like a girl and not a freak.

I ran my fingers over the dent in the hood. I wished I knew more about magic. I could probably fix that with a twitch of my nose.

I turned to say goodbye to Bram and stared at an empty road.

"You are definitely something more than human," I said.

Chapter 17

Before getting into the Impala, I used one of the gallon jugs of water in the trunk to sponge off the draugar blood. I couldn't drive around like this; I especially couldn't drive into a small western town and check in for the night looking as if I'd spent the day as an extra in the latest Quentin Tarantino movie.

After removing my ruined lime-green tank top and bra, I changed into fresh ones—this time in power red. Maybe the shade would wake me up.

I bought shirts, bras, and underwear by the bagful at Wal-Mart. They rarely lasted long enough to wear out. I'd learned quickly to purchase dark-colored jeans that could disguise myriad questionable body fluids. I'd also bought black sneakers after my white pair had first become pink when I washed them, and then fallen apart when I bleached them.

I'd had high hopes for finding a motel in Osage, the next town up the road, but it turned out to have a population between two and three hundred and little use for a motel. Luckily I saw the sign for a family-owned establishment near Upton that promised an Internet connection and a free breakfast.

I paid cash. Too many Nephilim knew me by name.

The federation did have a wide network in place—members in every walk of life and level of business and government—that could erase all trace of my transaction with a single phone call on my part. But they had better things to do with their time and talents. Besides, the Nephilim had a similar network. One never knew who might see the info first, or even intercept a phone call.

Though I was the leader of the light, I wasn't exactly sure how many members the federation had, who they were, or even what all they did. Ruthie had died too suddenly to tell me much of anything, and I'd been a little busy sticking my finger in the dike of the Apocalypse to take an administrative crash course.

But Ruthie had trained her people well—except for me—and they were used to working alone. They continued to do so with no input or management on my part. As a result, the federation had kept chugging along pretty smoothly, considering.

The motel clerk appeared as if he'd just come in from a three-week fly-fishing excursion. His face and arms were fried the shade of an overripe strawberry. He had to have a hundred mosquito bites. He still smelled of fish, and I could swear there were a few entrails hanging off his seed cap.

He couldn't stop staring at me. I wondered if I was the first non-Caucasian to walk through his door this year.

"Miss," he began.

"I'm Egyptian," I said in an attempt to stave off the usual questions about my nationality. Since I got them in Milwaukee—a town where around forty percent of the population was African American—I was certain I'd get them here.

"Oh. Ah. Well. Ain't that nice? I was gonna say you've got something there behind yer ear." He pointed.

I swiped a glob of draugar off my neck then casually wiped it on my jeans. "Deerfly." I hoped like hell they had them here.

"Bastards." He spit a brown stream of tobacco juice into a cup at his elbow.

I was a little embarrassed that I'd expected the guy to question if I was black. I'd been asked that all my life, and I hated it. Not because I didn't want to be seen as African American. Ruthie had been, after all, and I'd wanted nothing more than to be exactly like her—until I was.

No, it had bothered me then because I hadn't known who my parents were. I had no idea why I looked the way I did, and I hadn't wanted to be reminded of that. Of course once I'd met my mother, I'd only wanted a return to my blissful state of ignorance.

"You doin' some sightseeing?" the man asked.

"Mmm." I eyed the key in his hand. Why didn't he just hand it over?

" 'Cause if ye are, it's good ye aren't white."

My gaze flicked from the key to his face. "Excuse me?"

"There are a lot of places 'round here that are cursed for the white man."

"Sure there are."

He grinned, revealing tobacco-stained teeth. Why on earth would someone do that on purpose?

"You can hardly blame the Sioux for being teed off."

"Interesting position for a white man."

"My great-great-great-granny was Lakota."

My ears perked up as the curse got a whole lot more interesting. "Really?" I'd discovered that family legends often held the truth.

"Really. You know the government stole the Black Hills from the People."

"I heard something about that."

He grinned that terrible grin again. "They call the hills Paha Sapa, and they're sacred. In the Treaty of Fort Laramie the Sioux were given ownership. But then gold was discovered."

"And suddenly the land that was useless enough to give to the Indians wasn't so useless anymore."

"You've heard the story?"

"It's common enough. They found oil in Indian Territory. Shazaam. Not so Indian anymore."

The clerk nodded. "White men started pourin' into the Black Hills. Custer even led an expedition in 1874. Carved his name right into the peak of Inyan Kara. You can still see it. G. Custer. '74. According to my granny, the mountain was angry. Ever since then, any white man steps foot on Inyan Kara is cursed."

"You believe that?"

"Didn't work out too well for Custer."

"That's because he was a moron," I muttered.

"That too," the clerk agreed. "Split his force. Underestimated the enemy. Got hisself surrounded. Him a West Point man, too. Though he did graduate at the bottom of the class."

My regard for the clerk increased. I should know better than to judge by appearance. This guy knew a thing or two.

"Despite the protests of the Indians," he continued, "white men began to mine for gold. When the Cheyenne joined the Sioux and they all kicked some ass, the government said the Sioux had broken the treaty and took the Black Hills away."

"What about a reparation lawsuit?" I asked.

"*United States Versus the Sioux Nation of Indians,* 1980. Supreme Court ruled the Black Hills were illegally confiscated, and the Sioux should be paid what they were worth in 1874 plus interest— around a hundred and six million dollars." His eyes actually twinkled.

"Go on." I wanted to hear the rest almost as

much as he wanted to tell it to me.

"Sioux refused to accept the money. Wanted their sacred hills back."

"But most of it's divided into national parks."

"Few state parks, too. So them gettin' back their land wasn't happenin'."

"And the money?"

"Sits in the bank. Last I heard it had grown to over seven hundred fifty million dollars. And the Sioux won't touch it even though they're one of the poorest people in the country."

"What about the curse?"

"Stays in force until the hills again belong to the People."

"That could be a while."

He lowered his chin. "So it's good yer—what did ye say? Ethiopian?"

"Egyptian."

The clerk shrugged.

"You never answered me before. You believe the Black Hills are cursed?

"Maybe not all of them. But Inyan Kara…" His eyes got a faraway expression. "Yeah. I believe it."

"Why?"

"There've been plenty of hikers gone up and never come back down. Weird storms blowin' in from nowhere. Lightning blazing from a clear sky. Torrential rains and such. Probably been a dozen broken bones in the last year alone—legs, ankles, arms. Inyan Kara's got a bad reputation, and the landowners are real touchy 'bout who they let walk through. Gotta ask permission, maybe even sign somethin'. Lawsuits, you know."

The scourge of America. Lawsuits. And lawyers. The latter almost made demons look good.

Almost.

"Sounds to me like the place is in a bad-weather pattern, with a lot of dangerous slopes and stupid hikers. You don't really think the mountain can bring up a storm, do you?"

I didn't. But only because I knew what could.

"Guess not." The man smiled again. If he was going to continue with the chew, he should really stop. "But it's a good story, ain't it?"

"It is."

"Still goin' to see Inyan Kara?"

"I am. According to you, the mountain oughta love me."

"One more thing. Folks say they've seen..."

An old man? A young one? A ghost? A wraith? A spirit?

"A coyote."

I wasn't sure what to say.

"It's big," he continued. "Some think it's part wolf. It's also black. No one 'round here's ever seen a black coyote, though I hear tell they exist. Some claim it's a medicine man who can change shape."

I laughed, but the sound was forced. Because I thought it was a medicine man who could change shape, too. But changing into a coyote was disturbing. To the Navajo it's an insult to call anyone a coyote. In their folklore the animal is a disreputable character, one that does nasty things and cannot be trusted. They call the coyote *mah-ih,* one who roams. Which might explain how a Navajo shaman wound up in Lakota land.

"If you come across it," he continued, "be careful. Thing's been known to attack. Some thought the animal was rabid and went after it, but they never found a trace when they carried a gun. Smart bugger. People been seein' it for more years than a coyote could live. Myself, I think there's a pack of them up there."

Well, at least I knew who—I mean *what*—to search for.

"I'll be careful."

"You do that." The clerk tossed the key onto the counter then retreated through a door to the rear where a television blared, "Wheel. Of. Fortune!"

Another night, another motel room, I thought as I made use of the key. This one was little different from any other. Drab. Dank. Dark. The only color came from the god-awful painting of a pheasant that hung over the bed.

I suddenly realized how tired of it all I was. Or maybe I was just tired and being alone was making me depressed. I couldn't remember the last time I'd stayed in a motel alone. Maybe I hadn't.

I considered calling Megan, but that would only make me more miserable. I'd wind up missing her, missing the kids, the bar, my apartment, everything I'd left behind and hoped to return to. I was starting to suspect that I might never be able to stay more than a day or two in one place for the rest of my life. However long that might turn out to be.

The thought of sleeping with hidden draugar remains stuck in unknown places had me climbing into the water-stained tub despite my exhaustion. Who knew where more globs of blood and ash might lurk?

When I was done, I returned to the bedroom, which was far too quiet. In the mirror my face was drawn and pale—for me. For anyone else, the shade would be deep tan. My eyes appeared bluer than usual, probably because of the haunted expression that lived there.

The jeweled collar that circled my neck mocked me. So pretty and bright, a complete contrast with the ugly darkness it controlled. I wanted that darkness gone, along with the damn collar, but I didn't know if that were possible. I had a sneaking suspicion the darkness was a part of me now.

The turquoise that lay between my breasts seemed to pulse to the beat of my heart, calling me, mesmerizing me, and slowly I lifted my hand and touched it. In the glass just behind me, something moved, something low to the ground and dark.

My fingers clenched on the turquoise as I spun. "Sawyer?"

Nothing was there.

My head hung, the disappointment far too deep. What would I have done if Sawyer *had* been in the room—as a beast or as a man?

I rubbed the greenish blue rock with my thumb, and it warmed—from my hand or from the magic? The stone was a conduit, or at least it had been when Sawyer was alive. Now it was simply a stone.

Turning back, I froze.

Sawyer stood in the mirror.

Chapter 18

I closed my eyes then opened them again. He was still there.

He wasn't a reflection; he wasn't in the room. He was *in* the mirror.

I hadn't seen him like this since he'd died. Make that since *before* he'd died.

I didn't want to remember what he'd looked like trussed to a telephone pole with his heart torn out. Unfortunately what I wanted, I rarely got, and I'd seen it often enough both in my dreams and out of them.

His skin glistened bronze beneath a sun I couldn't see. Muscles rippled in his stomach, his chest, his arms, causing his tattoos to dance. His hair shone black, sleek, and loose; it flowed around his shoulders, blown by a wind too far away for me to feel. His gray eyes burned wherever they touched. Since I'd left my clothes in a heap on the bathroom floor, along with the towel, my body responded to the brush of his gaze as fiercely as if he'd run his fingers everywhere.

"I miss you," I whispered, and he held out his hand.

I reached forward, half afraid I'd put my palm to the cool glass and he'd vanish now like he had when he'd died. Instead my fingers squelched through the pane, seeming to disappear from here and appear over there. His closed around them, and Sawyer tugged me into the mirror.

I stumbled, and he caught me. He was warm, and he smelled so good—like the trees, the earth, the sun on the mountain—like himself. I wanted to rub my face all over him, feel his flesh against my cheek, his hair brush my eyelids, his scent becoming my own.

Glancing through the looking glass at the motel room, empty but for my duffel and keys, made me dizzy. Here the sun shone bright and warm in opposition to the moon sheen I'd left behind. That contrast made me realize that where I stood was the mirror image of where I'd been. I returned my attention to Sawyer, questions ready to tumble from my lips, and he kissed me.

He tasted of both day and night, salt and sugar, spicy yet sweet. He tasted like Sawyer, and all I wanted was to keep tasting him until the pain and the fear and the loneliness went away.

I filled my hands with his hair. The ebony strands felt like midnight—cool and dark, they flowed over my wrists, spilling the scent of the mountains that rose from the desert and the wind that whirled the waters of the sea.

His tongue brushed the seam of my lips,

causing gooseflesh to ripple across my back. He rubbed the prickle away with firm strokes of his hard, magic hands, then traced his nails across my shoulders, making the skin rise again.

Opening to him, I met his tongue with my own, dueling, teasing, chasing it back into his mouth for just one more taste. I scored his lip with my teeth, tempted to draw blood just to see if I could. A wraith wouldn't bleed, neither ghost nor spirit, just a man. But Sawyer had never been *just* anything in his life.

If I drew his blood would he disappear forever? If I tasted it would I? I didn't want to take that chance.

My hands were cold against his neck, and he shivered. I ran my palms over him as he'd done to me, and beneath my closed eyelids the images of his beasts flashed like a Vegas light show. If I wanted, I could become each of them. All I had to do was touch him and reach for the change.

Though there was another skinwalker on Inyan Kara, there would never be another with the power of Sawyer, the power of me. There was no one like us in the world.

He'd told me once how similar we were, and I'd denied it. The thought of being as cold, sarcastic, dangerous, and distant as he was had repelled me. For years Sawyer had terrified me. Probably because whenever I peered into his eyes I saw a reflection of myself. More recently I'd come to realize that our similarities connected us in a way I was connected to no one else. Only with Sawyer could I ever be completely me.

I tried to peer into his face, but the sunlight through the windows was too bright. I squinted, and he flicked his wrist. The curtains flew across the curtain rod with a muffled shriek.

The sun still peeked around the edges just enough that I could see myself at the center of his gray gaze, captured forever.

"What is this?" I asked. "Where are we?"

He didn't answer, and I began to wonder if he could. Like the Little Mermaid, had his voice been the price he'd had to pay to touch me one more time? What would I pay to touch him?

How about your soul?

Was this how Summer had lost hers? Feeling the pain of Jimmy's inevitable loss, knowing she could prevent it, being enticed with the promise of saving him. All she had to do was sell her immortal soul. Would I do the same to bring Sawyer back? Would I do it even for Jimmy?

"Kiss me," I whispered. "Kiss me and don't stop. Love me and don't talk."

I didn't want to hear any more whispers, not his and definitely not my own.

Sawyer didn't need to be told twice to have sex. Sawyer *was* sex. Temptation in perfect form.

He slid to his knees, his mouth, his hands caressing me as he went. His tongue circled my navel; his teeth scraped my hip. He pressed his thumb to the throbbing vein in my thigh, then he lowered his head, and his hair cascaded over my knee as he put his mouth to that vein and suckled.

I thought I might fall, but his palms held me firmly by the backs of my legs, the tips of his index fingers just brushing the swell of my rear, sliding across the sensitive skin below.

I steadied myself with a hand on his shoulder, the other cupping his head, urging him on. Who could have ever imagined that the press of lips, the spike of teeth, the laving of a tongue against the femoral artery could nearly make me come?

He inched upward, but I slid down. I wanted to kiss him again, to make this last. He'd be gone when we were done, and after tomorrow who knew if I'd ever see him again. The last ghost I'd raised had told me what I needed to know then taken the express train to eternity.

I both wanted that for Sawyer and feared it. He deserved peace; despite Jimmy's words, he deserved heaven. But once Sawyer went, he'd be lost to me. I doubted he'd get a weekend pass for a dream booty call.

We knelt face-to-face, so close in height our bodies aligned perfectly. His erection caressed the darker curls between my thighs. The mountain lion on his chest seemed to purr when my breasts brushed against it. Only a whisper apart, breath mingling, hands at our sides, our eyes stared intently into each other's.

I licked my lips, and my tongue caught the edge of his. A flame seemed to flare at the center of his eerie gray gaze, and he lifted one hand, clasped my neck, then crushed our mouths together.

My heart gave a single thud then began to race. Sawyer tensed, jerked back. His eyes flared first yellow, then orange, then the pupil at the center widened into the silhouette of a great bird in flight. For just an instant his face flickered—man, bird, man, bird.

Hissing, he yanked his palm away, shaking it as if he'd been burned, though I could see no evidence of it. When he lifted his eyes, they'd returned to their normal light gray.

"The shifting works both ways," I murmured.

Not only could I touch one of his tattoos and become the animal beneath, it appeared he could touch the phoenix on my neck and become one, too. That would have been an intriguing development if he weren't dead.

"Whatever," I said, and kissed him again.

He laughed, the vibration causing a shimmer to slide all the way from my lips to my toes.

We kissed for a long time. He could make me forget the now. Hell, he could make me forget my name. Too bad he couldn't make me forget the past; too bad he couldn't scourge it from my brain forever.

His mouth trailed across my neck to my breasts. Sawyer might be part beast, but he was all man. As lovely as kissing was, eventually he moved on.

I cupped his chin, lifted his face, smiled at his confusion. "Lie back."

A shove in the middle of his chest, a tiny flare of light and a slight shimmy of my form when I touched his mountain lion, then he tumbled onto the floor.

I wanted to walk my lips over his skin, rub my cheek against his flesh and memorize the texture, imprint the scent, though I knew that for the rest of my life when I smelled rain on the trees I'd smell him.

Closing my eyes I traced my mouth across his fluttering eyelids, the sharp slash of his nose, the spike of his cheekbones and chin. The curve of his neck tasted like the first blade of grass in spring— sweet and tart, green and earthy. When I kissed his biceps, his wolf howled in my head—agony, ecstasy, freedom and pain.

"Hush." I licked the tattoo from the tip of the wolf's tilted snout to the base of his curling tail.

The rumble of Sawyer's growl drew my lips to his chest. I avoided the lion in the center, concentrating on the flat, brown disks of his nipples. His nipples were softer, darker than the rest, and they tasted softer and darker, too. Like fine Belgian chocolate after a long stretch of generic candy bars.

I teased them until the tips had tightened to pebbled peaks then taunted them with my teeth. His fingers clenched in my hair, cupping my head, showing me that he wanted me to go on and on.

I ran my tongue down the ridge of his ribs, laid my cheek against the plane of his stomach. Felt his breath go in and out, lifting and lowering me, like the rock of the sea or the sway of the wind.

My own breath brushed his erection and he leaped. My lips curved as I raised my head, pressed a kiss to the soft skin, pulled hard and tight over his pelvis. I hovered, centimeters away from where he wanted me to be, his penis rising higher and higher, nearly brushing my chin, and then I pounced, running my tongue over the vein in his thigh as he'd run his over mine.

His back arched—pleasure or pain?—and his fingernails scraped the carpet as he clenched his hands. I rested my head against one thigh and smoothed my palm down the length of the other, swirling my index finger over the scattering of black hair. He had very little body hair, like most full-blooded Native Americans, or so I'd heard. There aren't many left to ask.

I explored his knees, pressing first my thumbs, then my tongue into the valleys. When I licked the seam at the back, then took a fold into my mouth and suckled, his breath caught as if he might come.

I raised my head, a brow. He breathed deeply—once, twice, again—before some of the tension slid away.

I gave the same attention to his feet, pressing my fingers here and there, testing his toes with my teeth until he moaned. Then I shimmied my way back up his body and licked the rattlesnake tattooed on his dick. I'd never been sure if that was a joke—if so, it had Sawyer's name all over it—or a way to keep a dangerous predator under wraps, so to speak.

I meant to take more time, give him a reward for being so patient, but I'd waited too long, touched him too much, and after that one leisurely lick and a single dip of my mouth over the head, he grabbed me by the elbows and dragged my lips to meet his.

He was wild now—his teeth nipping, catching, and pulling—first at my mouth, then at my neck, my breasts. The sharp draw on first one nipple then the next caused an answering tug much lower. I was so empty, and I desperately needed to be full.

As if he knew, his hands slid from my arms to my hips, over the curve until they rested at the backs of my thighs, then he lifted and separated, sliding within the warm, wet place that waited.

He stretched and filled me, claimed and completed me. Clenching my knees to his sides, I rode the tide. I reached for him and met his hands reaching for mine. We strove toward the place where we would splinter and then fall.

Thrusting together—almost—sliding apart—not quite. Together, apart, almost, not quite. And then—

At last.

Our hands clenched palm-to-palm, fingers grasping, thumbs caressing. I collapsed onto his chest, pressed my face into his neck, breathed in the desert mountain scent of him, felt his warmth, his breath, his touch. Exhaustion hovered, my eyes so heavy, my limbs the same.

"I don't want to go to sleep." I shifted so his hair cascaded over me, shielding me from the world.

If I slept, I'd wake up back there. I knew that as surely as I knew the taste of his skin. If I stayed awake would I remain here—wherever *here* was— forever?

What about the other side of that mirror? The world I'd pledged to protect. The other man I loved. The child I'd sworn to keep safe. Both places pulled at me, increasing the exhaustion I felt.

I resisted as long as I could. I listened to Sawyer breathing, focused on the steady in and out, the muffled thud of his heart—a heart I knew to be as silent now as Sawyer—beneath my own. I both wanted to stay and had to go.

Eventually, consciousness slipped away despite my efforts to fight it. When I opened my eyes, I lay facedown on the empty, lonely, cold motel bed— my head at the foot, my feet near the head—my hands clutching the sheets, my face hot and streaked with sweat, my body still trembling from the orgasm only he could give.

I turned over, my gaze drawn to the mirror. Was I here or was I there?

But the mirror reflected this room exactly, the fading darkness behind the curtains, the coming dawn. I'd have thought the entire thing a dream, that I'd never gone into the mirror at all, except—

Near my feet stood a wolf in every shade of midnight-blue and black and purple—with eyes of so light a gray they appeared to blaze like silver stars. A nonexistent wind ruffled his fur and whirled the scent of water and trees and earth through the room.

He appeared as solid as I was. I couldn't see through him; his paws made dents in the quilt; his weight lowered the bed below him.

Holding my breath, afraid to believe that he would still be there when I took my gaze from the mirror and turned, nevertheless I did.

The wolf remained—slick and solid as sin. I reached for him, and felt the silky sift of his coat, yet my fingers passed right through him.

And as they did, his body became smoke and disappeared.

Chapter 19

I swore I could still smell him—on the sheets, on my skin. I passed my hand over the bed where he'd stood, hoping to feel the warmth from where he'd lain, though that could easily be explained as my own body heat. What couldn't be explained was the tiny icon I found there.

Flicking on the bedside lamp, I shoved my hand beneath the glow. In the center of my palm lay a coyote carved in turquoise—a totem, a fetish, an amulet, a talisman, who knew? But it hadn't been here before, and I hadn't brought it with me.

My gaze fell on my laptop, and I was across the room booting it up before I took another breath. A few clicks of the keys and I was surfing for an answer.

I'd encountered amulets before; they protected the wearer from trouble. Talismans brought good fortune. But totems and fetishes I knew very little about.

I skimmed a few Web sites. Totems watched over a particular group of people—usually a family, a clan, or a tribe—and were carved to depict the animal spirit associated with them. Totems were most often used by the Ojibwe but had been found in European, African, and Australian cultures as well.

I discovered that while the Ojibwe had once dominated the Upper Midwest from northern Michigan through South Dakota, and could easily have left something like this in the area, though doubtfully on my bed, they did not carve totems out of turquoise. Turquoise was found somewhere else.

In the land of the Navajo—the Apache, the Zuni, and Pueblo, too, but considering I was dealing with a couple of Navajo skinwalkers, we'd just stick to Navajo carvings for the moment.

Navajo didn't carve totems but fetishes, ascribing mystical qualities to the inanimate objects. According to the light research I was able to do in ten minutes on the 'Net, a fetish gave the wearer increased powers. The carving was often kept in the medicine bundles of Navajo shamans and used in their ceremonies. A fetish made of turquoise was especially powerful, because the Navajo believed turquoise a sacred stone that increased communication between the wearer and the supernatural.

I rubbed the tiny coyote between my fingers. "In that case, I'll keep you close by."

When I left the motel, the sun had just crept past the long navy-blue line of the horizon, turning everything from violet to molten gold. I tucked the

fetish into the pocket of my jeans. Who knew why
Sawyer had left it, but I was certain I'd soon find out.
One thing I'd learned since becoming leader of the
light— everything happened for a reason. I might
not like the reason, but there was always a reason.

Since I'd taken care of the necessities by having
coffee in my room, I didn't bother to stop for
breakfast. All I wanted was to find the Old One and
do what needed to be done.

Less than an hour later I approached Inyan
Kara. I'd seen the mountain on the horizon within
minutes of leaving Upton behind. It wasn't hard
considering the land leading up to it was flat and
covered with low, patchy grass. Buildings rose here
and there—red, white, gray—and cattle dotted the
landscape like flies.

The mountain was surrounded by private land,
and as the clerk had indicated, I'd need permission
to climb it. I followed the arrow on a hand-painted
sign, knocked on the door of the house at the end of
a dry and dusty lane, then politely asked the elderly
woman who answered for her blessing.

She pursed her lips and eyed me from head to
foot. "You know the mountain is 'bout twelve square
miles?"

"Yes." I hadn't, but it didn't matter. I wasn't
going to examine every inch of it as she was
examining every inch of me. I just wanted to find
Sani.

She stepped onto the porch, her steel-gray braid

swaying across her thin back, then pointed toward the crest with a hand marred by age spots and raised blue veins. "Ridge is the shape of a horseshoe, with the peak in the middle. Real steep, that ridge. The peak's thousands of feet high, bare of grass and trees, slippery as all get-out. Big old canyon in between. You be careful."

"Yes, ma'am."

"Best be back before dark." She eyed my bare arms. "Gets cold on Inyan Kara when the sun goes down."

Since I did not plan to stay there after dark I had no problem agreeing.

"Whatcha want up there anyway?" she asked.

My mind went blank. For an instant I couldn't think if I should tell her the truth or a lie, then I couldn't recall what lies I'd told lately and to whom, which was the problem with lies. I decided to stick as close to the truth as I could.

"I heard there were black coyotes."

"You another one of them cryptozoologists? Had one here last week looking for a new species."

"Sure."

"Just so you know, none of them ever seen a black coyote." She went into the house and shut the door.

As I turned to leave, I murmured, "I will."

I drove as close to the mountain as I could get in the Impala then loaded a backpack with water, granola, crackers, and a jacket. I checked my cell phone, though I doubted I'd get much reception up there. Still, never leave sea level without it.

I found it a little strange that no one had called—not Jimmy, not Summer, not Megan or Luther. Then again, two out of three had their hands full with the baby from—

I paused. I'd been about to think *hell* but that was far too possible to joke about. At the back of my mind hovered the concern that Faith could be the daughter of the last leader of the darkness. For all I knew, she could become the next one. Or even something worse.

I headed up the sharp incline that composed one arm of the horseshoe ridge. The Norway pines provided welcome shade as the sun climbed ever higher. On several occasions a quick grab for a branch saved me from sliding, maybe even falling.

Reaching the top, I glanced into the gaping canyon then up to the peak. I really didn't want to climb that, but I'd do whatever I had to do to find the skinwalker.

If he was close by, if he even existed, he had to know I was here. I didn't sense anyone, or anything, following me, but that didn't mean they weren't.

"I'm supposed to be a sorcerer. So sorcer."

Too bad I didn't know how. I missed Sawyer for more reasons than one. He'd taught me a lot, but there'd been a lot still left to teach.

However, most of what I *had* learned about magic involved opening myself to the power within, focusing on what I wanted, and believing it could happen. Which wasn't as easy as it sounded.

I closed my eyes, stilled my mind, fixed the image of a coyote in the center—a black coyote—then…well the only way to describe it is that I reached, sending my desire into the world and trying to pull that desire back to me.

Nothing happened.

"Sometimes you need a spell. Eye of newt, sacrifice a goat." I shivered. Sometimes a goat wasn't a goat but a human. I'd seen both die for the sake of magic. I hadn't particularly cared for either option.

Since I was alone, with no goat and not a single eye of newt, I sat on a high, flat rock and drank half a bottle of water in a single gulp as I wondered what I should do. When I lowered my head, a black coyote stared at me from a few feet away.

Though I'd been hoping for just such an occurrence, the sight made me uneasy. I wasn't Navajo, not by blood, but I was a skinwalker by magic. I hadn't learned everything, but I had learned some things. Namely that the coyote is a bad omen as well as a symbol of black magic. Nevertheless, I needed his help.

"Sani?" I asked.

The coyote began to pant.

As the motel clerk had said, he was big. Maybe he *was* part wolf; more than likely he was merely part man.

"Can you shift? I don't have access to a

coyote..." I searched for a word to explain what I needed—a tattoo, a robe, something to spark the change. That I was even considering becoming a coyote showed how desperate I was. According to Sawyer, that just wasn't done.

The animal tilted his head so far to the right, he was nearly upside down. I sighed. When I was a wolf—or anything else—I could decipher plain English.

"Do you understand me?" His head bent in the other direction.

Either Sani couldn't or wouldn't shift, or this wasn't Sani.

If I were a coyote, we could "talk." In animal form talking was telepathy. But I'd have to become a coyote to do so. Tigers couldn't talk to wolves and birds couldn't talk to coyotes.

"Wait a second!" I got to my feet. The sudden exclamation and movement had the coyote skittering backward.

I tugged the fetish from my pocket, held it up to the shimmering, tree-shadowed sun. The coyote yipped and hurried forward.

"Think this will work?" I asked, but I knew it would. Why else did I have it?

If I was going to shift, I needed to lose the clothes. I narrowed my eyes at the coyote. "I don't suppose you'd consider turning around?" He lifted his lip and showed me his teeth. "That's what I thought."

In the past few months I'd become less shy about being naked, but I still wasn't wild about stripping in front of strangers. However, I needed to get past that and there was—

"No time like the present." I pulled my top over my head.

Less than a minute later, I stood naked in the dappled light. The coyote seemed far too interested in my breasts for a coyote.

Putting aside my unease, I curled my fingers around the coyote fetish, pressing the stone into my palm and waiting for the bright flash that preceded the change. The sun continued to flicker over my bare skin; the shadows made me shiver. I closed my eyes. Centering myself, emptying my mind, opening my heart, I reached for the change.

"That isn't going to work."

My eyes flew open. My gaze swept the tree line. Nothing there but the coyote. I spun around. Nothing behind me but the steep, forested ridge.

"Who's there?"

"Who do you think?"

The voice was deep and aged, with the odd cadence I associated with those who spoke English as their second language.

I turned back. The coyote remained the only living thing besides me within earshot.

Chapter 20

"I don't need to ask who sent you," he said.

A talking coyote. Terrific.

"No?" I couldn't seem to manage any more than that.

The coyote glanced behind me. "Where's Sawyer?"

"Ruthie Kane told me to come."

"Ruthie." His voice lowered to a caress. "How is she?"

"Dead."

The coyote yipped as if he'd been clipped in the butt with buckshot. "Impossible!"

"Not really."

"Someone with Ruthie's power never really dies."

"True that," I muttered. "She *is* dead, but she still..." I waved my hand. "Speaks."

"To you?"

"Not lately."

The coyote tilted his head again, studying me. Then his gaze dipped to my breasts. "You should put your clothes back on. It's been..." His head canted in the opposite direction, though his eyes stayed right where they were. "Decades since I saw a naked woman."

Crap. No wonder he'd been staring. Quickly I turned, earning a rumble of appreciation that I chose to ignore, and threw everything back on.

"You're Sani?" I faced the coyote again.

"Isn't that who you came here to see?"

"Question with a question, not really an answer."

"I am Sani." He dipped his head in a bow that would have been Old World, if he hadn't had a snout. "Now, where's Sawyer?"

"He's also a little...dead."

Sani blew air through his nose derisively. "Impossible."

"Do you know what impossible means?"

The coyote's eyes narrowed. "Skinwalkers do not die."

"Unless they choose to."

That shut him up. For a minute.

"Sawyer *chose* to die?"

I nodded, afraid my voice would break if I spoke.

"Must have been a woman." He eyed me again. Again, I remained silent. "How did you come to possess the fetish if Sawyer's dead?"

"Magic."

Sani snorted.

"You're a talking coyote and you don't believe

in magic? By the way, *why* are you a talking coyote?"

"Once, long ago, I trusted the wrong man."

"You and about a hundred thousand women a year."

He ignored me. "My home was stolen from me along with my human soul."

"How do you steal a human soul?"

"By stealing the icon where it rests when the human is in coyote form."

"This?" I held up the carved turquoise. "You're saying Sawyer stole your soul?"

"And my mountain."

"Mount Taylor?"

The coyote dipped his snout.

"Why?"

"Because he could."

I wanted to argue, but that *did* kind of sound like Sawyer.

"I've been told the Navajo don't trust the coyote."

Sani opened his mouth in a doggy grin. "What's your point?"

"Why would you become one?"

"Unlike Sawyer, some of us have little choice over what we become. I dreamed of the coyote when I was a boy. I embraced the form of my spirit animal and the magic it brought to me."

"Black magic," I said.

"We take what we are given."

"Oh, I'm sure you took it." And I knew exactly how. I couldn't throw stones. I'd murdered for my magic, too. "How did you end up on Inyan Kara?"

"I was banished from the Dinetah, from the Glittering World, from the home I loved and the mountain where I was born. I had to go somewhere, and this place called to me."

"I hear it's magic, too. For the Sioux."

"Magic is magic."

Not really, but I decided to let that pass.

"Weren't the Sioux annoyed?" They certainly hadn't taken kindly to the whites wandering all over these hills.

"A bit. But they had bigger problems than a trespassing Navajo. By the time they were free to deal with me, I was as much a part of the legend of Inyan Kara as they were."

"How many years have you been a coyote?"

"More years than I was ever a man."

"Ruthie said you couldn't leave Inyan Kara."

"Ruthie is often right." He tilted his nose into a bright beam of sunlight that reached through the trees, then huffed. "It doesn't matter." He shook his coat, giving the impression of a deep shiver. "Coyotes are skittish, and I've been one so long people make me nervous."

"What about me?"

His eyes, so dark a brown they nearly blended into his silky black fur, met mine. "We both know you aren't a person."

"What am I?"

"I would guess, since Ruthie has spoken to you, that you are the present leader of the light, and considering that tattoo on your neck, I'd say you are also a skinwalker."

As well as a dhampir, a vampire, a psychic, and a phoenix, but I figured he knew enough, so I shrugged. "How is it that you can talk?"

"Sawyer cast a spell, placed a curse."

"He made you a talking coyote? Why?"

"I was an outcast. I was never to fit in anywhere, with anyone or anything. I could not become human without my soul, but I wasn't a coyote, either. Not if I could talk."

Wow. Some curse.

"What did you do?" I asked.

"I trusted. I taught Sawyer all that I knew, and he used that knowledge against me."

There had to be more to it than that. But what if there wasn't? What if Sawyer had learned all he could from the Old One then taken his home and his soul and banished him to Inyan Kara just because he could? Sawyer had done a lot of things that were borderline. His right-and-wrong radar was not exactly spot-on. I blamed his mother.

On the other hand—

"Who did you kill?" I whispered.

Sani lifted his lip and showed me his teeth again. "We do not ask such things."

"Maybe *you* don't."

"Ask what you like. I will not answer."

I decided it didn't matter what Sani had done or even who he'd killed. I still had to do what I'd come here to do—raise Sawyer, get answers to my questions, then deal with the results. I could worry about the truth later. Or not at all.

"I told him one day he'd need my help," Sani continued. "And the only way he'd get it would be to give me back myself."

I held up the fetish again. "This is payment."

"Now you need only tell me for what."

"I want you to raise Sawyer's ghost."

"You can raise him yourself. All you must do is kill someone you love."

"Already did."

His eyes became shrewd. "Ruthie or Sawyer?" Before I could point out that *we didn't ask such things,* my mouth got the better of me and I snapped, "I'd never hurt Ruthie."

The coyote's mouth opened, a grin of sorts. "I'm beginning to like you for something other than your very nice breasts. Tell me more."

"No." One thing I would not discuss was Sawyer and how I'd killed him.

Sani emitted a disappointed sigh. "If you sacrificed someone you love, you're a sorcerer and a shape-shifter, a true skinwalker. You can raise a ghost."

"I tried. Couldn't do it."

"Odd."

"I've never raised anyone by myself before. I thought you could watch. Tell me if I'm doing something wrong."

Sani cast me a quick glance. "You know that sometimes a boost of power is needed."

"Yes."

"You're willing to do whatever's necessary to speak with him?"

I didn't hesitate. "Yes."

"You do love him."

"If I didn't I wouldn't be what I am."

"All right." The coyote headed for the trees. "Come along."

We climbed to the top of Inyan Kara. I was tempted several times to shift into a phoenix and meet him there, but it hardly seemed fair to let the old man-coyote clamber up alone.

At the apex lay a plateau. Rocky here, with dry brittle grass there, the only thing beautiful about the place was the view.

Devil's Tower and Bear Butte loomed nearby, and the plains seemed to stretch on forever— brilliant green and dusty gold giving way to neon blue dotted with white. I was mesmerized.

"Do you have something that belonged to him?" Sani asked.

"Damn."

"I thought you'd done this before."

"I have." Last time I'd used Sawyer's toothbrush. When the spell didn't work, I think I might have tossed it into the desert.

"Didn't he ever give you anything, girl? Or was your love completely one-sided?"

More than likely it had been. Sawyer didn't love. Not anymore. But he had given me something.

I lifted the turquoise from my neck. Then I laid the stone on the ground and drew a circle around it. Sani nodded his approval. "You never know where the dead have been, what they've done, who they've seen, or what they might have been offered."

The circle would contain them. We couldn't raise ghosts and let them wander through the earth like Jacob Marley.

"Now bring the storm," Sani ordered.

"What if I need help? What if I don't have enough power to do this alone?"

"I'll help." Desire flickered in his eyes.

I clenched my hands and forced myself not to run. Sex boosted my power, and if I needed more juice, Sani was eager enough. I didn't like it, but I'd asked for it, and I couldn't complain. I'd known that there'd come a day I'd have to do someone I did not want to do. Apparently that day was today.

Power surged through me along with frustration. I hated being forced to do anything. Fury sparked, and I went with it, throwing my hand toward the sky. The single bright white cloud opened and poured down rain. As the rain fell, the cloud turned from white, to gray, to black.

"Use both hands," Sani said.

I shot the other up to match the first, and the wind whirled in, kicking around dust and dry grass, tugging clouds over the distant horizon and drawing them toward us at high speed. The sun became shadowed, and the mountain beneath our feet stirred.

"Thunder!" the Old One cried, and the earth shook.

I was soaked to the skin, my hair plastered to my head; Sani's fur dripped. Within the circle, mud welled over my turquoise necklace, bubbling as if the rain were hot as lava.

Sani curled around my legs, rubbing his wet, musty coat against my pants; his muzzle nuzzled my thighs. I fought a shudder of disgust.

"Now the lightning," he whispered, his breath so hot against my crotch I thought steam might rise from my wet jeans.

I reached for the lightning, felt it crackle then fade.

"Again," Sani shouted.

I closed my eyes, imagined the bolts tearing from the sky, slamming into the ground; the fire would blaze and then die, the smoke would create a curtain, and when it disappeared Sawyer would be here.

I inched my fingers higher, reaching with all the power I had for a single, solitary flare.

Zzztt!

The smell of spent fireworks fell with the rain

but no lightning came. I lowered my arms, opened my eyes, and admitted the truth. "I can't."

Sani growled and sank his teeth into my hand.

Pain erupted, so deep I fell to my knees. "What. The. Fuck?"

The coyote's snout appeared in front of me, and he breathed in deeply, as if trying to catch a whiff of my pain. Then he licked my wet face and cocked his head. "No tears?"

"I never...cry," I managed. Except when Sawyer died. Fat lot of good that crying had done me. I'd learned long ago that tears were a sign of weakness, and the weak did not survive.

My uninjured hand crept toward the silver knife at my belt. Sani latched on to it before my fingers got anywhere near.

The wounds would heal quickly. But they still hurt enough to make me gasp, even when he released me.

"My power, little girl, lies in pain." His breath cascaded over my face; I caught the scent of my own blood and my demon howled. "You want to bring that lightning, give me some agony."

I gritted my teeth. "No."

"You said you'd do whatever was necessary."

"I thought you meant sex."

He laughed. "You'd rather have sex than cry?"

"Who wouldn't?"

His laughter died. "I'm not Sawyer."

Sawyer got a power boost from sex—like me.

That had seemed kind of sick. Until I met this guy.

His power lay in pain, which might be the reason, or at least one of them, that Sawyer had banished him. The old coyote was lucky Sawyer hadn't killed him. Of course, if he had, I'd be shit out of luck right now. How many true skinwalkers were trolling this earth? I didn't think very many.

"Fine." I screamed as if the pain in my hands wasn't fading by the second.

"Very good," he whispered, his voice breathless. He was enjoying this far too much. "Now try for that lightning again."

I stretched for the sky with one hand; Sani chewed on the other. I shrieked, and the lightning burst from the still-streaming clouds, slamming into the ground so close to us my scalp tingled.

The mountain trembled. Ozone sizzled. Smoke billowed from the black mark in the earth, and when it cleared—

The turquoise lay alone in the circle.

Chapter 21

Sani released my hand, and before I could stop myself I twitched my wrist. The coyote flew several feet and smacked into a tree.

"Whoops," I said.

He got to his feet and shook his head, stumbling sideways a bit. "Don't do that again."

"I thought you liked pain."

"Not my own."

The rain stopped; the clouds blew away on a heated wind. The thunder moved off to the east with the remnants of the lightning.

"Where the hell's Sawyer?"

The coyote crossed to the turquoise, albeit a little unsteadily. "That should have worked."

"It didn't."

He lifted his head. "You're sure he's dead?"

"Yes." And no.

"You don't sound sure. What happened?"

"He disappeared."

"Into thin air?"

"Maybe." I hadn't actually seen him go poof.

Sani cursed, using words I didn't know. "He's alive."

My heart leaped at the words, even though I knew they weren't true. "He can't be."

"Why not?"

I clapped my hands and thunder answered, flicked my hand and a nearby tree toppled over with a resounding crack. "*That's* why not."

"You gained your magic through his death. If he weren't truly dead, you wouldn't have it."

He sounded relieved. I wondered what Sani had done to Sawyer while he'd been teaching him. If that, as well as Sani's command of black magic, was why Sawyer had cursed him.

"If he were in the afterworld," Sani continued, "the land to the north and beneath the earth, he would be compelled to stand in the circle and answer the questions of the one who raised him."

"But he wasn't, so what does that mean?"

The coyote collapsed onto the ground with a huff then laid his chin on his paws. I scooped up the turquoise and flipped the chain over my head.

Sani raised his snout. "Have you dreamed of him?"

I started.

"You have!"

"I loved him. I killed him. You think I wouldn't dream of him?"

"What kind of dreams?" I looked away, but not before Sani saw the truth. "Sex dreams."

"It's Sawyer."

"*That's* how he's doing it." The coyote was on his feet, hair bristling.

"Doing what?"

"Skinwalkers possess an affinity for ghosts. Some say they have sex with the dead."

I'd heard that before. I hadn't liked it any better then.

"What do *you* say?" I asked.

"That at least one skinwalker has been having sex with the dead."

My stomach rolled. He meant me.

"Sawyer's power lies in sex," he said. "To enhance his magic in the past, I'd guess you've *helped* him."

Since that went without saying, I didn't say.

"He's enhanced that magic now by invading your dreams."

"He's *dead.* How can he enhance anything?"

"How many times has he come to you?"

"Three." That I remembered.

"Has he become more real each time?"

I thought of the first visit, when I hadn't seen him at all, only felt him, then last night when he'd been *there* enough to leave me a turquoise coyote.

"Yes."

"Have you begun to see him even when you aren't dreaming?"

To begin with, I'd only sensed him, then I could have sworn his fur brushed my legs. Later I'd touched him and then I'd caught a glimpse of him standing on my bed, caressed the warmth left behind by a body that could not be there.

"Yes," I said.

"He's between worlds."

"I don't know what that means."

"Only the most powerful of sorcerers could manage this much, and then only because the two of you have a connection that stretches the boundaries of earth and beyond. But he's going to need more assistance to take that final step."

"Assistance," I repeated. "As in more dream sex?"

"Can't hurt."

Except it did. Every time I dreamed of touching Sawyer in the night, then woke up alone in the morning, it hurt. A lot.

"If I do that" —or him— "eventually I'll bring Sawyer forth?"

"You're going to need help."

"That's why I'm here."

"More than I can give."

"But—"

"Sawyer's stuck between worlds," he repeated. "If he could come to you he would have." Sani gestured at the fading circle in the dirt.

"Who *can* help?"

The coyote's mouth lolled open. "First, payment must be made."

"What kind?" In my world, payment was seldom in currency I wanted to give.

"Sawyer left you that fetish for a reason, child."

"Oh! Right." I reached into my pocket and

pulled out the turquoise coyote. I let the icon rest in my palm and extended my hand, fighting not to flinch when Sani trotted closer.

But he merely snuffled the stone into his mouth, leaving a slash of snot behind. I was such a mess already it hardly mattered. A second later, the sky filled with silver light, and a man stood before me.

Perhaps eighteen or twenty, with inky, dark hair long enough to brush the curve of his naked backside. His skin was bronze all over, his muscles long and lean from centuries of running through the trees on four paws. His face was unlined, stark bones beneath wide cheeks, his eyes as black as his hair.

"Why do they call you Old One?" I asked.

"Because I am. Skinwalkers don't age."

"Sawyer was a child once." Or so he'd said. I wasn't quite sure I believed him.

"But he's been a young man for centuries. Though we're born like humans, we grow like magic. It is in our blood."

I thought of Faith, and I knew he was right. "And then?"

"We stop aging when the magic becomes ours."

So murder made us more than sorcerers. Murder made us forever young, too. I could see where some might consider this a pretty good trade. Some but not me. Unfortunately I hadn't had any choice in the matter.

"Are you going to leave the mountain now?" I asked, concerned that I'd just unleashed a very bad guy into the world, although, again, I hadn't had much choice.

Sani stared at the turquoise wolf between his fingers, then smiled and lifted his face to the sun. He yipped, just like a coyote, and moments later a gray female appeared in the shadow of the trees. Her doey brown gaze focused on Sani, but she didn't appear afraid.

He crossed to a large flat rock, dug a hole, laid the turquoise within and then covered it up. Passing his hand over the obviously disturbed dirt, he muttered a few words in Navajo, and the earth smoothed out as grass sprouted like springtime. There was so much I didn't know about what I was.

"No," Sani said.

It took me a second to remember what I'd asked. "You're staying?"

He glanced at the coyote in the trees, and his face softened. "For now."

Left unspoken were the words, *As long as she lives.* I swallowed against a sudden thickness in my throat. Love hurt.

Leaning forward, Sani placed his hand against the new grass. His outline shimmered and in a flash, he was a coyote again. His mate bounded out of the trees, jumping onto his back and then rolling onto hers, presenting her belly in perfect beta submission. She'd obviously never cared that he was different, that he wasn't completely a coyote. True love never did.

They began to run off.

"Hey!" I whistled.

Sani stopped then nuzzled his mate, who disappeared into the trees, before trotting back.

"Forget anything?"

He tilted his head.

I pointed at the rock where the fetish lay buried. "I paid, you talk."

For an instant I feared that giving Sani the icon had taken away his voice. But I guess once a talking coyote, always a talking coyote, because he spoke. "There is someone you must see, but it won't be easy."

"Wow. Not easy," I deadpanned. "That's new."

He ignored me. I guess age does grant wisdom.

"If you still want to bring Sawyer forth, only this man possesses the knowledge of how."

"Who is he, and where can I find him?"

"You'll find Mait in an old church near New Orleans."

New Orleans. The perfect place for someone who could raise a ghost.

"How near New Orleans?"

"Honey Island Swamp. Look for the crossroads."

"Can you be more specific?"

"No. But I doubt there are very many abandoned churches in the swamp at a crossroads."

"There better not be. This guy is a bokor?"

"He came from Haiti ages ago, but he's not a voodoo priest. He's more of a magical bodyguard, named after Mait-Carrefour—the god of magicians. He's a bringer of bad luck and the ruler of night demons."

"What is he?" I spread my hands. "A voodoo spirit? A god?"

"I'm not sure. He protects things. He makes magic. I've heard he's a necromancer as well."

I spread my hands wider.

"A witch who can raise the dead, usually for purposes of divination. Sometimes with the entrails of the dearly departed."

I couldn't wait to meet this guy.

"How does he do all this?" I asked.

"He uses a book of prophecy and magic."

I stilled. "What kind of book?"

"Grimoire."

The *Key of Solomon.*

Had something actually come easily?

"In it are spells that reveal mysteries beyond the understanding of humans, along with hints of how to win the coming war between good and evil. They say it was dictated by a demon to his offspring here on earth. Mait keeps it near him at all times, and protects those secrets with his life."

A chill wind seemed to sweep across the mountain, though not a single gust stirred the trees.

Not the *Key of Solomon.* The *Book of Samyaza.*

"How do you know about this?" I asked.

"I am not completely cut off from the world."

"Yet you didn't know that Ruthie or Sawyer was dead."

"I haven't exactly been in contact with those on the side of the light."

"Still, I'd think the forces of doom would be thrilled to inform you that we'd lost both our leader and a powerful ally."

Sani huffed breath through his nose. "I did know you'd lost your leader. When I was banished, however, Ruthie was but an underling."

Ruthie an underling? I couldn't imagine it.

I opened my mouth to ask about her past, about the previous leader of the light. Sani spoke instead. "And I have my doubts that Sawyer is dead, as well as whose side he's actually on."

I had doubts about that, too.

"Mait is protecting the grimoire," Sani continued. "He has killed everyone who has tried to take it from him."

"You think it's a good idea for me to visit a guy who keeps Satan's handbook on his nightstand?"

"I think that if you want to talk to Sawyer, you'll have to. Besides—" Sani's coyote shoulders rippled in a canine shrug. "—he can't kill *you*."

Even if he could, it didn't matter. I had to get my hands on that book—and not just to raise Sawyer. According to legend, whoever carried the *Book of Samyaza* was invincible.

Which made me wonder why—if they had it—

the Nephilim weren't already marching across the earth, laying waste to cities, and munching on the citizenry like a never-ending human buffet. I guess I'd just have to find out.

Sure, I was nervous. Not only was I going to meet with a half demon who'd been assigned by other half demons—or maybe a whole demon, who knew?—to protect what amounted to the Holy Grail of the Apocalypse, but I was being sent there by someone I trusted about as much as I'd once trusted Sawyer.

Sawyer had walked the line between good and evil, but Sani? I thought he lived over there in the dark. Why else would Sawyer have banished him?

Regardless of whether Sani was on our side or theirs, if the *Book of Samyaza* was in New Orleans and if it actually contained a spell to bring forth Sawyer's ghost, I'd go there and I'd take it. Someone had to.

In the distance, Sani's mate called. Sani fidgeted, looking in that direction, then back at me, then into the trees again. I needed to ask my questions before he gave in to the call of the wild.

"You're telling me there's a spell in the book that will raise a ghost?"

"No."

"Dammit, Sani! You just said—"

"The time for raising ghosts is past, at least with Sawyer."

"Past?" My voice came out faint, like a lost little

girl in the night.

"Sawyer has climbed out of the afterworld with your help. Now you must raise him completely or let him wander forever between here and there. Your choice."

"Raise him completely," I repeated. "As in…" My voice trailed off. I was more lost than ever.

"The spell in the *Book of Samyaza* doesn't raise ghosts," Sani said. "The spell raises the dead back to life."

Chapter 22

Silence settled over the mountain, broken only by the distant but insistent call of Sani's mate.

"You wanna run that by me again?" I asked.

"If Sawyer was a ghost, he'd have come when you called, told you what he hadn't, shown you what you needed to know, done whatever it was he had to do so that he could rest in peace. But he's more than a ghost, just as he was more than a man."

"This spell would make him a zombie? A vampire?"

The coyote shook his head.

"Revenant?" The human-like zombies my mother had raised. "Ghoul?" Raised by a witch or a demon to do an evil deed.

"You aren't listening. Sawyer would be alive again. Human." The coyote cocked his head. "Or as human as he gets."

"That's not—" I paused, unable to go on.

"Possible?"

"Good," I finished. "That's not good."

"Isn't getting Sawyer back what you wanted?"

In my land of impossible dreams, sure. But I'd also known it wouldn't happen. The most I'd hoped for was one more conversation. I'd ask Sawyer about Faith, his death, the *Key of Solomon,* his magic, he'd tell me everything, then he'd realize he was dead and go into the light, or the dark as the case may be. But to have him come back to life—

"I don't know if it's such a good idea to raise the dead."

As far as I knew, only those with more than a passing acquaintance with evil dragged people out of their graves.

"Good idea or not, you're going to need him." Sani disappeared into the trees.

I returned the way I'd come, descending first the mountain, then the ridge, then driving past the owner's house to let her know I hadn't fallen in a gorge and broken my neck. I toyed with the idea of staying at the same motel I'd slept in last night and starting fresh in the morning, but I had a good long stretch of daylight left so I headed for the nearest large airport, which was in Cheyenne.

I'd have to leave Summer's car in long-term parking and probably pay a fortune to fly to New Orleans and rent another car, but I really couldn't spare the time to drive the length of the Mississippi— as much fun as that might be.

My hands weren't steady; I solved that by clenching them so tightly on the wheel, they ached. Then I breathed in and out until the racing of my heart matched that purposeful cadence.

There was a spell to make the dead come to life.

I wasn't sure what to think about that.

My initial reaction—that it wasn't a good idea—was probably correct. However, Sani had said I'd need Sawyer, and I'd learned over the past few months that when a sorcerer predicted something, he or she was usually right.

I spent the four-plus-hour drive checking in by cell phone. As usual Megan made use of her caller ID to avoid one of her pet peeves, the word *hello.*

"Where are you? What are you doing? How's the baby?"

"Wyoming. Driving and I don't have a clue." Silence came over the line as she no doubt decided which answer to comment on first.

"Where's Faith?"

"With Jimmy, Summer, and Luther."

"And why don't you know how she is?"

"Because I was stupid enough to call you first."

"Liz," she said, exasperated. "Moms check on their children before anyone else."

"I'm not her mom," I said sharply, my stomach jittering and my chest tightening. I'd never had one of my own, had no idea how to be one to anyone else. Faith deserved better.

"Just because you didn't give birth to her doesn't mean you can't be a great mother. What about Ruthie?"

"I'm not Ruthie." Something I continued to prove with annoying regularity.

"The kid's going to need at least one parent. You

promised to take care of her, which means you're it."

"What if her real mom shows up?" And turns out to be a bone-marrow-sucking troll.

"You'll deal with that when and if it happens."

"I guess so." Note to self—look up how to kill bone-marrow-sucking trolls.

Silence descended for several seconds, then Megan said softly, "I saw the way you looked at her. The way you held her."

"Like I was going to drop her?"

An exasperated sigh whispered across the miles. "You know that bitchy, ass-kicking, demon-killing loner thing doesn't fly with me, don't you?"

I didn't answer. Because, yeah, I knew.

"The baby was getting to you," Megan continued. "You were falling for her. Just like you fell for Luther."

The fear at the back of my throat tasted like ashes. Which is what Faith and Luther would be if the Nephilim found out that I cared.

"You're wrong."

"Sure I am."

"So. Everything okay by you?" I asked.

"Dandy. Business is good. *My* kids are fine."

"How's Quinn?"

"The bartender?"

Among other things.

"Yeah, him," I said.

"He comes to work on time. Drops a lot, but he always pays for it."

Would Megan ever see any other man but Max? Should she? I didn't know the answer to those questions any more than I knew the answer to a lot of others.

"Why are you in Wyoming?" Megan asked.

Not only was the reason too complicated to explain, but the less Megan knew about what I did and where I went the better.

"Never mind," she said when I hesitated. "Just be careful."

"Always am."

"No, you're not." She hung up.

My next call was to Luther. He answered on the second ring. "Where are you?"

Faith cooed in the background. I could almost see her smiling. My chest tightened. Love or a heart attack? They probably felt the same.

"Where are you?" I countered.

"Summer's place."

"Faith okay?"

"You wanna talk to her?"

"No, that's—" I began, but he had already put the phone by her ear.

"It's Liz," Luther said. "Can you say Liz?"

"Ga!" Faith blasted in my eardrum.

"Ouch!"

"Ouch!" she screamed.

"Shh."

"Shh! Shh! Shhh!"

Hearing her voice made my chest loosen a little

yet, oddly enough, hurt even more.

Luther came back on the line. "She repeats everything."

"You don't say?" I switched the phone from one ear to the other. "She's advancing pretty quickly." And now that I'd talked to Sani I knew why. Magic in the blood. Poor kid.

"It's lucky we're living out near the rez where there aren't too many people, not to mention the sparkly dust Summer uses to make us fade into the landscape. If anyone human saw Faith one day and then a few days later..." He trailed off.

"I think homeschooling is in her future."

"If the world doesn't end first. How we doin' on that, by the way?"

"Better and better. I have a lead on the *Book of Samyaza.*"

"Shut up!"

"Shut up!" Faith echoed with the exact same inflection.

"Whoops," Luther said. "You want me to get Sanducci?"

"He's still there?"

"Yeah. Though he's getting twitchy. He's gonna have to kill something soon just for the hell of it."

"Summer?"

"I don't think he should kill her."

"I do."

"He doesn't let her out of his sight," Luther muttered.

"Good." She couldn't be trusted. So why did the news that Jimmy was keeping both eyes on her annoy the crap out of me?

"You want to tell him about the *Book of Samyaza*?" Luther asked.

"No. And don't you tell him, either."

"Why not?"

"I'm not sure it's true. I'll check it out and get back to you. Until then, keep your lip zipped. I don't need any help. You hear me?"

"I don't know how I could avoid hearing you when you're shouting in my ear."

"Do *not* tell Sanducci about the book or even that I called. Do *not* tell him where I'm going."

"I don't know where you're going."

"Thatta boy," I said, and ended the call.

Sanducci would be on board with getting the book. What he would not be on board with was the possibility of raising Sawyer back to life. Since I might have to do just that, I'd leave Sanducci out of it.

I had a short jump to Minneapolis, where I picked up a direct flight. Once I'd strapped myself into my window seat and nodded to my neighbors, who'd brought books and appeared ready to use them, I checked out for most of the trip. I had a doozy of a dream.

I'm in a city I don't recognize—though I know it's America and I'm not sure why—wandering among empty buildings. The only light comes from the moon, which is big and bright and full. The street is broken and torn, with large chunks of pavement and cobblestones tossed into piles, as if there's been an earthquake, or perhaps a monster sprung from the deep.

The buildings are made of stone, too, and they appear ancient, which narrows things down. There aren't a whole lot of ancient cities in America—and the ones there are—those built into the hills by the Anasazi, or the Pueblo's Mesa Verde, even Santa Fe—do not look like this. The architecture reminds me of photos I've seen of Savannah or St. Augustine; although I've never been to either of them, I can't believe they've ever been this deserted. If the Nephilim have their way, however, every city might become quite similar in the future.

The night is cool, but not cold, so either summer anywhere, or anytime in the South. I wear what I always wear—jeans and a knife, tank top and a gun, tennis shoes and silver bullets. Strangely, I'm not hiding. Instead I walk right down the center of the street, letting the keen silver light of the moon flow over me like gilded rain.

"You wanted me," I shout. "Here I am."

No one answers. I turn in a slow, wary circle, gaze touching on each building, the windows, the roof, the doors. Who, or what, am I searching for?

"Let her go!"

Laughter slithers through the air like a slug, leaving a damp and oily trail behind. Gooseflesh rises on my arms, and I shift my shoulders as the invisible bull's-eye pulses between them.

The rasp of my knife leaving the sheath thunders through the eerie silence. "We had a deal."

The laughter comes again, bringing to mind a cartoon red devil with a spiky black goatee and curling horns.

"Me for her," I say, though my voice is weaker. I'm starting to see what I've known all along—deals with the devil aren't deals at all.

A door creaks open a few yards ahead of me. A shadow moves inside. A thin white hand slides through the opening and beckons.

I swallow, my throat clicking with a cold, murky fear that nearly chokes me, and go in.

Jimmy hangs on the wall.

The laughter swirls through the room like a midwinter wind, but no one is here but us.

I want to run to him. I want to run away. Instead I stand there, just inside the doorway, and stare. They've crucified him.

Turning, I stumble outside and throw up. When there isn't anything left inside me but fury, I tighten my hand on my knife and return.

I stride across the room, my teeth clenched, and try to take the nails out of his feet. They're gold, of course, otherwise they wouldn't hold him at all.

He moans, opens his eyes, and, seeing me, curses. "Get out," he manages. "Take her and run."

"In hell," I say, and use my knife to yank out the

first nail.

Jimmy draws in a sharp breath. "Baby, where do you think we are?"

"Not hell. Not yet." Though you wouldn't know it by looking around. "Where's the kid?"

"I don't know."

Fear flickers. "She all right?"

"I think so. Saw her when I got here. Heard her crying since." He gentles his voice at my flinch. "They wouldn't hurt her. Permanently. But I don't think they ever plan to let her go. They need her dead almost as much as they need—"

"Me dead," I finish.

"You shouldn't be here. If they kill you, Doomsday's back. Is that what you want?"

"Of course not."

"Then why did you come?"

"For Faith. But I'll take you, too."

"Idiot."

"You're welcome," I say, and yank out another nail.

Jimmy's mouth tightens, and his face pales. But he doesn't pass out. It would take a lot more than this to kill a dhampir. "I had it covered, Lizzy. Me for her. That was the agreement."

I lift my gaze. "Same one I made."

"Double-dealing assholes," he says without heat.

I have his feet free and reach up to work on his right hand, sliding in the blood on the floor. My stomach lurches. The scent is nauseating.

Odd. Lately, the scent of blood has been anything but. I realize that my collar is gone.

I jerked in my sleep, bumped my head against the side of the plane, my elbow against the arm of my chair, and the image shimmied, almost fading. What did the absence of that collar mean?

Was this only a dream, not a prediction of the future? Because in any true future, if I wasn't wearing that collar I'd be licking Jimmy's blood not only from his wounds but the wall.

Was it a vision of loss or the hope for a future without a demon inside me? I had no idea, so I fought my way back into my head.

"You can't save me," Jimmy says.

"Of course I can. Saving people is what I do."

"You won't be able to save us both. You'll have to choose."

I hate choosing who lives and who dies. But the Nephilim seem to get their jollies out of making me do just that.

"I'm the most powerful being on this earth," I whisper.

Jimmy's eyes meet mine, and in them I recognize good-bye. "Won't be enough this time. You'd need two beings just like you if you wanted any kind of chance at all."

Two beings like me. Two.

I stifle a sob as I realize that the only way out of this is Sawyer, and Sawyer is dead.

Chapter 23

I came awake with a start, gasping, trembling.

"You okay?" A flight attendant leaned over me, the concern in her voice belied by the watchfulness in her eyes. If I so much as blinked funny, she was going to signal the nearest air marshal.

The woman next to me and the man next to her were leaning as far away from me as they could get with their seat belts on. Everyone else in the vicinity was staring.

"Fine." I wiped my face. My hand came away drenched with sweat. A bead ran down my cheek. The air from the vent couldn't stir my hair because every strand was plastered to my head.

"We're on our descent," the flight attendant said. "I'll get you a cup of water, but you'll have to hurry."

I nodded and glanced out the window. Lights reflected off pools of black water—swamps with gators, Lake Pontchartrain—and in the distance ships cruised down the winding Mississippi, which spilled into the sea. New Orleans was surrounded on three sides by water, which was both beautiful and foolish.

"I don't much care for flying, either," the woman to my right murmured, her voice so full of the South I could see Spanish moss on the trees and smell the magnolias in bloom. She patted my hand, withdrawing with a mew of distaste when her fingers slid on my slick skin.

"Sorry," I said.

She gave me a tight smile and went back to her book.

We landed at Louis Armstrong International Airport, and I retrieved my bag then rented a Jetta. I figured I might as well drive something I was familiar with, and I doubted they had any vintage Impalas.

The instant I walked out of the terminal New Orleans hit me in the face. August in the Crescent City, not the best idea in the world.

The humidity swirled around my head, clogging my nose and throat, making my limbs lethargic and my eyelids heavy. I practically dived into the car and cranked the air-conditioning to ice.

Though the sun was still up, it was falling steadily toward night. I checked into a hotel in the French Quarter. Certainly I could have stayed near the airport, but why? I was in New Orleans.

The last time I'd been here, I'd attended a bartenders' seminar. After spending the mornings inside a banquet room, we'd spent the both the afternoons and the evenings on the town. I had fond memories of New Orleans. Memories I hoped didn't tarnish too badly on this journey through.

I had no trouble getting a room in a tall, narrow hotel several streets from Bourbon. At this time of year, I could have gotten a room with a balcony that opened onto the legendary street itself, but I wanted to be far from the lights and the music.

I did have a balcony, but it gave me a view of a less traveled side street, just what I'd asked for. I wanted as few eyes as possible—preferably no eyes at all—to witness what I had planned for when the sun went down.

After a long, tepid shower and a change of clothes, I hustled to Bourbon Street and found a bar—ha, I couldn't *not* find a bar—that was showing a baseball game on a mammoth plasma TV, then I ordered a Sazerac—a traditional New Orleans cocktail with rye whiskey—and fried alligator, followed by a muffuletta. If I were still alive in the morning, I'd walk down to the river and buy beignets with strong, black chicory coffee.

What was it about this town that made me so hungry? Probably the food.

I strolled back to my hotel as the sun gave its last gasp. A few times I could have sworn I felt someone following me. Even though the tourist trade was nearly nonexistent at this time of year, there were still plenty of people on Bourbon Street, so people *were* following me. They couldn't help it. I was in front of them.

I ducked into a T-shirt shop, chose a few new

shirts since I'd had to toss so many lately, and kept my eyes open for suspicious characters. An exercise in futility. Everyone seemed suspicious around here.

Like the guy dressed as a jester playing a saxophone on one corner, or the girl who appeared pale enough to be empress of the undead selling ice cream from a cart across the street. Several soon-to-be senior citizens in full black leather chaps and vests strolled into a strip club. A drag queen in a sundress, black chest hair curling over the yellow bodice, strutted down the sidewalk walking a cat on a leash. The cat wore a Mardi Gras mask that matched the guy's dress. God, I loved this place.

It took me a while to find a shirt that wasn't pornographic. I could have walked over to the French Market and found something more appropriate, but now that the sun was down, I didn't have the time.

I ignored everything with variations of drink, drank, or drunk, boobs, party—you get the drift—and made do with three different colors of I FLEUR-DE-LIS NOLA. I also couldn't resist a tiny pink T-shirt that read: MARDI GRAS PRINCESS. I stuffed that one deep in the bottom of the bag.

As I walked out a young girl walked in. Her T-shirt proclaimed: THROW ME BEADS IF YOU WANT A LOOK AT THESE! I could barely read the words past all the multicolored coils around her neck—and it wasn't even Mardi Gras.

I headed away from the lights and the music, down a quieter side road. It wasn't long before footsteps echoed mine. When I glanced over my shoulder, however, I was alone.

As I continued, so did the footsteps. Closer and closer they came. My knife rested inside the fanny pack around my waist. Un-cool yes, but I couldn't exactly wear a knife on my belt on Bourbon Street. *Better loser-ish than dead*—that was my motto.

I walked a little faster, trying to give myself time to slide open the zipper and slip a hand within. My fingers closed around the hilt and I spun, grabbing the person behind me by the neck and slamming them against the nearest wall.

It was the Goth girl who'd been selling ice cream and the instant I touched her, I knew she was human. She'd been thinking about school. She was a student at Tulane. The vamp costume was just for show, for the tourists, to make a buck and pay her bills.

"Sorry." I let her go immediately, allowing the knife to drop out of sight within the pack. "You— uh—" I ran my hand through my hair, embarrassed.

"I scared you," she said. "Don't worry about it."

I knew better than anyone that if they looked like a vamp, they weren't. A little girl skipping rope in the sunshine was more likely to be hiding fangs than this one.

She rubbed her throat, eyes dark in her overly powdered face. "Can't be too careful around here."

"Something strange happen lately?"

She rolled her eyes. "It's New Orleans."

"Right." Something strange happened every day. "Sorry," I repeated.

"Forget it." She ducked into a courtyard. The gate clanged shut, then it locked behind her, and I was alone once more.

In my room, I turned off the A/C and opened the terrace doors. A breeze had risen along with a thick curved band of a moon and both spilled into my room, one languid and hot, the other cool, liquid silver. I lost my clothes, touched my neck, and changed.

Bright light, cold and heat, my body contorted, becoming something else. I experienced both the pain of the change and the pleasure at bursting forth. In an instant, I could fly.

I doubted anyone would notice a huge, multicolored bird banking over Bourbon Street. They had better things to discover on the ground. Even if they happened to glance up and see me, they'd blame the bourbon.

I sailed out of New Orleans, easily following the scent of brackish water, cypress and rot. The Honey Island Swamp is over seventy thousand acres huge, with more than half of that a government-protected wildlife refuge. There was no way I could check the place for an abandoned church at a crossroads on foot.

Even with wings it took me most of the night,

flying back and forth from one corner to the next in a tight grid pattern so as not to miss anything. Broken-down buildings abounded—not just in the swamp but everywhere across New Orleans—and upon landing I discovered that a lot of them were still occupied, and none of them was a church.

I was near to giving up, the sun just beginning to lighten the eastern horizon, turning the blue-black night a hazy purple, when I caught sight of a listing belfry and dived like the phoenix I was into the trees.

The instant I came within ten yards of the place, a screeching began, so loud and horrific I became disoriented and flew into the dripping Spanish moss of a cypress tree. Similar to a spider's web, but damp and musty, the tendrils clung to my brightly colored wings like a net.

Trapped, panicked fire shot from my beak, and the moss dissolved into nothing. But I wasn't safe yet. The screaming continued as dark, prehistorically huge bat-like creatures sailed out of the belfry. They were large enough to be pterodactyls, if pterodactyls weren't extinct. Of course *extinct* was just a word these days.

My breath was a flame, rolling over their darkly ethereal bodies, making them appear like Halloween decorations studded with tiny orange lights. Then the fire went out with a puff, and they kept coming.

I braced for impact, and one flew right through

me. I'd have thought it was a ghost-bird, except I felt its talons scrape my bowels, its beak peck at my liver. The pain was like being torn apart from the inside out. Two skimmed either side of me and wherever they touched, agony flared, as though their feathers were tipped with razor blades.

Tumbling toward the earth, I picked up speed as I fell, and the horrible winged creatures followed, shrieking so that my eardrums seemed to rupture and bleed. I hit the ground with a solid thump, and at last blessed silence was mine.

I awoke as a woman, the sun blaring into my eyes. I moaned, laying my arm across my face. I hurt all over.

"What the fuck was that?" I muttered.

"Night demons."

I sat up in a hurry, wincing as my head spun. I put my palm to my forehead to keep it from falling off.

A man leaned in the crumbling doorway of the church. Tall and muscular, his chest was bare, his sienna skin shining in the sun. At first I thought his ebony hair had been cropped brutally close to his scalp, but when he moved, straightening away from the doorjamb, the skin between the teenie-tiny braids that had been woven into his hair flashed. There appeared to be a design to their swirl, but from where I sat, I couldn't tell what it was.

The church did stand at a crossroads, but not the kind I'd been looking for. To me cross *roads* meant a street of some kind—paved or at least covered in gravel. In this case the "road" was a waterway in two directions, with the church perched on a small plot of land between a dirt trail and a creek so narrow only a canoe could pass.

"You are here for de book," the man said, his accent a melodic combination of France and Jamaica.

Should I lie or shouldn't I? I was never quite sure.

"De night demons know. They attack only those who are up to no good."

"And who would that be?"

"Nephilim, for de most part."

"The Nephilim are trying to steal the *Book of Samyaza*?" Why pretend I had no idea what he meant when I did, and he knew it?

He inclined his head. "To possess de book is to rule this world as well as de next."

"Then why aren't you?"

"I protect de book until our Prince comes."

"From what I hear, all the demons got sent back to hell."

"There will come another chance."

Unfortunately he was right. Doomsday, Armageddon, Apocalypse, they were inevitable. The only thing we could do was attempt to put them off until we were better prepared to win.

"Why you be so happy to see de Grigori sent back? You're as Nephilim as I am."

I would have known even without his confession. I felt a buzz in the air, the hum that made my teeth ache and screamed that evil was near. There was a darkness about him, so abysmal I could almost see it hovering like smoke.

Since I wasn't about to explain myself—to him or anyone else—I ignored his question to reiterate my own. "Why are you protecting a book for someone else when you could become the Prince of All You Survey?"

"We each have our parts to play. One of de reasons we haven't won yet is that we fight one another as much as we fight de light. I promised long ago to keep our *Book of Samyaza* safe for when de Prince would come."

A Nephilim that kept his word. The world really was coming to an end.

"What do you get if you do?"

He smiled, a brilliant white flash in his handsome, dark face. "Anything I desire."

His gaze wandered from my no doubt tousled head to my—eek!—bare feet. I was all-over bare, and from the expression on his face, he didn't have a problem with that.

"Come closer," he murmured, his voice a mesmerizing melody that compelled me to obey.

I took a single step before I managed to stop myself. "What are you?"

"Mait. Commander of de night demons."

"Which explains why they don't peck the crap

out of you whenever you get near the book."

"I am their god."

I didn't like that one bit. Commander *and* god. I needed to get that book out of his clutches and fast. No matter what Mait said, it was only a matter of time until he got sick of waiting for the Prince to come and decided the Prince was here and it was him.

His tongue swept his lips; his emerald gaze refused to leave my breasts. I crossed my arms, and he smirked.

"Come here," he said again.

This time I was prepared and held my ground. "No, thanks." He might be beautiful to behold, but if I got too close I'd be sorry.

"I want to touch you."

"And I don't want to be touched."

He lifted his face, breathed in the dawn. "Your scent is enticing; you are so many things. Strong and dangerous, soft and smooth and round. You'll be so warm inside." His head fell back, his chest muscles tightened and flexed. From the bulge in his khaki cotton pants, he was having a great time without me. "First I will satisfy my lust and then my hunger."

"What kind of hunger?" With creatures like him, it could be anything.

"I thirst for fear, terror, for de darkness only I can bring."

"You 'eat' fear?"

"Mmmm. I doubt I'll sleep again until I've had you."

I prepared for a fight. I wasn't going to let this guy "have" anything. But he stayed where he was, and I began to wonder.

"If you want me so bad why don't you—" I bit my lip, considering. "You stuck in there?"

His head came up; his eyes flashed fury, darkening to evergreen, and I laughed. "No wonder you aren't marching at the head of the army of doom. You can't leave."

"Yet."

"What does that mean?"

He merely smiled and didn't answer.

"Where are your night demons now?" I lifted my face to the sky.

"At night they protect this place. In de daylight, I do."

"How long have you been here?"

His gaze lowered to my breasts again. "A long, long time."

Oh, brother.

"Would you like to see de *Book of Samyaza*?" he asked.

"Sure."

Once again, it couldn't be this easy.

"All you need do is fuck me."

And it wasn't.

There was no way I could sleep with this guy for the book. He was a Nephilim. I'd been warned. I could absorb his evil along with his strengths—whatever they were. For all I knew, I might even be trapped in this place with him forever.

"How about we do it my way?" I asked.

"We can do it any way that you like." His voice roughened in anticipation.

I flicked my hand, hoping I could knock him senseless on the first try. No such luck.

He uttered a few words that didn't sound like French—maybe Latin, maybe Greek—and something that felt very much like the fist of a giant smacked me in the chest and sent me flying backward several feet. I landed on my ass with a thud.

"Care to try again?" Mait asked.

"What exactly are you?" I climbed to my feet, but I stayed right where I was. The farther away the better.

"God of night demons, protector of de book."

"You threw my power back at me."

"Not me. The spell."

My gaze narrowed. "From the book?"

"What else am I to do while I'm waiting for another Nephilim to arrive?"

I didn't think he was supposed to be reading the book and trying out the spells. Then again, I would have been.

"What else can you do?"

He smiled and went inside.

Shifting into a phoenix, I followed. In this form

I could fly through the doorway, snatch the book out of his hands, or wherever it might be, and leave. If he tried anything, I'd fling fire at him. If he flung it back, it wouldn't matter. I was a firebird. I didn't burn.

I never got the chance to see what he'd do; I never got close enough to see anything at all, at least not the *Book of Samyaza.*

Three feet from the door, I hit a wall. I'd say it was literal, except there was nothing there. Nevertheless, I slammed into a tall, wide, immovable object and fluttered to the ground with the worst headache I'd had since I'd blown my brains out with my own gun. Don't ask.

Luckily I didn't lose consciousness. I fluttered my wings until I was upright then stumbled sideways on woozy talons.

Mait leaned through the empty window. "I possess de power of protection. Around anything or anyone I can build a wall that cannot be breached."

I let out my breath in an annoyed huff and fire swirled outward, running up the invisible barrier, then back down, hitting the ground and disappearing in a puff of dirt and black smoke.

"You have failed." Mait turned away, dismissing me as if I were no more powerful than the last Nephilim to try.

Chapter 24

I cut my losses. I needed to learn more about Mait. I could stand in the swamp until I was as old as he was and never figure out how to break through his invisible, enchanted wall.

I had no doubt it could be broken. One of the many things I'd learned since I'd become the new me was that everything had a weakness. Nothing and no one was indestructible. Just look at Sawyer. Not a scratch on him but tattoos for centuries, and then I was born. Had he known the first time he saw me that I'd be the death of him? If so, then why had he ever left me alive?

I returned to town as a phoenix. This might be New Orleans, but I still didn't think I'd make it from the Honey Island Swamp to the French Quarter, naked, without drawing a crowd or at least a cop.

Less than half an hour later, I landed on the terrace, shifted, and went inside. I scared the shit out of the maid.

"Eeek!" she squeaked as I strode in from the balcony.

"Whoops." I snatched my clothes off the floor.

"I knocked," she managed. "You didn't answer."

"Don't worry about it."

"I could lose my job."

"Not if we keep this between us, all right? You didn't come in when I was naked," I said.

And a woman-sized bird didn't just land on the balcony.

She nodded eagerly, her eyes too calm and her manner too normal for her to have seen anything but me walking in off the terrace.

"I'll just—" I edged toward the bathroom.

"Of course." She inched toward the door. "I'll come back later."

As soon as she left, I flipped the security latch and booted up my computer. I went first to the members-only, password-protected, super-secret Web site of the federation.

Members logged in and entered what information they'd gleaned on every Nephilim and breed combination they came across—specifically how to kill them. Unfortunately the federation was down to a skeleton crew, most of them doing the best they could to stem the demon tide but instead being washed away by the flood. Which meant not too many had the time to add new information to the database.

On Mait I didn't find much, so I was forced to go about this the old-fashioned way—trial and error by Google search. My luck there wasn't any better.

I rubbed my eyes. I needed a shower, coffee, and

food, in that order. Then I'd make some calls.

The hot water felt heavenly on skin that had been stretched and released, sprouted feathers then regrown skin. My shoulders were a little sore from flying.

My stomach growling and my head beginning to pound with a lack-of-caffeine headache, I wasn't paying attention when I strode back into the room sans towel. My only warning was a slight shimmy in the air.

I rammed my elbow backward. The blow should have sent whatever had snuck up on me flying into, if not through, a wall. Instead that elbow was grabbed so hard my bones crunched, and I was spun like a top. An instant before my eyes registered the sight of him, my nose caught his scent—cinnamon and soap.

"Sanducci."

Jimmy wrapped his arms around me, one hand circling both wrists and holding them still at the small of my back. "You gonna hit me, Lizzy?"

My breasts crushed against his thin overwashed T-shirt—this one with jagged red lettering I'd had no time to read. With his knuckles teasing the curve of my ass and my mouth a mere inch below his, I couldn't help but whisper, "You want me to?"

Lust flared in his eyes. It had always been like this between us. One touch, one word, one whiff and we were lost.

His neck was so close, the warmth of his skin

drew me in, making it impossible not to press my face to the curve and just breathe. His scent flooded me with memories—first kiss, first love, first time. He'd been everything.

That scent was also betrayal and heartache, mistrust, murder, and mayhem. Jimmy was both danger and safety, hatred and love, violence and the first gentleness I'd ever known in a man. For the rest of my life whenever I smelled heated skin and fresh soap, or tasted hot cinnamon toast, I'd think of Jimmy Sanducci.

His cheek touched my hair. His thumb stroked the tip of my tailbone, and I couldn't help it. I licked his neck.

Without any warning, Jimmy shoulder-checked me into the doorjamb. I managed to grab it before my spine, or the back of my head, connected.

"I like my jugular just the way it is," he said. "Intact."

I didn't bother to explain that I'd been more interested in kissing than killing him at the time. The same couldn't be said of right now.

"Vampires who live in log cabins shouldn't throw burning stakes," I muttered.

"What?"

Yeah, that hadn't made much sense, but—

"If you weren't thinking with your dick you might have gotten the allusion."

He still appeared confused.

"Glass houses and stones, dumb-ass. You're a

vampire, just like me."

"*I* wasn't licking your neck," he said.

"No, you were too busy grabbing my ass."

I walked across the room, purposely brushing his arm with my breast as I passed and sat on the bed. I didn't bother to get dressed. He'd seen it all before. I wanted him to remember what he might never see again if he kept it up.

"What are you doing here?"

"Same thing you are."

Somehow I doubted that.

"I didn't—" I paused in the middle of saying I hadn't told anyone what I was doing, because I *had* told one person. "I am going to kick Luther's bony behind."

Jimmy's gaze began to drift below my neck. Then he stiffened, turned, and strode to the still-open veranda doors. I stifled a smirk. I was getting to him.

"Wasn't Luther," he said.

"Ruthie." Jimmy didn't answer what hadn't been a question. "What did she say?"

"That I'd better haul myself down here to help you before she blistered my backside with a paddle."

Ruthie continued to threaten us as she had when we were children even though we hadn't been children since...

I sighed. Jimmy and I had never really been children.

Ruthie had made a game of thinking up

colorful ways to intimidate us into doing what she wanted. She'd rarely laid a hand on us, and when she had, we'd deserved it. In truth, every kid who'd ever spent a moment with Ruthie Kane would have done anything she asked just because *she'd* asked.

Take Jimmy for instance. Ruthie had told him to break my heart, and he'd run off to do it so fast, the door hadn't even brushed his ass on his way out of my life. I needed to get over that.

Eventually.

"I don't need help," I said.

"Ruthie disagrees."

"Ruthie can kiss—"

"Ah-ah-ah." Jimmy glanced over his shoulder, then just as quickly back out the window at the increasingly steamy day. "She knows all and sees all."

"Not really." In her new incarnation, Ruthie seemed to know a little and only see enough to be a pain in my butt. "Ruthie sent you to help me." I straightened as if someone had goosed me. "What about Summer? You didn't just leave her—"

"No," Jimmy interrupted.

"Tell me you didn't bring her along."

"Definitely no."

"You're supposed to be watching her." I began to pace. "She can't be trusted."

"Neither can you."

My hands curled into fists. I wanted to slug him, but then I usually did. "What's to keep her from—?"

"What do you think she's going to do?" Jimmy spun, hands clenched just like mine. "She sold her soul for me. You think she's going to make that sacrifice worthless by selling us out?"

"I think she'd sell anyone to save you," I said quietly.

He sighed. "I think she would, too."

Have I mentioned that Summer's a little obsessed?

"I locked her in a room, put rowan across the exits," he continued.

Rowan repelled fairy magic. It could also kill them, along with cold steel. I'd started keeping both in my duffel. Never could tell when I might need some.

"I bet she loved that."

"*Love* isn't quite the word I'd use."

I'd seen what lurked behind Summer's pretty face, and it was frightening. I wondered if Jimmy'd seen it this time, and if he had, would he at last let me kill her like I wanted to?

"Luther wasn't happy, either. He thought he could keep an eye on her."

I snorted.

Jimmy's gaze lowered to my breasts as they jiggled. "You wanna put on some clothes?"

"If it bothers you."

Jimmy's hands clenched tighter. Pretty soon blood was going to run between his fingers.

I found clean underwear, yesterday's jeans, and

one of my new shirts. I purposely left the bras in the bag. It was too damn hot.

Once dressed I faced Jimmy, and my gaze touched on his T-shirt. Red letters on a gray background revealed that: ALL I REALLY NEEDED TO KNOW I LEARNED FROM STEPHEN KING.

Someday that might even be funny.

"Let's walk and talk," I said. "If I don't get coffee, I *might* go for your jugular."

Jimmy's dark hair fell over one eye, and he shoved it back impatiently before following me into the hall.

"Luther thinks he's a big boy now," I said as we made our way to street level.

"He's big enough. He's just not mean enough."

"You've never seen him go lion. Although..." I shrugged. "He isn't exactly a man-eater then, either."

"He will be. It's only a matter of time."

I understood what Jimmy wasn't saying. The more horror Luther saw, the simpler it would be for him to kill. It happened to us all—I glanced at Sanducci's stunning profile—some much sooner than others.

As we stepped onto the street, the heat hit us in the face like a blanket that had had been soaked in the river—heavy, damp, musty-mold. When I tried to breathe, the air not only burned my throat but seemed to fill it with cotton balls as well.

"You sure you want coffee?"

"I'm sure." I headed for Decatur at a pace mere

mortals dared not go.

Despite being in a hurry to get to a cup of chicory coffee and a plateful of fried dough, I glanced into the windows of the storefronts along the way. I couldn't help it. A shrunken head shared space with a gloriously bedecked Mardi Gras mask; Catholic religious icons stood right next to a selection of voodoo dolls. All I had to say was—New Orleans.

Suddenly I stopped, and Jimmy slammed into me so hard he threw me forward. I caught myself, palms against the glass, nose brushing the cool, clear pane.

I'd never seen the photograph before, but I knew Jimmy had taken it. I didn't need to touch it and "see"; I didn't need to ask; I didn't need to hear his answer. I just knew.

The portrait wasn't even his usual fare. Instead a little boy, stark in black and white, stared out. The smudge of dirt on his face matched the shade of his eyes; his filthy shirt might once have been as light as his crew cut. A fly sat on his pale hair and another on his shoulder. The camera had caught him in the act of blowing air upward; his lower lip jutted out; his bangs scattered. The fly stayed put.

Had he been playing in the mud or living on the street? The picture was both the cutest and the saddest thing I'd ever seen.

My eyes met Jimmy's in the glass, and he reached for me. "Wait, Lizzy—"

I sidestepped and opened the door. Inside were more photos like the first. All in black and white, mostly of kids, each one asked a question, told a story, tore at my heart.

Perhaps because of his supernatural ability—Jimmy saw what others did not—he had always been beyond talented. Sanducci was famous, and he deserved to be. However, none of the pictures he'd taken for money deserved to be in the same room with these.

"Why didn't you ever show me?"

An emotion flitted across his face, one I couldn't put a finger on before he glanced away. "Baby, I'll show you anything you want." He put his hand on his taut stomach and rubbed, tugging his shirt up, trying to distract me with a six-pack.

"Don't." I put my hand on his arm. He jerked it away but not before I'd seen the truth. He might pretend the photos meant nothing, but I knew better. Each one held a tiny piece of his soul.

"May I help—?"

I turned, and the eyes of the slim, white-haired man widened. "It's you."

I shot Jimmy a glare. "Show me," I ordered, and the salesman scurried toward the back.

"Fuck," Jimmy said, but he followed.

I stepped into a separate room and slowly turned in a circle staring at so many varied versions of me, I got dizzy. Also black-and-white, these shone with one huge difference from the others—the brilliant, sapphire blue of my eyes.

Talk about artsy. But they didn't seem contrived. Instead their beauty was haunting.

Me right after I'd come to Ruthie's—twelve years old, far too skinny, yet already developing and horrified by it. My legs stuck out like kindling beneath a skirt that was too big; my shoulders were all bones; my breasts softly curved beneath a sweater that looked to drown me. A child hovering, both eager and petrified, at the cliff edge of womanhood.

Me on the balance beam in high school, my pole-dancer body outlined in a skintight leotard, the expression on my face reflecting my love of the first thing I'd ever been any good at.

The next a silhouette in the second-floor window of Ruthie's place. My window. I was lifting my arms, taking off my shirt. My skin appeared gilded by moonlight. I had my head turned just enough so the camera caught my face. I'd been thinking of him.

"Perv."

"Lizzy, let's—"

I lifted my hand to make him stop, and he backed up as if I might hit him, which caused the salesman to cast us a quick frown.

"Great," I whispered furiously. "Now he thinks I beat you."

"You do," Jimmy said.

I narrowed my eyes. "I might."

In the subsequent image, glancing back at the camera, I walked down the stairs at Ruthie's. My shirt was twisted, my skirt wrinkled from being hiked to my waist, my hair—long now—was ratty, messy, as if I'd been dancing outside in a tornado. But I was smiling just a little, a smile that said, *There's no one in the world but you.*

I expected the next photo to reveal the gap in years between when Jimmy had left and when he'd come back. Instead I took one glance and caught my breath.

Me sitting in the window, rain cascading down the glass, making it seem as if tears ran down my face. I'd just discovered Jimmy was gone.

The next picture made my heart lurch. Me in my uniform, frisking some skid, kicking his legs apart as he leaned over the Milwaukee Police Department cruiser. My hair was short—I'd chopped it off, impatient with the gum perps kept spitting into it—and my mouth was the thin, frustrated line of every city cop.

Several more photographs followed—all taken during the period when Jimmy had been lost to me. Me laughing at one of the Murphys' barbecues, testifying in court, wearing a ball gown to some charity event and black to Max's funeral. The photo of me alone at the grave after everyone else had gone brought that day back so sharply my eyes burned.

Jimmy had been there. He'd watched over me. I

wasn't sure if I should be happy or sad, glad or really, really mad.

"I don't like the idea of people hanging pictures of my life on their living room walls."

"These aren't available for purchase," the salesman said hurriedly. "This is our showroom." He pointed to several signs that said NOT FOR SALE spaced every few feet between the displays. I hadn't even noticed them.

Jimmy had moved to the back window, where he appeared fascinated beyond all understanding with the view of the alley behind the gallery.

"You thought they were here because of the colorization?" the man asked.

"Not exactly," I said.

Anyone with a heart could see that the difference in the portraits stemmed from a difference in the photographer. He'd cared about his other subjects, but this one—

This one he'd loved.

Chapter 25

A final image hung to the right of the door. Taken only a few months ago at the dairy farm where Jimmy had once worked, it showed me asleep on a cot in the tack room. The setting sun cast through the windows above, bathing me in soft, pale light.

The glaring absence of any photos since told a tale that shattered my heart, even though I'd suspected the truth for a while now. Jimmy's love was gone. Too bad mine wasn't.

I vacated the gallery as fast as I could, leaving Jimmy behind. Once outside I retraced my path to the hotel. My stomach was pitching too violently to even think about coffee.

Discovering Jimmy's love for me portrayed so vividly for the world was upsetting enough. Realizing that love was gone was like losing him again the way I had at eighteen.

"Lizzy!"

Jimmy chased me down the sidewalk. There was no point in trying to outrun him. In human form we had the same powers. And shifting into a phoenix in the middle of the day in the center of the street wasn't something I was willing to do, even to get away from him.

I let Jimmy catch up, and we walked a few blocks in silence before he spoke. "I'm sorry. I knew some of the pictures were in New Orleans and one of the shows—"

"Whoa." I stopped, pulling him to the side. "There are more of those out there?"

"I—uh—needed money. I haven't been able to work as much as I used to with all the—" He waved one long-fingered hand.

"Chaos?" I supplied. "Death? Destruction? Murder? Rape?"

"I would have said something about the New Orleans gallery before we left."

"Really?"

He glanced up at the blistering sun. "Maybe. I don't know. I didn't come here for that."

"Why did you come here?"

His gaze met mine. "You know why."

"Because Ruthie told you to, and you always do what Ruthie says."

Something flickered in his eyes, something angry, something violent. "Don't you?"

"Yeah." I began walking toward the hotel again. "I don't know what else to do."

My quiet admission deflated him, and he fell in step beside me. We remained silent until we reached my room again. I took the single chair near a small table in the corner.

Jimmy sat on the bed. "Did you find the skinwalker you went looking for?"

"I did."

"I'll assume he helped you raise Sawyer, who then sent you here."

"No," I said. "According to Sani, Sawyer's between worlds."

"How did that happen?" Before I could answer, understanding dawned in Sanducci's eyes. "You helped him."

"I didn't mean to."

"You've never done anything you didn't want to do in your entire life."

"You're wrong," I said. "And you of all people should know it."

Just as Jimmy had done things he had never shared with me, I'd done things I'd never shared with him. When you're eight years old with nowhere to go and nothing to eat it's surprising what you'll agree to.

"I shouldn't have said that," he murmured.

"You think?"

He ignored my jab, probably because it came out sounding less like sarcasm and more like a serious question from the child I'd once been—scared to death but determined to let no one know it.

"You didn't want to kill Sawyer."

Surprise knocked all the words right out of me. Jimmy had been referring not to my childhood but to Sawyer. I had to take a few seconds to switch gears. When I did, I told him the truth.

"I wanted to kill Sawyer more than I ever wanted to do anything in my life."

His face, which had been etched with shock and concern, smoothed out. "That was the demon, not you."

"The blood was on my hands." It had also been on my feet, my face, pretty much everywhere.

"When the demon's driving, you aren't really you."

"I know that here." I pointed to my head. "But here?" I laid my hand over my heart. "If good is stronger than evil, if love is stronger than hate, if I'm any kind of leader, I should have been able to stop myself."

"Lizzy." Jimmy shook his head.

"I realize that's foolish. I know I had to do it. But still his death haunts me."

"Probably always will."

Because I was hoping to find a way to end my eternal guilt, I didn't answer. Jimmy would never go for it. He'd do everything he could to stop me from getting Sawyer back. So I wouldn't tell him.

I wasn't going to lie. Not that I wasn't capable of it. But in this case, I didn't have to. A half-truth would do the trick.

"Sawyer's past the point of raising his ghost," I said. "I tried. Sani tried. No dice."

"Oh, well." Jimmy shrugged. "Tough break."

"Yeah. But Sani did give me a tip on something else."

"What's that?"

"The Book of Samyaza."

Jimmy rolled his eyes. "Again with the book. Have you forgotten that no one's ever seen the thing?"

"We will."

He tilted his head. "When?"

"As soon as you help me steal it."

"I don't think it's a very bright idea to steal Satan's instruction booklet."

"I think it's the best idea I've had in months."

"You sure about that?"

I wasn't sure about anything—except that we had to get that book.

"This skinwalker," Jimmy said. "How did he know Sawyer?"

"Sani trained him."

"How is it that I've never heard of the guy? Where has he been? Why isn't he helping us?"

"He's a little...trapped on the mountain." Or he had been. I didn't think it was advisable to admit that I'd set him free.

"Sawyer cursed him."

"I'm sure he deserved it."

"Unfortunately, most people tend to get pissy when they're cursed, regardless of what they did to deserve it. You think Sani gave you good intel?"

I hadn't thought. I'd just believed. And since I'd

had the dream, vision, whatever about Jimmy hanging from that wall—

I turned away so he wouldn't see my face, clasped my fingers together so he wouldn't see my hands shake. I could stop all that, but I had to have Sawyer's help, and no one, not even Sanducci, was going to prevent me from getting it.

"This Nephilim is keeping the *Book of Samyaza* safe for the Antichrist," I said. "If we walk away, if we let the Prince of 666 possess it, he'll be—"

"Invincible. I know." Jimmy bit his lip, thinking.

I kept my mouth shut. Sanducci would come around to my point of view. Because as many arguments as there were against taking the book, the only truth that mattered was this: We could not allow the Nephilim to keep it.

"All right. I'll help you, but only if we do the *plenus luna malum* spell first."

Plenus luna malum translated to "full moon evil"—a sex spell that confined evil beneath the moon. In other words, every month when the full moon rose Jimmy and I would be unable to control our vampire tendencies because we would have pushed all that violence into the single night when the moon grew round.

I fingered my collar. Once the spell was performed I could take the thing off because every other night of the month I'd be normal. Almost.

At first glance, the spell seemed like an excellent idea. However, upon further examination, the difficulties were apparent. If our vampires were only accessible one night a month, then any big bad getting its jollies from stomping on Tokyo would just *keep* stomping until the full moon rose and Jimmy and I were strong enough to kill it.

Also, when the vampire was confined to a single night it became stronger and more vicious, and when it was released the only way to control it was with powerful magic. The kind of magic only a few beings possessed—like Sawyer and me. If I was batshit at the time and Sawyer was dead, we were going to have problems.

Another very good reason for raising him.

"Why should we perform the spell before we steal the book?" I asked. "We might need the extra push of a badass vampire to get it."

"We can handle things."

"Still, it might be better to wait until we have the book before we confine our demons." Just in case.

"We should *not* get anywhere near the *Book of Samyaza* with demons inside us. Who knows what a manuscript dictated by Satan might do to them."

I didn't like the images that tumbled through my brain at his words. We *didn't* know. We might touch the cover and suddenly be compelled to remove our controls and join the other side. If the Nephilim owned Jimmy and me, plus that book, the world was more screwed than usual.

"You've been begging to reconfine your vampire

since I let it out, but Ruthie said no. What changed her mind?"

Jimmy didn't answer.

"You never asked her."

He shrugged.

"She isn't going to like it."

"I thought you were in charge now."

"I thought I was, too." But every day I discovered how delusional that thought was.

"If you want that book," Jimmy said, "then we do the spell."

"You'd really let the Nephilim keep it if I don't agree?"

He looked me straight in the eye. "I really would."

He seemed serious, but there was only one way to find out for sure. Quick as a March wind, I brushed my hand along his, and got a flash of him and Summer rolling across the sheets naked. I snatched my fingers back. "You did that on purpose."

"Stay out of my head. I've got a lot of stuff in there you don't want to see."

Of that I had no doubt.

"Fine. I agree. But there's just one problem. I don't know the *plenus luna malum* spell."

Jimmy's lips curved. "I do."

"How did you—?" I began, and then I knew. "Summer."

She'd do anything he asked.

"She didn't tell me, I—" He pulled a piece of paper out of his pocket. "—figured I might need it later and wrote it down."

"Why didn't you just tell her to do you again?"

"I'm having trust issues. Call me silly, but I'd prefer not to let the soul-selling fairy perform an encore of sexual magic on me."

"When do we do this?"

"Beneath the moon." Jimmy glanced at the window. Sun poured through the glass like honey. "Tonight."

"Okay." I was suddenly uneasy. This was a sex spell. Jimmy and I hadn't had sex since—

My mind shied away from those memories. We'd been having a lot of vamp sex lately. Extremely good, but also violent. Blood and lust, pain and desire were, for a vampire, all rolled together so tightly as to be indistinguishable.

"After we—" I couldn't finish. "You know. Then we'll deal with Mait."

"Mait? The sosye?"

"Huh?"

"The wizard," he translated. "Haitian?"

"Yes. I thought he was a sorcerer."

"Sorcerer." Jimmy flipped one hand palm up. "Wizard." He flipped it palm down. "Same difference."

"You know him?"

"He's the one who got away."

"From what?"

"Me," he snapped.

"That happens?"

"Har-har."

"Well, you did say he was the *one.* You didn't go after him? Hunt him down like a dog. Devote your life. Become obsessed. Never give up, never give in."

"Fuck you," Jimmy said.

"We'll get to that."

He winced, and I almost felt bad. Then he opened his mouth…and I felt worse. "It was the first year I was away from—"

He looked out the window, suddenly fascinated with the freckles of golden sunlight on the wrought-iron balcony.

"Ruthie," I supplied. "The first year you were away from Ruthie."

"Yeah. I was in training."

It appeared that he was having a hard time going on, so I helped him again. Training for DKs and seers meant—

"Sawyer."

Jimmy had never admitted outright that he'd trained with Sawyer, though I'd gotten hints of it from things he'd said. I wasn't sure what had happened between them, but whatever it had been there remained an unrelenting animosity that I'd never been able to get to the bottom of with either one.

"You were in training with Sawyer," I pressed.

Jimmy cleared his throat. "You know how that was."

This time *I* winced. For me, training with Sawyer had been a bizarre combination of hand-to-hand combat, magic, and sex. I didn't think Jimmy's had been similar, but if it had that would explain why Jimmy never stopped wanting him dead.

"Constant running, swimming, jumping, fighting. Very little food. No sleep. And weird stuff happening all the time."

My chest feeling less strangled when he didn't mention seduction, sex, or worse.

"He said I was ready, and he sent me after a sosye."

"Mait. What happened?"

"Guy kicked my ass and left me for dead."

"If he meant for you to be dead, you would be."

"He didn't know what I was."

In other words Mait had killed Jimmy once, and for a dhampir once is not enough.

"How do you kill a sosye?" I asked.

"Charmed dagger through the left eye."

"Ew." Still— "Doesn't seem that difficult."

"You wanna try it?"

I was probably going to have to.

"You'll have better luck than me," Jimmy said.

"Why's that?"

"Magic. You've got it."

"So does Mait. He had no trouble shoving what magic I tried right back in my face. I might possess the power, but I don't possess a clue of how to use it."

"That's okay."

"No," I said. "It really isn't."

I'd killed for this power. I should at least be able to do something beyond smacking people without even touching them. Although that *was* handy.

"There's a charm that will protect you," Jimmy said.

"From the protection demon?"

"I've been studying ways to take this guy out for years. I know what I'm doing."

I guess he had been obsessed, and that obsession made Jimmy the best choice to help with Mait. Which was probably why Ruthie had sent him.

"I always wondered if Sawyer wanted Mait to get away."

"Why would he want that?"

"Who knows with him."

"Maybe you were supposed to check out the background of a sosye," I said. "Make sure you knew all you needed to before you skipped off to stick him in the eye with a dagger."

"I'm a DK. I'm supposed to follow the instructions of my seer without question. Dicking around will get innocent people killed."

"What if Mait was a test of your abilities? Sawyer couldn't exactly let the guy die if he was helping train federation members."

"Nephilim who help?" Jimmy snorted. "Since when?"

"I don't know. But Mait *didn't* kill you. There's

gotta be a reason. Just like there's a reason Sawyer didn't tell you all you needed to know."

"Besides him wanting me dead?"

"He didn't even know you yet." Not that knowing Sanducci ever prevented anyone from wanting him dead.

"He knew enough."

I wondered what that meant, but knew better than to ask.

"I still think Mait was a training test. He was probably a friend of Sawyer's."

"A Nephilim friend of Sawyer's who's now protecting evil's version of *The Idiot's Guide to the Apocalypse*." Jimmy scratched his chin, which had taken on a bluish tinge from at least two days' growth of beard. "Strangely enough, that's an explanation I can get behind. I was never quite certain Sawyer wasn't playing both sides of this war."

I hadn't been, either, until he'd died for us.

But I was never going to convince Jimmy that Sawyer was anything other than an enigma, so I wasn't going to try.

"What do you know about sosyes?" I asked.

"Haitian wizards. They command night demons, which are—"

"Creepy shadow birds that fly right through you and peck your insides raw."

"You've met."

"Oh, yeah. How do we kill them?"

"Mait dies, they do."

"Otherwise?"

"They don't."

"Of course not. Go on."

"A sosye is part witch and part loa, a voodoo god."

"If he's Nephilim he's part *demon*," I pointed out.

"In the old days, people had to have a word they used to refer to those beings with supernatural powers. Sometimes they called them gods. In Mait's case, his father was Kalfu, ruler of the night spirits."

"Otherwise known as night demons."

"Yep," Jimmy said. "According to legend, Kalfu is the grand master of charms and sorceries. He's the origin of darkness. He upsets the natural order, thwarts fate. Basically he is chaos. He protects the gate between this world and the next."

"And his son?"

"Controls the malevolent spirits of the night as well as the displaced souls of the next world."

"He can raise ghosts," I clarified.

"And thanks to his mother he can perform magic."

"Which is how he threw up the protection spell around the old church. Unlike his father, he's protecting a book instead of a gate."

"For all we know," Jimmy said, "the book *is* the gate."

Chapter 26

"There are things I need to get for tonight." Jimmy stood.

"You want me to come?" I asked, but he was already shutting the door.

Since I was so tired I ached with it, I decided to "rest my eyes" until Sanducci got back. No sooner had I closed them than I was out. Where I went it was dark, and I was alone. But not for long. Something was coming. Friend or foe?

Sawyer? I whispered into the darkness.

A chill wind brushed my face—tree bark and ice, heat and hay. The air smelled like him, but then again, it didn't.

Are you close?

Fur brushed my knee. I reached out, but my hand found nothing. Nearby a growl, but it didn't sound like Sawyer.

I sat up with a gasp. Jimmy stood at the small table to the left of the terrace. Orange, pewter, fuchsia, and slate fought for control of the horizon. Dusk was on its way.

"What time is it?"

"Eight."

I was dopey with sleep. I felt like I'd only closed my eyes and then opened them again. In truth I'd been unconscious for hours.

The scent of food made my stomach growl. "What did you bring?"

Jimmy drew wrapped parcels from the bag on the table. "Po' boys."

I bit my lip to keep from making *yummy* noises. A po' boy was a shrimp, oyster, beef, or whatever sandwich wrapped inside the best baguette in the country. Sanducci had good taste. Although it was almost as hard to find bad food in New Orleans as it had been to find the *Book of Samyaza* at all.

A second bag sat on the dresser. I lifted my chin in its direction. "You found your sun-dried pig's nostrils?"

"I found everything I needed. Here, it isn't much of a problem."

"Voodoo Wal-Mart?"

"Right." He took a bite of his roast beef po' boy. The scent of hot mustard wafted my way, and I dug in to my own shrimp version.

When the food was gone along with the soft drinks we'd used to wash everything down, I asked, "What exactly *did* you need?"

Jimmy shoved the empty wrappings into the bag. "A priestess to provide the materials for the gris-gris."

"You found a bona fide voodoo priestess?"

"This is New Orleans. You can't swing a cat and not hit a voodoo priestess."

I'd just take his word for it. "What's a gris-gris?"

"Combination of both black and white magic. The most powerful charm there is."

"Isn't a priestess a practitioner of white magic? A bokor practices black?"

"Technically. But a voodoo priestess or priest studies both sides. They believe the only way to thwart evil is to understand it."

Had to agree with that. "This gris-gris will prevent Mait's magic from harming us?"

"Yes."

I guess it made sense to use a voodoo charm of protection against the son of a voodoo god that protected things. If sense could be made of any of this.

"How did Mait come to exist?" I asked.

It never hurt to know the history of a Nephilim. Sometimes the past was the only thing we had to keep us alive in the present.

"Legend says his mother—a mambo, or priestess who became a bokor—summoned Kalfu with black magic, then compelled him to give her a child."

I shivered despite the steaming heat that still poured in through the open balcony doors. I couldn't imagine why anyone would want to do that. The idea of allowing a demon to not only touch you but impregnate you—

Actually I *could* imagine it, but I really wished I'd stop.

"Where's Kalfu now?"

"The lowest level of hell with all the other fiends."

To make a Nephilim like Mait required a Grigori and a human. Kalfu, being a Grigori, was confined. At the moment.

"What about the voodoo witch mom?" She might be the human part of the equation, but in this story she'd behaved as badly as any demon.

"Dead," Jimmy said.

"You're sure?"

"I'm sure." Jimmy tossed the trash into the wastebasket in the corner.

"You killed her."

He didn't answer. He didn't have to.

"Lizzy," Jimmy murmured, and when I glanced at him he gestured to the window.

The moon was coming up.

"Could you do one thing?" he asked.

"I'm sure I'll have to do more than one."

His exhale was short, sharp, and annoyed. I couldn't blame him.

"Can you take that off?" He pointed to the turquoise that still lay between my breasts. It had always driven Jimmy insane. The stone was a constant reminder of the bond between Sawyer and me.

Without another word, I lifted the necklace over my head and set it aside.

Jimmy and I had never had a problem having sex. The problem had always been trying *not* to have it. Of course things had changed since the last time we'd had anything but vampire sex. I wondered if Jimmy would be able to perform. He not only didn't love me anymore, lately he didn't even seem to like me.

He opened the brown paper bag on the dresser and began to remove items. Candles, incense, and two tiny burlap sacks, which he set away from the rest. The gris-gris, I assumed.

"Candles and incense," I said. "How… seventies."

Jimmy's cough sounded like smothered laughter, but when his dark eyes met mine in the mirror on the wall not a hint of amusement remained. "Both the candles and incense contain dragon's blood."

"There be dragons?"

Jimmy gave me a look. We both knew there were dragons. We'd killed quite a few, and I was certain there were more where they'd come from.

"Dragon's blood is an herb," he said. "In the candles it ensures that whatever we put in, we get out." He held up a hand to stall my questions. "I'll explain later. In the incense it cleanses negative entities or influences."

Jimmy picked up a green candle and set it on

the table. "Green for changes and renewal." He set a red candle on one side of the bed and a pink on the other.

"And those?"

"Sex stuff." He wouldn't meet my eyes.

I didn't push it. I couldn't.

Next came the incense—small cones that Jimmy set on equally small dishes next to the candles, lighting one before he moved on to the next. "Tea tree for cures. Spearmint for freedom, power, and peace. Bay for protection and exorcism."

Listening to Sanducci recite the magical powers of scents and colors was a little like hearing a professional wrestler share his favorite recipe for canapes.

"You learned all this from Summer?" I asked. "She doesn't seem like an incense-and-candle gal."

Jimmy went to the window and stared at the sky, neatly avoiding my eyes again. He didn't want to talk about Summer. Neither did I.

The candles glowed golden, at odds with the cool silver spray of the moon. The incense mixed with the scent of the night, and I felt a little floaty.

"During the spell," Jimmy said, "we'll order our demons beneath the full moon, banish them from our souls, ask for protection and peace."

"What we put in, we get out. When do we do this?"

"I'll—" He cleared his throat. "I'll let you know."

Silence settled over us. Jimmy continued to

peer upward. I continued to stand several feet away, breathing in candle wax and incense.

"Should we...?" I paused, uncertain what to say.

"We probably shouldn't, but that never stopped us before."

I found myself smiling. That had been the perfect thing to say.

I crossed the room and slipped my arms around him, laying my head against his back. I half expected him to tense, but he'd been waiting for me.

Jimmy was taller than me, so my cheek pressed to his shoulder blade, my breasts at his rib cage, my hips just below his. I spread my palms against a firm, flat stomach. His heat pulsed through the soft, worn material of his T-shirt.

We'd embraced like this dozens of times. It brought back so many memories, as did the faint scent of cinnamon that wafted from his skin. If I closed my eyes, I could convince myself we were kids again, before we'd hurt each other, before we'd killed. Or at least before I had.

I'd never loved anyone the way I'd loved Jimmy Sanducci. I doubted I ever could. I'd trusted him utterly, believed in him completely, wanted him with that crazed burn of bursting teenage hormones. When he'd broken my heart, he'd broken it forever. I would never be able to trust, or believe, or love quite like that again.

Even with him.

Chapter 27

"Jimmy."

He spun and kissed me. There was nothing gentle about that kiss, nothing of our childhood except the flavor. Jimmy tasted like danger—always had.

His tongue plunged, mine met it halfway, and they tangled. My hands swooped under his T-shirt. His skin seemed to scald mine, and I only wanted more.

I traced my palms over the ridges in his stomach, moaning when the muscles clenched. I wanted to lick them as they rippled, feel the movement with my tongue. My thumb circled his navel then traced lower, slipping below his belt and caressing the smooth hot head of him.

He arched and his hips advanced and retreated, advanced and retreated, rubbing my thumb over and back, over and back. Memory flashed, illuminating a path we'd blazed many times before.

I used my fingernail on his tip, nothing more than a tickle, but he gasped, capturing my breath into his mouth. Once we'd lain for hours, nose-to-nose, staring into each other's eyes, breathing each other's breath.

I wish we could stay like this forever, I'd whispered.

Even then, Jimmy had kissed me and said nothing at all.

His long-fingered, clever hands rode my hips then swept across my stomach. I was hot, but he was hotter. When his skin touched mine I half expected steam to rise.

I tore off my shirt, tossing it aside and drawing his dark head nearer. He filled his palms with my breasts and despite the admirable size of his hands they overflowed his grasp.

Though my skin was as dark as his, in the moonlight I seemed carved of marble, his fingers like onyx. He stared at my chest, his hands, tilting his head, watching the candles flicker gold across the stark white globes and tendrils of black.

I knew that expression. He was wondering where he'd left his camera.

"Later." I cupped my palms over his knuckles, showing him what he already knew.

Together our thumbs slid right and then left, right and then left across my nipples. My head fell back, and he feasted. My hands clenched in his hair then slid to his shoulders and held on. As he suckled, my knees weakened. Without support I would fall.

Memories flickered through his mind before he

cut them off. Jimmy had become almost as adept at keeping me out as I'd become at not seeing in. Right now I had no desire to see his secrets or the past. The only desire I had was for him.

His erection pressed against my belly, pulsing and alive. I wanted to climb up high, hook my ankles behind his back, and welcome him home. I'd lifted myself onto my tiptoes, begun to slide my leg up his. Only then did I realize he still wore all his clothes, and I still wore half of mine.

"Off." I tugged at his zipper.

He lifted his head, mouth glistening, eyes glazed. An instant later, he began to return to what he was doing, and I scraped his stomach with my nails.

His breath drew in on a hiss. "Sheesh, Lizzy," he said, but he focused.

I stepped back, and my fingers went to my own zipper. "Race you." I yanked it down as he reached for the hem of his shirt.

I beat him. I usually did, even when I wasn't ahead by a T-shirt.

He kicked away his jeans, and I held up my hand to keep him from tackling me. I wanted to look at him for just a minute. Who knew if I'd ever get to look at him this way again.

Sanducci had a beautiful face. His body, long and lean, a runner's body, glistened like copper beneath the moon. Because he was a breed and could heal most everything, there wasn't a single scar to mar his perfect flesh.

Soft, dark curls dusted his legs; an equally dark trail led from the matt of hair between his thighs to his navel. I let my gaze wander higher, across his toned chest and biceps. His shoulders were broader than his hips, but not by much, his muscles taut not bulky.

The only thing that tarnished his perfection was his vampire control—a cock ring—which, in comparison, made my dog collar seem like a gift from Tiffany's.

I'd had to employ a fairy god with enough magic to override Summer's sex spell. That fairy god, known as the Dagda, had possessed a slightly sick sense of humor, and he hadn't much cared for Jimmy. Hence the cock ring. At least Sanducci's was hidden from view most of the time, unlike mine.

A cock ring was supposed to increase the amount of time a man could maintain an erection. Not that Jimmy'd ever had any problem. Nevertheless, I bet he couldn't wait to get it off, and I couldn't blame him. He had to hate it even more than I hated my poodley neckwear.

Every time my eyes brushed his erection, it leaped. When I licked my lips, caught my breath, his penis darkened as even more blood raced there.

"Lizzy." His voice was choked, a little desperate. If he didn't lie down soon, he'd probably faint.

I held out my hand and tugged him with me onto the bed. He lay nestled between my thighs; I felt the beat of his heart both there and against my chest. When he kissed me, the rhythm echoed in his lips. I closed my eyes and became caught up in the music. Time slowed as we relearned every dip and curve with lips and tongue and teeth.

Tangling our legs, I flipped him onto his back, rising above, taking control. His eyes glittered in the candlelight, for an instant reminding me of the red that would glow there if his demon took the wheel.

But the glow was gold; the eyes were Jimmy's. I cupped his cheek, slid my thumb over his cheekbone, and it came away wet.

"Sweat," he said, his voice rough with arousal. "You're a lot of work."

Then he smiled, and my heart tumbled slowly toward my stomach. I was going to love him until the day that I died. I just couldn't help myself.

Afraid I might cry, though I never cried, I leaned forward and kissed him again. He let me. But not for long.

I straddled his hips; his erection rode my buttocks. The cock ring pressed in interesting, innovative places. Very nice, but not quite nice enough.

I wiggled, trying to find a way to make the frantic need abate. Jimmy cursed and dumped me onto my back. Before I could complain, he slid inside me, and that frantic need turned into a frantic pace.

"Okay." He pressed his forehead to mine, even as he pressed himself deep within. "Listen."

"Shhh," I hissed, concentrating on the beat down below.

"Lizzy!" He pulled almost all the way out, leaving only his tip perched at the edge.

I arched, reaching for him with my body, clutching his buttocks. He captured my wrists, yanked them above my head, and held them there with one hand. I could have gotten away, but I really didn't want to.

"Focus, baby."

The word *baby* made my eyes snap open. I'd never liked it when he called me that. Once he'd stopped, I'd only wanted him to start again.

Our eyes so close I felt his eyelashes brush mine when he blinked, our breath mingled as our bodies yearned.

"We have to say the words as we—" He paused. "We should come together. You understand?"

"Orgasm," I managed. "At the same time."

"Right."

"That's part of the spell?"

"There's power in it."

"I'll say." I'd been here before, though not with Jimmy. Sawyer had said nearly the same thing the night he'd given me the ability to shape-shift. I decided to keep that tidbit to myself.

"We'll have to stay right on the verge, say the words, then—" He thrust forward just enough to make my eyes cross.

"Not going to be easy."

"Name something that is. Ready?"

I nodded, and he started again, slow and steady, in and out. Our gazes remained locked. In his I saw echoes of our past. No one knew me like he did. No one could.

"Faster," I whispered.

"Touch me." He let go of my hands.

My palms skimmed his back, showed him the rhythm. Every time he slid in, our lips met, when he slid out, they parted. I'd never had sex with my eyes wide open. It was interesting. Where before I'd always known he was close by the slowing of his hips, the racing of his breath, the slight but telltale swelling within, now I saw the future in his eyes.

He stilled. I squirmed. He nipped my lip. "Don't," he managed, then licked the swell.

I saw blood on his tongue, and my damnable demon awoke. It didn't want to be confined and began to promise all sorts of tempting things.

"I order the vampire within to live only beneath the fullest of moons," Jimmy said.

I was busy trying to ignore my demon's promise to give me anything, anyone, at any time that I wished.

"Say it!"

His urgency got through and I repeated his words. As the word *moons* slipped from my lips, the demon's whisper faded.

Jimmy rewarded me with a slow, single stroke. All the way out then a deep plunge home. I moaned.

"I banish you from my soul, my body and mind."

I wanted another stroke like that so bad, I'd have said just about anything. I repeated his words and was again rewarded.

"Give me protection; give me peace."

I asked for the same, though I had little hope of actually getting it. I thought that was the end and lifted my hips, drawing him ever deeper. Jimmy cursed.

"Hold on. One. More. Thing." Sweat dripped from his forehead onto mine. *"Ci e niente che possiate fare che mi rendera l'arresto che lo ama."*

"Latin?" I asked. "Since when—?"

"Just say it," he managed between clenched teeth. "Hurry."

The orgasm rolled between us like a thunderstorm across the horizon. He tried to stop it, but it was too late. I felt him pulse, and I tightened around him. As the winds broke over us, I whispered: *"Ci e niente che possiate fare che mi rendera l'arresto che lo ama."*

The last word left my lips, and the candles died with an audible puff. Silence fell like a cool dark sea. We were both damp with sweat—the scent salty yet somehow sweet.

"Is that good?" I asked. "Or bad."

He rolled to the side, keeping hold of my hand as he always used to, and we both stared at the ceiling where the light of the moon now flickered and danced all alone.

"I don't know," he said.

Jimmy turned his head; I turned mine. Our noses brushed, and I was nearly overcome with the urge to kiss him and not stop kissing him until we made love for real, though what had just happened had felt more real than anything had for a long, long time.

"The only way to know if the spell worked is to take off—" With one finger, Jimmy traced my neck just above the collar.

The urge to kiss him, the warm, fuzzy, maybe-he-still-loves-me feeling vanished in a wash of cold sweat.

"You want to go first?" he asked.

"Why don't we take them off together?"

"If the spell didn't work, one of us has to stay sane enough to wrestle the control back on."

I swallowed, discovered I suddenly couldn't talk, and settled for a nod.

Jimmy sat up. "You first or me?"

I sat up, too. The moon cast just enough light to see the glow of his eyes but only the shadow of the rest of him.

I held out a hand. "Two out of three? Rock, paper, scissors?"

"Sure."

We began to count—*one, two*—swinging our fists up and down.

"Wait!" Jimmy stopped mid-three and so did I. "Does the winner go first or does the loser?"

That was a toughie. Being the first to know you were free—partially—of a bloodsucking evil thing was good. Then again, being the first to go bugfuck and try to kill the other, only to be forcibly latched back in to an embarrassing, bespelled control, was bad.

"I can't decide."

"Okay." Jimmy bit his lip for a second, scowling—a little boy faced with an impossible problem—then shrugged. "Winner should always go first."

"Works for me." This was basically the toss of a coin. Fate would decide. Or God, depending on what you believed. Either way, it was out of my hands.

We played the game as we had when children—fast and furious, no time to think, to reason, to plan a strategy.

One, two, three—I won. *One, two, three*—he did. *One, two, three*—

Jimmy's eyes met mine, and his lips quirked. "Congratulations."

"Ass."

"Sticks and stones. You still have to go first."

"Fine." I tugged on the catch. After a minor struggle—for obvious reasons the thing wasn't easy to remove—the collar loosened and tumbled free.

I watched it fall to the bed, the paste jewels catching the moonlight and turning every color of night. The control bounced on the mattress and lay still.

I waited for the change to rush over me.

Chapter 28

"Wanna tear out my throat?" Jimmy asked. "Bathe in the blood? Drink me so dry I blow away on the next stiff breeze?"

"Not right now," I said. "Maybe later."

He reached for his cock ring.

"Hold on."

"You wanna do it?" He lay back on the bed, putting his arms behind his head. "Be my guest."

"Don't screw with me now, Sanducci. I am in no mood."

He sat up. "Figures."

"Shhh." I tilted my head, listening, waiting for the voice of evil to whisper…something. I didn't think it was there, yet still I… "Sense it," I said.

Jimmy's temporary lightness fled. "We'll never be free of the vampire. I told you that when you insisted on becoming one. We can put it beneath the moon" —he met my gaze, holding it— "but you know what that means."

"We'll be even more bloodthirsty on that single night." If such a thing were possible. "I wish there were a way to know for sure."

"Know what?"

"That it's gone." I waved my hand before he could correct me. "Or contained beneath the moon and not just hiding in here" —I rapped my skull with my knuckles— "waiting for you to take your control off, and then we can party."

"I know a way." He got off the bed and started rooting through my duffel.

"Hey!" I said, but he ignored me. Since there really wasn't anything secret in there, I let him.

Jimmy pulled out a small plastic bag, reached in, and held up Ruthie's crucifix. The sight of it made my eyes sting. I'd missed wearing that almost as much as I missed hearing her voice.

Wait. I should be able to hear Ruthie's voice again—as soon as she had something to say.

Jimmy sat next to me on the bed. He held up his hand, and the chain unfurled. The tiny cross with the tiny hanging man twirled right and then left.

Jimmy leaned in. His hair brushed my face. I closed my eyes and waited. Would I go up in flames or wouldn't I?

Seconds later his fingers brushed my hair as he slipped the chain over my head. Jimmy sat back, letting the crucifix fall between my breasts, then drawing his thumb over the cross, pressing it more firmly against my skin. "All clear."

I let out a whoosh of breath. "Your turn."

But Jimmy wasn't wasting any time. His fingers

had already encircled the cock ring as well as his cock. The sight made me swallow against a sudden flare of lust.

He twisted his wrist; the circlet widened with a metallic *snick* and slid off. Sanducci stared at the ring resting on his open palm. Then he crunched it just by closing his fist.

"I *hated* this." He threw it out the window.

"You preferred being..." I made claws with my hands and hissed.

"Of course not!" Jimmy began to dress. "But that just made me feel like a—a—what do you call a guy in a harem?"

"A eunuch?"

He cast me a glance. "Very funny."

"A harem boy?"

"All right. That made me feel like a harem boy, you know?"

Unfortunately I did. When Jimmy had been under the power of his creepy vampire father, he'd made me his sex slave, complete with the Barbara Eden genie outfit. It had *not* been a good look for me.

Jimmy saw my face and cursed softly. "Sorry."

I waved the word away. "We can't spend the rest of our lives apologizing to each other."

For one thing, there was going to be a lot more we'd have to apologize for in the future. I was sure of it.

"Is that why you had the Dagda put a cock ring on me? Revenge?"

"I didn't tell him what to use. It was his idea of a joke."

"Seemed more like *your* idea of a joke."

Maybe we *were* going to have to keep apologizing for the rest of our lives.

"Believe me or don't believe me. I'm not going to keep begging you to." I put on my clothes. "We need to deal with Mait."

"Now?"

I glanced at the clock. Midnight. "We should go during the daytime. Unless you know how to disable those night demons."

Jimmy shook his head. "Considering Mait is the son of the origin of darkness, I vote for daytime, too."

I didn't care for Kalfu's title. The last time I'd had anything to do with "the darkness" I'd wound up a vampire.

"We should get some sleep," Jimmy said.

My gaze went to the bed. The bedspread lay on the floor and the sheets appeared to have been slept in by a kid with untreated ADHD. Believe me, I'd known quite a few, had to share a mattress with some of them in foster care. They kicked like mules and even asleep, their legs and arms rarely stopped moving.

"It's big enough for both of us," I said, and Jimmy jumped as if I'd stuck him with a pin.

I straightened the sheets, leaning over to pick up the bedspread just as a latch clicked. My gaze flicked around the empty room even as I headed for the door. But when I opened it, Jimmy was already gone. I wasn't surprised.

I could catch him, but why? He obviously didn't want to stay. He'd be back with the dawn. He couldn't go after Mait without me. Jimmy didn't know where the Nephilim was.

Though I longed to throw my control over the balcony as Jimmy had thrown his, I knew there might come a day when I needed to put the collar back on. I shoved the thing to the bottom of my duffel, picked up Sawyer's turquoise, and looped the chain over my neck, tucking the stone beneath my shirt along with Ruthie's crucifix. Then I stripped off my jeans and tried to get some sleep.

Next thing I knew light had just begun to creep across the sky. The breeze through the balcony window felt morning-cool and smelled like the fresh water I heard splashing out of the hoses and washing away the filth on the streets below.

Sanducci slouched in a chair by the terrace. I could have been annoyed that he'd disappeared last night; I could have started the day bitchy. But he'd brought coffee and beignets.

I crossed the room and snatched the nearest cup, taking a healthy swig despite the waft of steam that billowed up and nearly blinded me when I removed the top. Then I grabbed a beignet and stuffed most of it in my mouth—they were small— letting the sugar and the deep-fried dough soothe me until I almost felt human. "Where'd you go last night?"

Jimmy reached into his back pocket and slapped a lethal-looking silver dagger onto the table. The weapon was small, but from the way the sun sparked off the edges, it was sharp, the grip black, grooved, all business. No fancy jewels or cutesy dragon faces to mess up the aim.

"Charmed?" I asked.

"Wouldn't be much good if it wasn't."

I thought it might be good enough for most things, if you stuck them just right. But we weren't interested in most things. This dagger was for Mait.

"Where'd you get it?"

"Charmed dagger shop."

"That's a legitimate question. What if I need a charmed dagger at some point in the future?" Knowing my future, I was sure that I would.

"You've got one." He flicked his finger at the table.

"Do *you* have one?"

He shook his head.

"Why not?"

"They aren't cheap, Lizzy. Besides, we only need one. I'll grab the book, you stab the Nephilim."

"How come I have to stab the Nephilim?" I whined.

"Mait and I have a history. If he sees me coming, we're screwed."

"I thought the gris-gris would repel his magic."

"They will. But he's a big guy, and he fights dirty."

"So do you."

"You'll have a better chance of sliding in and—" Jimmy made a stabbing motion with his fist toward his eye. I resisted the urge to gag. I did not do well with eyes. They were yucky.

That sounds girlie. But I *am* a girl.

Which didn't mean I wouldn't do what I had to. I'd also do everything I could to get out of it first.

"Why do you think I'll be able to get close to him?" I asked. "I'm not huge, and my dirty fighting isn't the best."

I'd always had a hard time with it, probably because I'd been kicked when I was down so often as a kid whenever I tried to do it myself, I hesitated. I needed to get over that, but I wasn't sure how.

"Besides," I continued, "the first time Mait saw me, he knew I was there for the book."

"Anyone who shows up is there for the book."

"They couldn't be out for a stroll?"

"In New Orleans? In August? In the *swamp*?"

"All right."

"You won't have to fight him."

"You think he'll just let us walk in and grab the *Book of Samyaza*?"

"I think he won't notice me grabbing it if you're seducing him."

I choked on my coffee, which went down the wrong pipe and made me cough as if I were in the throes of death. For a while I wanted to be. At last I managed a hoarse, "If I'm doing what?"

"This guy's been stuck in an abandoned church for a very long time. He's desperate to get some."

"Well, he isn't getting any from me! He's a Nephilim."

"I didn't tell you to sleep with him."

"You said *seduce*."

"I meant offer but don't deliver. I'm sure you know how."

My eyes narrowed. I'd certainly never offered him anything I hadn't delivered.

"I'll just fight him. I've got skills."

"You won't have your powers." At my frown, Jimmy lifted a gris-gris. "Once we walk in with these, it's a no-magic zone for everyone."

"You couldn't buy a gris-gris that puts a hex on evil magic and leaves the good guys' juice alone?"

"What *is* evil?" he murmured.

"Don't start with the existential bullshit!"

"It's a legitimate question." He repeated back my own earlier comment, and my head felt as if it might explode. Only Sanducci had this effect on me.

"You think a bag of seeds and grass can tell the difference between good and evil?" he asked. "Especially when the bad guys believe what they're doing needs to be done. Haven't you ever heard the saying: *A villain is the hero of his own story*?"

"No."

"Think about it. Mait was given the task of

protecting that book. He's going to protect it by any means necessary. Is that an evil deed?"

"Hell, yeah!"

"In your opinion."

"In everyone's opinion."

"Mait's just following orders."

"From Lucifer," I said. "You think because the guards at Dachau were 'just following orders,' they aren't roasting above an open flame directly to the left of Hitler?"

"Probably." Jimmy sighed. "The fact remains that the gris-gris will put a stop to any magic—good or bad—so seduction is your best bet. Get in close, make sure I've got the book, then" —he made the same jabbing motion toward his eye, and I flinched— "nail him."

Chapter 29

"Got the gris-gris?" Jimmy asked as he stepped out of the car near the swamp.

"Check. You?"

"Roger."

"Dagger?" Jimmy continued, as if I were new at this.

I patted the back pocket of my jeans. I'd donned the tightest pair I could find, along with a well-washed white tank so see-through the shade of my skin made it appear beige. I hadn't bothered with a bra. Why try to be subtle? I'd never been any good at it.

I'd left the turquoise and the crucifix at the hotel. No need to remind Mait whose side I was on until I had to.

"Okay then." Jimmy rocked back on his heels, glanced at the sky.

"Synchronize our watches?"

He lowered his head, lifted a brow. "You aren't wearing one."

"I'm not wearing much." I walked into the overgrowth.

Despite the early hour, I was dripping sweat by the time I reached the church. Mait had said he was on duty in the daytime, so I'd assumed night demons only demoned at night. Since no evil bat-like shadows dived from the sky and tried to eviscerate me, I appeared to be right.

"Mait?"

He appeared in the doorway so fast, I thought he might have been waiting for me. Probably just waiting for someone, anyone. If I had to live alone in an abandoned church in the swamp with only nasty demon birds and Lucifer's Bible for company, I'd hover around the doorway, too.

"Back for de book?" he asked, gazing on my breasts, which might as well have been bare for all the good my old, white, wet shirt provided for cover.

I didn't answer. He wasn't listening anyway. Instead I walked toward him, making sure I put a little bounce in my step that transferred to my chest.

Ba-booommmmm. Ba-booommmm.

"Mait," I said in what I hoped was a tempting voice.

Jimmy's idea of sending me to seduce someone, probably not the best idea he'd ever had. I was more of the *Jump him if you want him* school. But if I did that now, I'd have to follow through, and that wasn't happening.

A few more ba-boom steps and I came close enough to see the symbol depicted by the tiny braids across Mait's skull. A cross of two straight lines, combined with another cross that ended in a curlicue and tilted toward two o'clock, all with the same center—an *X* and a *T*—crossroad upon a crossroad. Very powerful magic.

I ran my finger along it, attempting to get inside his head, but either the gris-gris was strong enough to block my psychometry or his mind was too full of breasts for anything else.

Since I'd never considered my psychometric talent a form of magic—I'd been born with the talent; being psychic was part of me, not something I'd earned or taken or learned—I voted for the latter.

Mait snatched my wrist. "How did you get past de protection spell?"

I smiled despite the pain of his fingers crunching my bones. "I'll tell you later."

"Tell me now."

I needed to ramp up the seduction. At this rate, Mait was going to know Jimmy was coming long before he arrived. I had maybe five minutes to make Mait see, hear, and breathe nothing but me.

I tugged on my wrist and he let go, though he stayed close enough to grab me again if he needed to. I slid my fingers into my front pocket, pushing my chest out in the process.

The shirt had begun to dry in the heat, the salt from my skin causing the material to stiffen. When it rubbed against my nipples so did they.

"Mmm." I wiggled so the shirt shimmied some more. "I've got a little—"

With difficulty he pulled his eyes from my chest. Every one of my fingers was outlined inside of the faded denim pocket of my too-tight jeans. All of them pointed toward my crotch. Mait licked his lips, and I stifled a smile. This wasn't so hard.

I pulled my hand out just as slowly as I'd put it in. "Gris-gris." I held up the bag.

He snatched at it, but I'd been expecting that and put my hands behind my back. He got very interested in my boobs again. He *hadn't* had any in a very long time.

"Ah-ah," I singsonged. "No magic but what we make, okay?"

Sheesh, had I actually *said* that?

"Okay," he echoed, and I knew I had him.

How the guy could think the woman he'd met first as a phoenix and the woman I pretended to be now were one and the same without a complete personality transplant was a mystery. Then again, considering that all the blood in his head was now in his pants, maybe not such a mystery after all.

Why anyone believed it was a good idea to lock up people all alone yet expect them to be incorruptible, I hadn't a clue. Either the person would go stark raving mad or, if we were talking about a guy, he'd be easily compromised by a pair of great breasts in a thin white tank top.

A flash of movement caught my attention. *Jimmy!* Luckily Mait had his back to the room and his nose practically buried in my breasts.

"You can touch them if you like."

His hands crushed; his mouth suckled. I used his inattention to shove the gris-gris into my front pocket.

I must have made all the right noises, all the right moves, because Mait never hesitated in his adoration of my breasts. I retreated to my special place, one I'd fashioned when I was young and there'd been times I'd had to check out or lose my mind.

I'd learned I couldn't check out completely. Monsters—be they half demon or entirely human—liked to get some response. If they didn't, they only tried harder and kept at it longer.

Mait began to slide his erection against the skintight crotch of my jeans. I gasped at the sudden rush of nausea. But I'd had practice; I could make the gasp sound like anything. My head fell back as if I were in the throes of passion, when in truth I couldn't bear to see his face.

Mait's hands left my chest and grabbed my ass, lifting me onto his thigh. He held me there as he rocked his leg to the rhythm of his mouth at my breast. Jimmy'd better hurry up or I might nail this guy one way before he nailed me in another.

My jeans vibrated. Mait lifted his head. His mouth was wet, his eyes slightly unfocused, their brilliant green exquisite against the mocha of his skin.

"What is that?"

I smiled, though the expression felt as if it

would crack my frozen face. "Cell phone." The prearranged signal. Jimmy had the book. Time for me to end this guy and run. "I'll turn it off."

Slipping my fingers into my pocket, I clicked the OFF button. When I brought them back out, I held the dagger just out of sight.

"Would you like to come in?" Mait asked.

"Definitely."

Better to kill him out of sight than in the doorway. The longer the Nephilim remained unaware that we had their book, the better.

Mait flexed the muscles in his thigh. They rolled against my clitoris. My stomach clenched so hard I nearly doubled over. I'd thought I might have a problem sticking him in the eye with the dagger. I didn't think so anymore.

I climbed off his leg, glanced toward the church, and saw Jimmy through one of the holes in the crumbling walls. So did Mait.

"Who de hell are you?" he demanded. Then his eyes narrowed, and he roared, "Sanducci!"

Mait started forward. I brought the knife up toward his nearest eye. I might have made it if I hadn't at the same moment registered what Jimmy was doing.

Burning the Book of Samyaza.

The realization caused me to hesitate, and that hesitation cost me. As Jimmy had said, Mait was a big guy and he fought dirty. He didn't even look in my direction as he backhanded me across the cheekbone. Pain exploded. It felt as if he'd just poked out *my* eye.

I stumbled, disoriented, and he spun, catching me in the chest with his bare foot. I flew into the doorjamb. The force snapped my head against the corner and down I went. I didn't get back up.

"What have you done?" Mait shouted.

"Bastard burned the book," I mumbled as the whole world spun.

I should have seen it coming. Would have if I'd trusted Sanducci less and touched him with the intent of picking his brain a little more. That's what I got for being polite.

Dizziness washed over me, and I thought I might pass out. I wanted to. Then I wouldn't have to think about what Jimmy had just done.

Destroyed the only hope I had of getting Sawyer back alive.

Chapter 30

I was supposed to have a dagger in my hand, but I didn't. I glanced around; I couldn't see it anywhere. Checked my back pockets. Nothing. Front pockets. Nothing.

Spots flickered in front of my eyes. White. Black. Red. They chased one another like amoebas across a microscope slide. Watching them only made me dizzier, so I turned my attention to Mait just as he let out a furious shout and sprinted for Jimmy.

"No," I whispered. I didn't seem to have any volume to my voice or strength in my limbs. I'd been hit harder than this before. What was *wrong* with me?

The two men came together like deer during rut. Though they didn't butt racks, they did slam chests, then they wrapped their arms around each other and grappled.

Mait was a hair taller, a tad wider, and while he might be strong and fight dirty, Jimmy fought dirtier and had been doing so since he was very young. Mait, on the other hand, had been relying on magic for too long. It showed.

Jimmy wrestled him to the ground and attempted to get his arm around Mait's neck. Not that it would do much good. Jimmy had no weapon, or at least none that would work.

"Lizzy!" Jimmy shouted. "The dagger!"

I shook my head hard enough to rattle my brains some more. The pain sobered me, and I began to crawl, first looking then feeling for the missing knife. I couldn't find it.

"Lizzy!"

It was hard to tell who was winning; they looked like a double man pretzel, all wound together, fingers searching for a better hold, arms bulging, legs flailing.

"It's gone."

Jimmy flicked me a glance, and Mait slammed his elbow into his nose. The crunch echoed throughout the abandoned church. Blood spouted; Jimmy lost his grip. Mait leaped to his feet and ran.

Making a grab for him, I wound up on my face in the dirt. I slapped my palm to the phoenix tattoo. If I could shift, I'd heal, and then I'd catch him. Wouldn't be any trouble at all.

Except the gris-gris still blocked my magic.

I pulled the thing out of my pocket, then threw it as far as I could.

Jimmy cursed and bled. I crept over to him and felt his pockets until I found his gris-gris, then I tossed that away, too.

I began to lift my hand again, but Jimmy

grabbed it before I got there. "Don't bother," he said, his voice thick with pain and blood.

"I can catch him."

He shook his head then, cursing, winced. "The instant he got far enough from the gris-gris, his magic came back." He pulled himself to his feet then helped me to mine. I managed not to fall back down. "He's long gone."

"I thought he was confined."

"To protect the book." Jimmy met my eyes.

"But you burned it, and released him." I couldn't help it, I slapped Jimmy across his bloody face. "What were you thinking?"

The slap resounded in the sudden silence that followed. The imprint of my fingers appeared, dark splotches on his already dark and splotched skin. I hated the sight; nevertheless, I wanted to hit him again.

"I was thinking that the book was trouble. Nothing good could come from it." His gaze bored into mine. "Nothing."

I wasn't so sure about that.

"You insisted that we push our vampires beneath the moon so we wouldn't be tempted to steal the *Book of Samyaza.* But we could have used those demons, or at least one of them, to end Mait."

"I'll end Mait. Don't worry about that."

"Yeah, you've been having great luck so far," I muttered, earning an exasperated glare from Sanducci. "If you were going to burn the damn thing anyway, what was the point of the full moon evil spell?"

"We aren't the only problem. Anyone who has that book is dangerous. Anyone could be tempted by the secrets inside it. You were."

An icy breeze seemed to stir the wings of my phoenix tattoo. "What's that supposed to mean?"

"I'm not stupid, Lizzy."

"So *you* say."

His lips tightened. I couldn't blame him. "Do you remember when your mother was raising revenants?"

I blinked at the seemingly random change in subject. "I don't think I'm ever gonna forget Mommy or her army of the undead."

"They were an Apocalyptic portent."

"And now they're dust."

"Which leaves plenty of room for the next undead army."

"There's more than one?"

"Without a phoenix to raise revenants—"

"*I'm* a phoenix."

"You plan on raising some?"

"*Hell* no!"

The dead my mother had raised, while looking completely human, had not acted human. They'd given me the creeps.

"Besides," I admitted. "I don't really know how."

"I don't think it's brain surgery."

"It isn't."

Jimmy's eyes widened. "You tried it?"

"Don't get all bent out of shape, nothing happened."

Jimmy let out a long breath and rubbed his eyes as if they ached. "What were you thinking?"

In the days following Sawyer's death I hadn't been thinking about much but getting him back. I'd tried everything I knew. But I hadn't known how to raise a revenant, so I did a little research.

"The power isn't active until I've been raised from the grave like she was," I said. "And I'm not planning on dying anytime soon."

Jimmy lowered his hand and his gaze met mine. He was disappointed in me, but that was nothing new.

"Without a phoenix to raise revenants," he repeated, "the forces of darkness are going to have to find another way. According to the rumors, the way was written in that book."

I stared at him for several seconds. "You knew all along why I wanted it?"

"You can't raise the dead. You'll be playing right into their hands. It's better that the *Book of Samyaza* is ashes."

"I wasn't going to raise an army. Just—" My throat closed off; I couldn't say Sawyer's name.

"Did it ever occur to you that performing a spell in a book written by Beelzebub might not be the brightest idea for *any* reason?"

I forced myself to speak past the painful lump. "We need him."

"No," he said. "You do."

"Sawyer's one of the most powerful beings on this earth."

"Now you are."

"Two's always better than one." And according to my vision, two was what I would need.

"Not when one has died and been brought back to life through evil means," Jimmy said. "You have no idea what he'll come back like."

"He'll come back like himself."

"You sure about that?"

"You've always hated him."

"So did you once."

Had I? Those days seemed so long ago. After I'd gotten to know Sawyer, to understand him, and I realized why he was the way he was, things had changed. I'd changed.

I didn't want to raise Sawyer to assuage my guilt for killing him, or because Faith needed a father, or even because I missed him so much—though all of those things were true—but because Sawyer had power, wisdom, and knowledge beyond my own and everyone else's. I didn't think we could win without him. And that was without taking into account my dream of a crucified Jimmy and a missing little girl.

"None of this matters now," I said. "The book is gone."

Along with all its secrets.

The two of us searched awhile longer for the dagger but had no luck. There were so many holes in the floor, so many piles of old wood and stone, the weapon could be anywhere.

"You're sure you brought it?"

"You know, I'm not exactly new at this." I'd had it in my hand. Too bad I hadn't used it.

My dizziness passed. I began to attribute it more to being upset over the loss of Sawyer and what that would mean to us all than the love tap Mait had given me. The pain was already gone, and according to Jimmy the black eye was fading.

We were sweaty and panting by the time we reached the car. The air-conditioning felt heavenly, and I let it blow in my face all the way to the hotel.

Once there, I went directly into the bathroom and locked the door. Not that a door would keep Sanducci out if he wanted to get in. But the sound of my locking it might. Jimmy would never go where he wasn't wanted.

I let tepid water beat on my head and soothe the frantic pounding of my pulse. I was both furious and frightened. We were going to have to make do without Sawyer, and I wasn't sure how.

I slammed my palm against the wall. Something crunched. I opened one eye. I'd put a crack in the tile.

"Suck it up," I muttered. "Did you think the Apocalypse was going to be easy?"

No. But I'd thought I'd have more help.

I half expected Jimmy to be gone by the time I came out—either to beg, borrow, or steal another dagger or to get a lead on Mait. But he wasn't.

As I crossed to the dresser and slipped first Ruthie's crucifix, then Sawyer's turquoise, over my head, I caught a glimpse of myself in the mirror. For an instant I panicked, thinking my collar had fallen off.

I braced against the evil that would wash over me along with the unquenchable desire to kill everything I saw. Not that bracing would help. When the evil was free, there was nothing I could do about it. When the evil was me, I didn't want to.

Fast on the heels of panic came relief. The demon was gone—at least until the next full moon.

"Do you have to do that?" Jimmy asked.

"What?" I turned.

"Rub his turquoise as if you were rubbing—" Jimmy crossed to the balcony, staring out at the setting sun.

I glanced down. I *had* been rubbing the turquoise as if I were rubbing—

"Sawyer," I whispered, and my hand clenched around the stone. I listened, hoping for some kind of answer, but there was nothing. Would there ever be anything again?

Anger sparked, and since anger was always better than agony, I went with it, crossing the room until I stood just inside the terrace doors.

"Sanducci."

He faced me, expression tense, mouth tight.

"You were supposed to grab the book and run."

I shoved him in the chest.

"You were supposed to kill Mait." He shoved me right back.

"Why didn't you?" I demanded.

"Why didn't *you?*"

We stood nose-to-nose, just like when we were kids. If I weren't careful, he'd kick me in the shin and take my last cookie.

"We had a plan. You should have followed through."

"Did you really think I was going to put that book into your hands?"

I had. My mistake.

"Why didn't you take it somewhere and burn it?" Somewhere that I could have snatched it. "Why wait until Mait recognized you and everything went to hell?"

"I didn't wait. I signaled for you to kill him." He looked me up and down as if I were someone he'd just met and did not like. "You were close enough."

"That was the plan! Your plan. At least I stuck to it."

"Until you *didn't* kill him."

"I'm supposed to be the leader of the light. You're my *second.* That means you take orders from me, and I ordered you to bring me that book."

His eyes flared. For an instant I saw again the vampire he could become. Then he stalked to the door. "What are you going to do about it, *mistress?* Kill me?"

I took a step toward him—the fury inside making me think that sounded like a damn fine idea—but he stepped into the hallway and slammed the door. I didn't bother to follow; I knew he'd be gone.

This time I didn't think he'd be back.

Chapter 31

As night came, rain pattered on the terrace. I should have packed my things and headed for New Mexico, but I was tired, and sad, and depressed. Watching the rain fall on New Orleans wasn't helping.

I'd tried to call Luther then Summer, but no one answered. Not uncommon. Residing in the shadow of Mount Taylor often screwed up cell reception. Living in an enchanted cottage didn't help, either. If I still couldn't reach them by late tomorrow morning I'd start to worry, and by then I'd be halfway home.

I listened to the storm as I sipped the rich red wine I'd ordered from room service. Eventually my exhaustion, combined with the alcohol, made me nod, so I dropped all my clothes on the floor and crawled into bed. The rhythm of the rain followed me into the darkness.

I badly wanted to talk to Sawyer. Instead I got Ruthie. I should have been happier about it. I'd been wishing Ruthie back since I'd lost her.

When I spoke to Ruthie in my dreams I went to

her. The house with the white picket fence wasn't the one she'd lived in, and died in, but I knew it was hers just the same. Even before I strolled up the walk, and she opened the door.

"Lizbeth." Ruthie spread wide her arms.

Despite being skinny, with elbows, knees, and hips like razors, Ruthie gave the best hugs in this world as well as the next. God, I had missed them.

How being hugged by a woman who was built like a bag of bones could be so soft and gentle, I had no idea. But as I stepped into Ruthie's embrace my exhaustion fled, my sadness lifted, and I felt again like I could do anything. She'd always had that effect on me.

Ruthie rubbed my back, murmuring nonsense into my hair as she held me. As always, I pulled away first, never her. Which might just *be* the secret to those hugs.

She kept hold of my hand, hers thin and heavily veined—but still as strong as her heart, which I'd felt thumping steadily against my chest despite her being dead nearly three months now. She drew me inside and closed the door.

"I'm so glad you're back," I said.

Ruthie smiled, white teeth flashing against the rich coffee hue of her face, her puffy, graying Afro swaying as she shook her head. "Been here all the time, child. You were the one who was gone."

"Not gone. Not really."

"Occupied?" She shrugged. "Don't matter now.

Plenty of time for me to come and visit between every full moon." Ruthie's eyes narrowed. "Though I don't recall telling you it was okay to confine that demon."

Annoyance flickered. It hadn't been my idea, and besides— "I didn't realize I had to ask. Isn't that what being 'the leader' means?"

"You don't think you need my help?"

The annoyance died, like a flame in a high wind. "I didn't say that." I needed all the help I could get.

"Come on." She moved down the hall toward her sunny kitchen.

On the table sat two cups of tea. I wasn't a fan, but Ruthie was, so I took a seat. Beyond the big windows at the back of the house, children played in the steadily changing yard, first with a huge play set made of wood. Then a large field appeared and the kids—all shapes and sizes—chose sides for some kind of game.

Ruthie's place today was as full of lost souls as it had been when she was alive. The only difference now was that everyone in her house—except for me—was dead.

Every time I came to Ruthie's heaven, guilt pulsed. Lately every time I came, the kids were in residence because I'd failed to save them.

I took a swallow of tea. Refreshingly minty. I still didn't like it.

"Why am I here?" I asked.

"I thought you missed me."

"I did, but—" I shrugged.

"You'd rather see Sawyer."

"Yeah." I took a deep breath. "Thanks to Sanducci, I won't be."

Ruthie took a sip of tea and didn't answer.

"Right?"

She set down her cup then stared out the window. Her charges were kicking a soccer ball—back and forth, back and forth.

"Ruthie?" I tried again. "Why am I here?"

"Trouble's comin'," she said.

"If I had a nickel for every time I've heard that."

"You're gonna have to live with the choices you make; you're gonna have to make them on your own. And soon."

"When? What?"

I didn't like making decisions that saved or ended people's lives, that could, in the long run, mean the beginning of the end of the world. Especially since half the time I had no clue what I was doing.

"You're right," she said. "You've come for a reason. There's somethin' I've gotta tell you."

Fear trickled over me, leaving behind icy sweat and a thick nasty taste at the base of my throat. "Jimmy—" I began, then— "Luther."

I started to get dizzy, realized I wasn't breathing, then did with a huge, loud gasp on the word, "Faith!"

Ruthie snapped her fingers in front of my face.

"Focus, Lizbeth!"

It wasn't easy, but I got it together. "I'm okay."

"If the Nephilim believe you have a weakness" —she narrowed her eyes— "or three. They'll use it."

I knew that. Had been warned over and over not to care too much. But I couldn't help it.

"What's wrong?" I asked.

"Everything." Ruthie touched the center of my forehead with her thumb.

My eyes crossed, I blinked, and in that instant I was somewhere else.

A dark, deserted street—sidewalk broken, a few streetlights, too. The air thick and hot; it still smelled of rain.

"New Orleans." I'd know that scent anywhere.

Rows of buildings seemed to hunch with age. Ahead I could just make out the towering spires of a church, and across the way—

"Saint Louis Number One."

The oldest existing cemetery in New Orleans, and a very dangerous place to visit after dark. Good thing I wasn't really there.

St. Louis Cemetery Number One had been built on what had once been Storyville, the only legal red-light district in the country. The place was a lot quieter now. Although as I watched, lightning began to sizzle and thunder to rumble. Both seemed to be focused directly above the cemetery. A low, deep voice lifted from beyond the white brick walls—a voice I recognized.

"Mait." I started for the gate.

He did say he'd been reading the book.

Was that Ruthie's voice, or my own? And what did it mean?

The gate was closed, locked, but that didn't matter. I wished to be within and I was.

I'd been here before, but in the daylight and on a tour. The place had been spooky then, now it was downright unearthly.

Since New Orleans had been built below sea level, they buried people aboveground; otherwise their coffins popped up and floated away during the rainy season.

Interestingly enough, the cemeteries were the most desegregated places in the city. In death, folks were separated by religion, not race, and every single one was treated the same.

After a year and a day spent on a shelf inside a brick monument, quaintly called an oven, their remains were dumped into a well with whoever had been there before to make room for the next occupant. Though St. Louis Number One spanned only a single block, it was the resting place of more than a hundred thousand souls.

White monuments shown luminescent in the moonlight. Shadows danced across the rock-strewn ground. Here the outline of an angel perched atop a tall thin crypt. There the ghostly form of the Virgin cast by a statue surrounded with sunburned grass.

I followed the sound of Mait's voice. He wasn't trying to be quiet. No one was really here but him.

"Arise!" he shouted.

The figure of a man darted toward the gate. At first I thought it was Mait; then I heard the sosye speak again nearby. "Not all has been lost."

Two more silhouettes sprinted between the crypts. The gate rattled. I peeked around a statue. Mait clapped once, and something creaked—very *Addams Family*— followed by the rhythm of retreating footsteps. A quick glance toward Rampart Street revealed the gate now stood wide open as half a dozen figures scooted through then scattered in different directions.

Damn. He had been reading the book.

I watched, both repelled and enthralled, as Mait set his hand against another glistening white tomb and murmured, "Arise."

I waited for the door to open, or perhaps for the stone to fall away. Maybe smoke would trail out of a crack and form the shape of the undead, becoming more and more solid until the newly risen spirit could cause the footsteps I'd so recently heard as it ran away to Samyaza-only-knew where.

Instead, another human-sized shadow flitted between the tombs and out through the gate. Now you don't see him, abracadabra, now you do.

The heated, overripe night suddenly felt far too cool. No matter what we did, we couldn't seem to get ahead in our battle against the forces of darkness. I knew everything was inevitable, but sheesh, couldn't we just once catch a break?

Burn the book to keep them from raising another army of the undead only to discover that the keeper of the book had memorized the freaking thing.

The next instant I sat across from Ruthie at the kitchen table. Her tea was gone; mine was cold.

"All he has to say is 'arise' and they do? What kind of spell is that?" I asked.

Ruthie's dark eyes contemplated me for several seconds, as if she was trying to decide if she should tell me the truth or not. Then she sighed. "The spell in the *Book of Samyaza* doesn't raise the dead, child, it creates someone who can."

Chapter 32

Me of the pithy comebacks stared at Ruthie and said, "Huh?"

"Mait has the ability to raise the dead."

The light in my brain finally flickered. "Armageddon here we come. What else was in that book?"

"We're never gonna know."

Maybe I *was* glad Jimmy had burned it. But what about Ruthie?

"Did you tell him to burn the book?" I asked.

"Me?" She seemed genuinely surprised.

I didn't buy it. "Did you?"

Ruthie shook her head. "Didn't know you'd found the thing until it went up in flames."

"You and me both. Just once I'd like to find out something before it's too late to stop it."

"Who said it's too late?"

I tapped my temple. "I just saw the guy raising zombies—"

"Not zombies," Ruthie corrected. "People."

"People?"

"You saw what he did. Were the beings that Mait raised shambling, moaning, dropping body parts across the ground as they ran?"

"No." That they were running at all was a pretty neat trick considering. "They moved normally. Silently. I didn't see them well enough to know if they had rotten ears and fingers, but—"

"They didn't," she said. "They won't need to eat human flesh to survive, either."

"Always a plus. What *will* they eat?"

"Same thing they always did. Mait raised them to life."

"He can raise anything?"

"Anything with human blood."

"Nephilim, too, then?"

"In theory," Ruthie said.

"I bet he makes that theory into a fact real soon."

The Grigori wouldn't even need to escape Tartarus to replenish their Nephilim army. All they'd have to do was raise their cohorts back to life and everything the federation had done would be erased; all those who'd died for this cause would have died in vain.

"Not on my watch." I was *so* going to kill this guy. But first he and I would have a chat.

Ruthie stared at me, waiting to hear more questions, or perhaps just my plan. I didn't have one, but I would. I always did. I liked plans.

"Once these beings are raised they're exactly as

they were before they died?" I asked. Maybe Sawyer wasn't gone forever after all. Which, considering what we were up against, was *such* good news.

"I doubt anyone's been dead would come back exactly the same."

"But you just said—"

"Physically yes. Mentally?" Ruthie shrugged. "They were dead. No tellin' how that affected their minds."

"Terrific. We've got crazy un-zombies running around New Orleans."

"Not yet. You saw the future."

I frowned. "How far in the future?"

Ruthie's sober dark eyes met mine. "Mait's been cooped up in that church for a while. Right now I'd say he's gettin' lap dances on Bourbon."

I stood so fast my chair skidded back and nearly fell over.

"Calm down. *Sit* down," she ordered.

"If he's on Bourbon, I could grab him tonight. No one would even notice."

Not that it would matter if they did. It would just be easier if they didn't.

"It's August in New Orleans, Lizbeth, not Mardi Gras. Someone would notice."

She was right. I sat down. "I can't afford to let him slip away."

"You know where he'll be."

"I'll stake out the cemetery," I said.

"I would."

"Just to be safe, how do I kill an un-zombie zombie?"

"No special way. They're the same, physically, as when they died the first time."

"Plain old murder then."

"Lizbeth," Ruthie said on a sigh.

"I need to know. What if something happens on the way to the cemetery? What if I fall and I can't get up? What if Mait does his dirty deed and raises a hundred thousand souls? Then what?"

"Chaos."

"Worse. The only reason to raise the dead is to create an army for the final battle."

"And they gathered them together to the place called in Hebrew, Armageddon," Ruthie quoted.

Everyone's heard about Armageddon—and I don't mean the Bruce Willis movie, but the OK Corral of the Apocalypse. Technically Armageddon is where the last battle between good and evil should take place.

As stated in Revelation 16:16, the word *harmageddon* means "the mount of Megiddo," literally the mountain of slaughter, and it's located in northern Israel. More than two hundred battles have been fought on that extended plain near the mount. Napoleon once called it "the most natural battleground on the whole earth." He believed all the armies of the world could maneuver across such a vast space, and from the photos I've seen they could. From what I've read, they'll have to.

Sounds like I paid attention the day they taught Revelation, doesn't it? Wrong. I looked it up last week.

"I need to get to Mait before he stops practicing on people and starts bringing back half demons."

"He won't," Ruthie said. "At least not right away."

"Of course he will. What good is an army of humans who can easily be demolished by anyone with supernatural powers?"

"We don't much like to kill people, Lizbeth. We're supposed to protect them."

"Which makes them the perfect foot soldiers." I rubbed at the pulse pounding between my eyes. "Why would human beings fight for the dark side?"

"What would you do for someone who raised you from the dead?"

I dropped my hand. "There's a price."

"Ain't there always?"

"Yeah."

"Remember that." Ruthie held my gaze. "Nothing on this earth ever comes for free."

"So the risen dead will pay their debt on the front lines."

"*They were trampled in the winepress outside the city,*" Ruthie quoted again, "*and blood flowed out of the press, rising as high as the horses' bridles for a distance of sixteen hundred stadia.*"

"You wanna translate?" When she started talking about stadia, my head just spun.

"In the final battle blood will rise as high as a horse's bridle."

The last time I'd stood next to a horse, the bridle'd been as high as my chin.

"A stadia is like a furlong," Ruthie continued. "Sixteen hundred stadia would be about a hundred and eighty miles."

"Blood as high as a horse's bridle across a distance of a hundred and eighty miles," I repeated.

Ruthie spread her bony, bird-like fingers. "So it was written."

Since a lot of what was written had come to pass, my stomach pitched like the Red Sea. Prophecy is tricky, but once it starts to make sense, things fall into place like the last few pieces in a very big puzzle.

"Nephilim would be ashes," I murmured. "No blood." Which only lent weight to Ruthie's belief that Mait would raise humans—at first.

"For centuries scholars argued over the meaning of Revelation nine-sixteen," Ruthie said. *"And the number of the army of the horsemen were two hundred thousand thousand."*

"Two hundred million."

"The number was too big to be taken literally for a very long time. But then came a nation with not only a huge population, but a mammoth standing army with uncountable reserves."

"China."

"Yes. The force will come out of the east, and

the population in what is now considered the east is more than three billion."

"The scholars focused on China," I said. "But they were wrong."

"Wouldn't be the first time."

"What about the *coming out of the east* part?"

"East is relative, child. March east-to-west and bam," she smacked her palms together, "you've got an army from the east. All the Bible really says is that the big ol' army will march across the Euphrates."

"Which happens to be east of Israel."

"Last time I looked," Ruthie agreed.

"I gotta go."

"Hold on." Ruthie laid her hand over mine. "The book is gone. The only being capable of bringing back the dead is Mait. You know what that means?"

"Charmed dagger to the left eye and fast."

"You also have to consider what's best for the world in the long run, not what's best for any one person right this minute."

"What are you trying to say?"

"You wanna raise Sawyer."

I didn't bother to lie. Not to Ruthie. "So?"

"No one comes back the same, Lizbeth."

"You sent me to Sani to learn how to raise ghosts."

"I sent you to Sani because I was told to send you to Sani."

That made me pause. Though Ruthie often

behaved as if she were the lead singer in our rock-and-roll end times band, she wasn't. She took her orders from the biggest voice of all—the one that had serenaded Moses on Mount Sinai. Or at least that's what she told me.

And if she wasn't telling the truth about that... well, I was in bigger trouble than I'd ever get out of.

"There's a reason—"

"For everything," I finished, having heard it before. I didn't much care for being ordered around without an explanation, but I was used to it. No matter how much I disliked operating half blind, the truth remained—I had to have faith. In more ways than one.

"Sani knew where the book was," Ruthie said.

"Why didn't you know? Why didn't *anyone* know what Mait was up to before he was up to it?"

"The spell of protection cloaked everything."

"Then how did Sani know where to find the book?"

"Sani isn't one of us. He's one of them."

I wasn't surprised. Still... "Why would he tell me—" I paused as my brain answered the question before Ruthie could. "Payment."

The twists and turns of fate, or God's will, or prophecy were far too complicated for a mere dumb-ass like me.

"Perhaps," Ruthie said.

"Don't we need Sawyer?" I asked.

"Is it need or is it want, child?"

"He's... My voice trailed off. I'd been going to

say *necessary,* but instead I said, "Powerful."

"So are you."

"Two's better than one," I repeated.

"Is it?"

When she started answering my questions with questions, I always got a headache.

"You're telling me I shouldn't get him back?"

"Yes," Ruthie said. "That's exactly what I'm telling you."

Since Ruthie's motto had always been—*Do whatever you have to do to win*—I was shocked nearly speechless.

"Jimmy was right to burn the book," she said. "The temptation is too great."

"I'm not a four-year-old with a box of chocolates. I can control myself."

She didn't look convinced and I saw red. I pushed back from the table, and this time my chair did fall over. The *thwack* of the wood against the tile made me flinch, but I left it where it lay.

"You think I'll be tempted to force Mait to raise Sawyer before I stick a dagger in his pretty green eye?"

Ruthie lifted a brow, which was all it took for me to pick up the chair.

"Sit," she ordered again, but I couldn't. Instead I paced to the window. The kids were now playing basketball on a full cement court, complete with a painted three-point arc, free-throw line, and boundaries.

"Mait knows better than to give us back one of

our most powerful players," Ruthie said quietly. "You won't be able to force him to do anything."

"Wanna bet?"

"Payment must be made. Always. You can't reverse death without consequences. And sometimes those consequences are for the raiser and not the raisee."

"You think I'm afraid?"

"No." Her dark solemn eyes caught and held mine. "I am. You're the leader of the light. The choices you make aren't your own. You have to be sure the sacrifice is worth the reward. Weigh the effect of what you do on the future. And if you don't know what that effect will be…" She let out a long, sad breath. "Best not to do anything at all."

She was right, and I knew it.

I lowered my head, staring at the worn kitchen tile as I blinked several times hard and fast. Deciding to let Sawyer lie was like killing him all over again.

Ruthie remained silent while I got hold of myself. It never took me very long. I'd been getting hold of myself all my life.

"You know where I can get a charmed dagger?"

Ruthie searched my face. She must have been satisfied with what she saw there because she smiled softly. "You're a sorcerer, charm one yourself."

"I don't know how."

"Learn." She snapped her fingers, and I woke up in my room.

The storm had passed, leaving the air smelling cool, fresh, and clean. At least until the sun rose and heated the streets and the overgrowth until they again smelled a little like garbage.

I glanced at the clock. Middle of the night. I couldn't exactly call the local charmed dagger shop, even if I knew the number. It was times like these that I really missed Xander Whitelaw. The professor had been able to find out just about anything.

I stared at the ceiling and suddenly remembered something—really someone—so I scrambled out of bed, tore through my backpack, and found the slip of paper with a cell number.

Bram answered on the first ring, and he sounded wide-awake. " 'Lo?"

"This is Liz."

"Liz who?"

"From the cemetery." When he didn't say anything, I continued, "You meet a lot of women named Liz near cemeteries?"

"You never told me your last name."

I wasn't sharing the name *Phoenix* when Bram had dreamed of a great, multicolored bird. That would be a good way to gain a very lethal stalker. I had enough things trying to kill me already.

"Neither did you," I pointed out.

"You're right," he agreed, but he didn't tell me his name. "What can I do for you?"

"Know how to charm a dagger?"

"You've run into a sorcerer who needs killing."

He *did* know his Nephilim. "Can you help me?"

"What type of sorcerer?"

"Sosye."

"Haitian. Okay. Get a piece of paper. Draw a square. Within the square write what you want to happen. Then use the sharp instrument—"

"Any sharp instrument?" I asked. "Doesn't it have to be a dagger?"

"Anything sharp enough to kill should work. Use it to slice the paper into small pieces as you repeat, 'I want to be successful in all my undertakings.' "

"Then?"

"Kill the thing."

"That's it?"

"You think there should be goat's blood and moonlit holy water?"

Since there usually was…

"Seems too simple."

"Not if you don't know what to do, and most charmers won't tell you. Cuts down on their income."

"How did you find out?"

"The usual way."

My usual way would be to touch someone and pick his or her mind. If that didn't work, I'd beat it out of them. Which was probably Bram's MO, too.

"One more thing," Bram said. "Witches, sorcerers, wizards—anything magic—sometimes they don't die just right."

"What are you trying to tell me?"

"What if you stick the sosye and he doesn't die?"

"Yeah," I agreed, "what if?"

"It's a witch," Bram said. "Burn it."

I did what he'd said. Paper. Square. *Mait dead* written in the middle. I used my silver knife to slice it into teenie-tiny pieces as I said the words out loud: "I want to be successful in all my undertakings."

When I lifted the knife after the last slice, a rain-scented wind swirled in and scattered the pieces everywhere like confetti. For an instant the blade glowed red, but the flare died so fast I couldn't be sure it had actually happened.

Three AM. I needed to move. For all I knew, Mait might already be on his way to the cemetery.

I hid the charmed knife in my un-cool fanny pack. I should really replace that with…what? A Coach weapon carrier? A Louis Vuitton dagger sheath. Yeah, that would be *so* me.

I walked down Bourbon toward St. Louis Number One. If I was lucky I'd see Mait in one of the strip clubs; then I could follow him somewhere dark and isolated where I would do what needed to be done.

Of course that scenario was much, much too easy. So easy that I was only half searching for him as I strolled past each open doorway. When I actually saw him I'd taken several steps down the sidewalk before I realized it.

He was getting a lap dance, all right, and

preoccupied enough not to notice me when I ducked in for a closer look then ducked quickly back out. I moved across the street, ordered a virgin margarita in a to-go cup, then pretended to peer in the shop windows while I waited. I'd only taken one sip when my phone rang.

I glanced at the caller ID. Luther. My heart did a tiny panic dance as I flipped it open. "Hey, kid—"

"Come quick, Liz." His voice was choked, either with tears or because someone was choking him. I didn't like either choice.

"What's wrong?"

"Faith," he began, then gasped, either with pain or a sob.

"Luther!" The fear his last word had brought nearly made it impossible for me to speak at all. "Is—is someone there with you?"

"Yes." My hand clenched on the phone, and the plastic crackled. I forced myself to loosen my hold. "Summer," he finished. "Summer's here."

"No one else? No one…bad?"

"Not anymore."

Oh, God. I didn't realize until someone cursed at me that I'd dropped the margarita all over the sidewalk.

"Where's Faith?" I shouted, ignoring the stares I got, even on Bourbon Street.

"They took her."

Chapter 33

"Jimmy," I managed.

"He went after her."

Ah, hell. The dream. I guess it *had* been a vision. "Who was it?"

"I don't know. I didn't see—"

"Dammit!" I'd confined my demon beneath the moon, so Ruthie had come back to me, leaving Luther alone. It hadn't even occurred to me to let the kid know. I was as much to blame for this as anyone.

I inched into a small space between the bar and a T-shirt shop where I could still watch the front door of the strip club, but I was out of the way. "What the hell happened, Luther?"

The phone thumped and crackled. "Don't yell at him!"

Summer.

"I wasn't yelling." Although now that I had her on the line, I might. "What happened?" I repeated.

"Not a clue."

"You're a fairy!"

Now I did shout and earned a few nasty looks and one snarl from a passerby. That had sounded pretty bad.

"You live in an enchanted castle," I continued more quietly.

"Cottage," she corrected.

"What-fucking-ever. No one was supposed to get in."

"Surprise," she said. "They did."

"I'm going to kill you."

"You know, the more you threaten that, the less it scares me?"

"Not a threat this time, Tinker Bell. A promise."

"Spare me your wannabe John Wayne dialogue. We need to find the baby and Jimmy."

"You think?"

"Fuck you," she said, but there was no heat in her words.

She was scared. I could smell it from here, and she hadn't even seen what I had.

"Tell me exactly what went on." I figured she'd give me more 'tude, but she didn't. Which only proved how scared she was.

"Jimmy got a call. He left. I went to check on Faith; she was gone."

"Jimmy could have taken her."

"And not told us? Why?"

Why did Sanducci do anything?

"No sign of a break-in?" I asked. "No hint of a spell?"

"Nothing," Summer answered.

"Strange."

"I expect a little more than 'strange' from the

damned leader of the light."

"Damned is right," I muttered, as an idea began to form.

"I'll do anything to get him—I mean *them*— back," Summer said.

Mait strolled out of the strip club toward St. Louis Number One.

"So will I," I said, and followed.

Ruthie had said payment must be made, and I knew that was true. She'd also said that the dead couldn't be raised without consequences.

I didn't care. Two of the four people left on this earth whom I cared about were in trouble, and I could save them. All I had to do was embrace the darkness. Again.

I'd done it before, wound up a vampire. I wondered what doing it this time would make me.

Never sleep with a Nephilim.

"Shut up," I told Sawyer, though I knew he wasn't really there. The only way he'd ever *be* there was if I did whatever I had to do to get him back.

Summer had accused me of being unable to love enough. Would I choose a fate worse than death, the worst thing I could imagine, pledge eternity in the flames just to save someone I loved? I hadn't known the answer then, but now I did.

If I did this I could spare them all.

Theoretically.

I swallowed. I could do it. I'd just close my eyes and think of—

"England," I whispered as Mait turned onto Toulouse Street.

I'd been willing to give up Sawyer, had believed I was doing the right thing. However, I wasn't willing to let his daughter go, or Jimmy, either. That was too much to ask. If I had to sacrifice my body, my mind, my life—so be it.

Having made the decision, I was suddenly calm. Which gave me a near hyper-focus. Everything around me receded—the music, the lights, the people— except for Mait, who seemed to be shrouded in a silvery gray sheen that set him apart from everyone else.

I needed to draw him away somewhere quiet and secluded where I could first seduce him, then kill him.

Yeah, I *was* one of the good guys.

After toying with several versions of what to do next—buy a disguise, accost him in a dark alley, lie—I realized the truth. All I had to do was let him catch me. He was a Nephilim. Nature would take its course.

I didn't try to be quiet, didn't really try to hide, and a few blocks from St. Louis Number One I no longer saw Mait ahead of me. As I passed a thin alleyway, a dark hand reached out and yanked me in.

"What do you think you are doin'?" Mait's emerald eyes shone despite the lack of light between the buildings.

"Following you."

"And why would that be? You and your friend already took all that I had."

Not all.

"He wasn't my friend," I said. "He was a double-crossing snake." Since he was, my words rang true.

Mait tilted his head, and the shadow of the moon cast over his face. He was really quite beautiful. Maybe this wouldn't be so bad.

Mait's lips curved. My answering smile froze when he slammed me against the nearest wall hard enough to rattle my teeth and a few more of my brains.

"Perhaps you were lookin' for dis?" He held Jimmy's charmed dagger against my throat. No wonder we hadn't been able to find it. "You meant to kill me."

I met his eyes and didn't answer. Why lie?

His teeth flashed. He lifted the flat of the blade and slid it first down my cheek then along the curve of my neck. "Afraid?"

Not of the knife.

"You made a promise." The weapon continued its path, over my right breast, down my ribs, my hips, then across my stomach and back up the other side. "One you did not keep. But we will remedy dat."

He stepped in close, his body brushing mine. His *remedy* poked me in the stomach. I tried to jerk away, and ended up smacking my tailbone against the bricks.

I hissed in a pained breath, and Mait laughed. "Do you think you might cry? I like it when dey cry." He leaned over and licked my cheekbone. His breath smelled like Bourbon Street, or maybe that was just bourbon—and rot. "I *will* have you."

Since that was what I'd planned all along, I should have been happier about it. However, I was starting to catch a vibe. Mait liked to force women. He liked to hurt them, to make them cry. I could use that.

"No," I said, my voice breaking right on cue. "Let me go."

I fought, but my struggles only rubbed us together harder and faster, which was how he began to breathe, and so did I.

His free hand captured my wrists, drawing them above my head, pressing them against the wall, which settled our bodies into more perfect alignment. He lowered his head, nuzzling my neck, breathing in as if to memorize my scent forever, then took a fold of my skin into his mouth and worried it between tongue and teeth until pain and pleasure meshed.

"You will like it," he whispered. "Dis I promise."

I wiggled again, as if trying to slip away. In truth, I was becoming aroused. I didn't want to, but I needed to. To steal his magic required more than the act, it required fulfillment. To absorb the power, I needed to open myself, accept him, and—

Hell, basically, I needed to come.

My breath caught as he slit my shirt down the front. Moist, muggy air swirled against exposed skin. Placing the tip of the knife at the center of my chest, he flicked his wrist and cut my bra in half so that my breasts spilled free.

Mait murmured something in another language, his gaze captured by the copper-tipped globes. The weapon clattered to the ground; my arms tumbled to my sides as he filled both hands with soft, round flesh.

He was rough. He no doubt needed to be. He was one of those who had to hurt, perhaps be hurt, but he couldn't hurt me.

He teased me—gentle to sharp, tongue to teeth. Grabbing my hand, he pressed it to his erection. When had he released his pants so that they pooled at his ankles?

Locking our fingers together, he curled his palm around mine so that I held the head between my thumb and forefinger, then he slid back and forth, back and forth. From the depth of his moans, he was close to coming.

I shook my head, tried to focus. I couldn't jack him off. There'd be nothing left for me. However, if I told him what I wanted, he probably wouldn't give it to me. Nephilim were like that. I'd have to beg for the exact opposite.

"Go ahead," I urged, moving my hand faster. "You know that you want to."

His motions slowed, his moans stopped, and his eyes snapped open. "Not yet," he growled, and ripped at the fastenings of my jeans.

From that moment on things moved quickly, which was fine by me. The sooner the better. I wanted this done.

I tried to close my eyes and think of England. Problem was, I needed to come, and England just didn't do it for me.

I didn't want to think of Jimmy or Sawyer. I couldn't bear to pair what we'd had with the memory of Mait. Even though I'd chosen this, even though I was doing it for them, tonight wasn't a night to remember.

Instead, I let my mind go blank, let my body take over. If he hadn't been a half-demon stranger I'd followed into a dark alley, I might consider Mait decent in bed. Against the wall, not so much. Still, when I didn't think, when I forced myself only to feel, things happened.

Mait flexed and released, flexed and released, sliding in and out, filling me, emptying me. I lost track of time. The guy had the stamina of a racehorse.

Minutes, hours, days later, he pressed his forehead to mine. "I cannot until you do."

I'd met guys like him before—in handcuffs.

While most rapists wanted to assuage their pain by causing someone else's, vent their anger, show their dominance—some liked to pretend it wasn't rape by making the woman participate. Some couldn't get off unless they managed to "satisfy" the object of their twisted affection.

I hated those guys. The women who were assaulted by them were more traumatized than the ones attacked by any of the others. Maybe because the asshole made them believe they must have wanted it, wanted him, otherwise why would they have climaxed?

Mait licked the tip of his thumb and, holding my gaze, slipped his hand between us and unerringly found the right place. He continued to stare into my eyes as he rolled his thumb in a circle, all the while sliding in and out, faster and faster until—

I came.

My body convulsed, tightening around him. His breath caught; his eyes went blank. In them I saw myself—my face stark, blue eyes wide, framed against the dark stones of the building like the sacrifice I'd made of myself.

I couldn't watch. As I continued to quiver in reaction, I shut my eyes against the night and as the orgasm drained away, lightning flashed from a clear sky, leaving behind an ozone-scented wind. The flare of power as it passed between us was like boiling oil in the blood—painful but also exhilarating. Magic so often was.

I pushed aside thoughts of what I'd done—time enough for those later, or not, I hoped—and focused on what I needed to do. My eyes opened, though they very badly wanted to stay closed, just as Mait released me.

My legs slid down; my feet touched the ground. I bit my lip until it bled, refusing to crumble. When he bent to grab his pants, I slid my hand into the fanny pack that had twisted around my waist almost to my back, and removed the charmed knife.

As he straightened, I jabbed the point toward his eye. I hadn't even cleared the protection of my thigh when he grabbed my wrist and twisted. I was strong, near invincible, but I couldn't keep my fingers clenched against that move, and the knife clattered to the pavement.

At first, I panicked, thinking he was too close to fight, especially with my pants around my ankles. Then my free hand flicked, and he flew, smashing into the opposite wall before landing on the ground. Since he was a Nephilim, he got right back up.

I wasted no time, grabbing my jeans, searching for the weapon. It was gone.

"Lookin' for dis?" Mait held my knife in one hand and the dagger Jimmy had bought in the other. "One of a sosye's powers is that things come when summoned."

"Really?" I put out my hand, and Jimmy's dagger flew across the short distance between us. I snatched it out of the air. "Like that?"

He rattled off several French-sounding curses, ending with "Empath." He spat that like a curse, too.

If I hadn't already planned to kill him, I'd have to now. The sexual empathy was a secret I liked to keep from the dark side.

Reaching out, I tried to take the other knife, too, but he was ready for me and held on tight. I wished momentarily I didn't have to fight shirtless, but since I had no choice, and maybe it would distract him, I tightened my hold on the dagger and moved forward.

I'd never been in a knife fight. Close encounters were more Jimmy's style. Sanducci was king of the sharp shiny things. I was better with my hands, my feet, a club, a gun. Not that I couldn't *use* a knife. How hard was it? Pointy end went into the bad guy. But when we both had knives, and we both had superpowers, things got dicey.

He cut me; I cut him. I healed my wounds; he healed his. We could have kept at it for days. Then I aimed a fancy roundhouse kick toward his chest, and Mait saw my tattoo.

"You're a—" My heel met his sternum and he flew. "Skinwalker," he said right before he hit the wall, cracked his head, landed on the ground, and the knife in his hand slid across the pavement. "You'll never die."

"Never say never," I muttered. "But certainly not today."

I landed on his chest, the tip of my dagger speeding toward his left eye.

That thing I have about eyes?

Turns out, I didn't have it anymore.

Chapter 34

"What you doin' back there?"

The deserted street was deserted no longer.

"Mind your bizness," I shouted, doing my best impression of a crack addict. As a big-city cop, I'd known plenty of them.

The guy moved on, grumbling; I needed to move on, too. Except the body wasn't ashes yet, and I didn't dare leave until it was. Most Nephilim aren't any clean up trouble at all—killed the right way they burst into dust. Not Mait. Maybe being a god had something to do with it. Or, as Bram had said, he was also a witch. He needed to burn.

Burning a body isn't as easy as you'd think. Luckily I had supernatural fire literally at my—

"Talon-tips," I said.

An instant later I was a phoenix and could shoot fire in a steady, blistering stream until the only sound in the alley was the crackling of the flames.

When nothing remained of Mait, former god of the night demons, but ashes, I beat my huge, multicolored wings until every last particle had swirled away. Then I clasped the dagger in one talon, my knife in the other, and flew into the fading night.

Dawn threatened when I circled the hotel then landed on the terrace. As I'd done before, I went straight to the bathroom and took a shower. It didn't help. I might be able to wash the scent of Nephilim from my skin, but I wasn't ever going to be able to wash the memory of what I'd done from my brain.

And there was going to be payback. I just knew it.

So far I didn't feel evil. That had to be good, right? Maybe I'd get lucky and absorb only Mait's magic without the accompanying vice.

Yeah, that would happen.

My phone was ringing when I came out. I snatched it up, glancing at the caller ID—*Luther*—even as I brought it to my ear.

"Did you find her?"

"You done made your choice," Ruthie said.

Why was Ruthie *calling* me?

Then everything connected, and I sat down heavily on the bed. Ruthie was talking through Luther, because I'd just embraced evil again.

"I had to," I began. "I saw—" I paused, not wanting to tell her what I'd seen, as if putting the horror into words might just make it happen, if it hadn't already. "Something," I finished.

"Figured that or you wouldn't have done what you done. I told you'd there'd be consequences."

"I'll pay whatever I have to."

"Not much choice 'bout that." Ruthie gave a deep sorry sigh. "What you done, Lizbeth, I fear for you."

I feared for me, too, but I feared more for Jimmy and Faith. I'd do it again if I had to. I just hoped I never had to.

"You go on back to the Dinetah."

"No. I have to—"

"Sawyer ain't goin' anywhere."

She was trying to keep me from raising him. She had to know that, eventually, I would. I had to.

"The boy is frightened. Summer's losin' her mind. You go on back, find out what's what."

I opened my mouth to argue; what came out was, "Yes, ma'am."

I caught the first plane to Albuquerque, rented a Bronco, and drove to Summer's place. At heart it was an Irish cottage, and there were times the terrain around it appeared like the rolling emerald hills of that land. There were other times when the cottage became a castle, complete with a moat.

The gargoyles remained regardless of what shape the house took. Their job was to guard against evil. So what had they been doing when Faith disappeared? I planned to find out.

As I drove up, the cottage shimmered, shifted, became a ranch house with a wraparound wooden porch. Several horses whinnied from the corral. On closer inspection, I was certain they'd be revealed as half horse and half something else—gargoyles on alert. It was all glamour, courtesy of the fairy.

I climbed out of the truck, eyeing the statues in the yard. Gargoyles could turn to stone at will. They could also turn back, take to the air, and protect the innocent from demons.

Since I was no longer innocent, did in fact have a few demons in me, I walked warily between the bizarre figures. Half lion-half eagle, part man-part hawk, woman and wolf, several of them shifted in my direction, the light of the moon flashing off their flat, black eyes. They were watching me. I couldn't blame them.

The door opened; light spilled out, casting the silhouettes of a short female and a tall male onto the ground.

"Liz," Luther said. "Thank God."

Summer snorted.

It was good to be back.

I tromped across the porch, the weathered boards that weren't really there creaking beneath my weight. "No castle?" I lifted my hand to the gorgeous night sky, painted every shade of blue and orange and pink. "Turrets, moat, patrolling sentries?"

"There's nothing left to protect." Luther turned away. As usual his jeans sagged off his bony behind, the waistband of his boxers—red and black plaid—playing hide-and-seek with the frayed tail of a UNLV REBELS T-shirt.

I was close enough to catch Summer's wince, and for an instant I felt sorry for her. Then she opened her mouth. "What did you do to him this time?"

"Him, who?" I asked, but I knew. With Summer, it was always about Jimmy.

"He was mad, sad."

"Jimmy hasn't been happy for a long time now."

Had he *ever* been happy? Yes. I had too. Before we knew the truth.

"Because of you," she said.

"What else is new?" I tried to move past her and into the house, but she remained in the doorway. I could make her move, but then there'd be a catfight, and when you're talking supernatural cats, it usually got ugly. Even though I wanted to pop her in her perfectly pert nose, I didn't.

"We need to work together," I said. "We've got the same goal. Find the kid, find Jimmy."

"In that order?"

"Yes. Sanducci can take care of himself. Faith..."

"Can't," Summer finished.

Luther, still standing in the hall, said a word I didn't much care hearing from his mouth, but I decided to let it pass. I had bigger problems than a teenage boy's cursing.

Summer let me in. I nodded my thanks. Best to make nice for the time being.

For a change she wasn't wearing her circulation-inhibiting jeans and slutty, fringed halter top, though the alternative wasn't much better. White shorts so tiny I couldn't guess their size; they made her slim, smooth, perfect legs appear longer than they could possibly be. The pink shirt bared her flat stomach, revealing a belly button ring I had a hard time not yanking out.

Inside, the decor reflected the western ranch motif of the exterior. The walls were the color of the sky at dawn, the tile the shade of the earth. The paintings appeared to be Georgia O'Keeffe. The houseplants were cacti—huge, fat, gorgeous specimens.

"I like this," I said.

"I don't care," she replied.

So much for making nice.

"Any news?"

Summer shook her head.

"Did you try Jimmy's cell?" I had, but I figured he was avoiding me.

"What do you think?" she snapped. "Every call goes directly to voice mail."

"Making nice only works if we both make it."

"You've been making nice?"

"I haven't slugged you yet."

"The night's young," she muttered, and I laughed.

Sometimes our banter took a turn like this, and we ended up smiling at each other. Then we'd remember we didn't get along; we'd remember why, and the verbal and physical jabs would return. I liked to think that in different circumstances Summer and I might have become friends. As things stood, Jimmy would always lie between us.

"What are you going to do?" Summer asked. "How are we going to find them? Who do you think took them?"

"We don't know that anyone took Jimmy."

"I do." She tilted her chin. "He wouldn't stop answering his phone, unless he *couldn't* answer it."

I wasn't so sure about that. But I was more concerned with Faith at the moment. Someone had already tried to kill her. I was terrified that she hadn't been taken and hidden, but taken and killed. The only thing keeping me from gibbering in a corner, besides the fact that I rarely gibbered, was the memory of my vision. In it, Faith had been alive.

"You think the same guys who came for her the last time came this time?" Luther asked, and despite the steadiness of his voice I knew how scared he was by the tremor in his lips.

"It wasn't them."

I didn't point out that those guys would have killed her. I think he knew it anyway.

And I knew I needed more help than I had to make certain we got Jimmy and Faith back alive.

"Can I have a few minutes to myself?" I asked.

I certainly didn't plan on raising my first dead man with an audience.

Summer glanced at Luther, who had moved into the living room and now sat on a leather sofa the shade of sand pretending to watch TV.

He lifted one shoulder then lowered it. "I'm not movin'."

"I didn't mean that." I turned to Summer. "Can you show me which room is mine?"

"You're *staying* here?"

"Ruthie said I should." She hadn't, but Summer didn't know that.

"Well, she didn't tell me." Summer stomped as loudly as she could in bare feet down a hall that led toward the back of the house. As we walked, the corridor lengthened in front of us, doors appearing on either side.

I'd seen her do this before. She could change a cottage into a castle in the blink of an eye. She could also add rooms and floors without even waving her hand.

We turned into another long corridor, and she stopped, throwing open a door to our right. The room looked like a cell on Prison Block A.

I assumed Summer could also decorate with her imagination. Hence the cold gray walls, the metal cot with the uber-thin, stained mattress, and an army-green blanket that appeared as soft as a Brillo Pad.

"Thanks." I was unable to keep the sarcasm from my voice.

She smirked and turned away. I stepped into the room, which gave off an unpleasant chill, and shut the door, then I reached for a lock that wasn't.

"Lock!" I shouted, and in the next instant one appeared.

Summer could no doubt unlock the door just as

easily, but oh, well, this shouldn't take long. At least it hadn't for Mait.

Since I'd absorbed his powers, I hadn't felt any different from before. Sure, I could stretch out my hand and make stuff come to me, but I didn't feel any stronger in a mystical, necromancer-y kind of way. And shouldn't I?

What if it was a lie—the gift of raising the dead? I'd only seen Mait do so in a dream. Certainly Ruthie had corroborated his talents, but Ruthie couldn't be right about everything, all the time, could she? Had I risked my soul for nothing?

Panic threatened and since panic would help no one, I took a deep breath, closing my eyes, trying to calm myself. Just the familiar, meditative act made my training kick in. My mind opened. I reached for the power, and it was mine. Energy flowed through me, along with all the knowledge. Suddenly I knew exactly what to do and how to do it.

So simple. Such strength. I could raise everyone we'd lost. Ruthie, Xander. What was to stop me? *Who* could stop me? Who would dare?

I slapped myself in the face. The sting brought me back.

"Focus," I said. "You did this for Sawyer and *only* Sawyer."

But what if it worked?

I shoved the tempting thought aside and did what I'd sacrificed so much to be able to do.

Mait had touched the graves, but that was

because he hadn't known those he was raising. I knew Sawyer— probably better than anyone. All I had to do was think of him and call him home.

"Come back," I whispered, and then I waited.

For his touch, his voice, his scent. Nothing happened.

I tried again. Open. Reach. Beg. "Please, come back to me."

I remained alone in an empty room.

I was doing this right. Unlike the time when I'd attempted to raise his ghost—a spell boosted by magic and therefore easily screwed up with the wrong twitch of a finger or the switching of a single word—the power to raise the dead was part of me. I could feel the ability to lift Sawyer out of death and back to life in my mind, my heart, my very soul.

From somewhere in the house came a vicious growl, followed by several heavy thumps and the breaking of glass.

I was at the door in an instant. I jerked on it three times before I remembered the lock. Then I was running down the hall and skidding into the living room where three people now stood instead of two.

"I knew I could do it."

"Are you insane?" Summer asked, her tone almost conversational.

I ignored her, so glad to see Sawyer my legs wobbled.

"Thank God." I started forward.

"Wait." Something in Luther's voice stopped me. Luther's shining amber eyes were fixed on Sawyer; his nostrils flared, every muscle tensed. The kid's kinky curls stirred in an impossible breeze. "Ruthie says, 'Skinwalker.' "

"We know." I didn't pause to wonder why Ruthie was telling us twice—something she never did—but moved toward Sawyer again. I stopped a few feet away when the breeze that wasn't brought me his scent.

Not trees and grass, wind and water with a hint of smoke, but ashes, embers, hot coals and flames.

"Sawyer?"

His head cocked as if he recognized the name, or maybe my voice, and I took a good look at him. He had tattoos in all the right places, and I could see each one since, as usual, he was naked. But his skin was pale, his eyes dark—the gray irises vanished beneath the dilated ebony of his pupils— his hair, usually straight and sleek, was tangled with sweat. He appeared almost feral, even before the low, savage snarl rumbled free.

Quick as a snake he struck, snatching me by the throat and slamming me against the nearest wall. My head cracked; I saw stars. My feet dangled several inches off the ground as Sawyer held me aloft with just one hand. He'd always been freakishly strong.

"Put her down!" Summer ordered.

He flicked his other wrist and tossed her

through the front window.

A movement caught my eye. Luther. Sneaking up from the rear, in his hand a silver knife that would do nothing but piss Sawyer off. He appeared pissed off enough already.

"No," I croaked, only to have Sawyer tighten his fingers until I saw shiny black dots.

Luther froze.

"Who—" Sawyer tapped my head against the wall for emphasis. "—are you?"

His voice was hoarse, as if he'd been screaming for days and only just gotten back the power of speech.

"Liz." Luther spoke as if he were talking to a wild, crazed animal, and the way Sawyer appeared right now, I thought that was a damn good idea. "She's Liz Phoenix. Don't you remember?"

Sawyer peered into my face, and recognition flickered in his eerie black eyes. I tried to smile, to speak, but both were impossible. What I really needed to do was breathe.

"I remember you," he murmured.

Then he tore out my throat.

Chapter 35

I guess I deserved it. Tit for tat. I kill you; you kill me. Revenge. Payback. Whatever.

It wasn't as if I could die. Not yet. I had too many things left to do.

The arterial blood spray hit Sawyer right between the eyes. I wondered if he would have let me go otherwise.

I crumpled to the floor, blacked out for a second or two. A boom like a cannon brought me back. I caught the scent of ozone, sensed movement, then the dead silence was broken by a lion's roar. I tried to get up, to stop Luther from following. Sawyer wasn't himself. He'd been dangerous before; he'd be lethal now.

And I'd brought him back to life.

My attempt to gain my feet only made my throat wound bleed worse, and I fainted this time for real. I don't know how long I was out. I'd figured I would go dreamwalking, where I'd find answers to my most desperate questions—and I had a lot of them. But in the darkness there was only more darkness, and when I awoke even more questions.

"What have you done?"

Both Luther and Summer stood over me. I was so glad to see the kid in one piece I reached for his hand. He put both behind his back.

I swallowed. My throat appeared to be working just fine. "What I had to."

I patted my neck. Sore, but I'd healed enough to move, though the blood was still slick and plentiful. Not only was I going to need a shower and new clothes, but if Summer hadn't been a fairy, she'd need a wet vac and new wallpaper.

"You sold your soul to raise him." Summer had glass in her hair; her shorts were torn. Other than that—not a mark on her.

Bitch.

"I didn't sell anything." I sat up, holding on to my head with both hands when it pounded like a snare drum. "I took."

Understanding flickered in Summer's eyes. "You fucked a Nephilim."

I didn't bother to answer. I didn't *want* to answer. I didn't really need to.

"You *are* crazy."

"We need him."

"Not like that we don't," Summer muttered.

I didn't answer because I feared she was right.

"I never would have figured you for a whore," she said.

"No? I pegged you as one right away."

Summer snarled, the "otherness" beneath her pretty face escaping.

Luther stepped between us. "Stop." The voice was Ruthie's.

"You have got to be kidding me." Summer shoved Luther's shoulder, but she was looking at me. "You and Jimmy do the horizontal bop, shove your demons beneath the moon, and you turn around and snatch another one? Why did you bother? Did you just *have* to do him to prove you still could?"

I began to understand her hostility. Not that she'd ever been exactly friendly, but she was really on a roll tonight. Sanducci must have told her that we'd confined our demons.

"Moron."

"Watch it." Summer's hands clenched.

I was going to say *not you* then figured, *why bother?* "When Jimmy and I performed the spell I had no idea how to get Sawyer back."

"You have the guts to condemn me over what I did for Jimmy, but you did a lot worse."

"Worse?" I lifted one hand, palm up near my face. "Sell my soul?" I put the other, palm up, near my hip. "Screw a Nephilim?" Then I changed their positions a few times. "Yeah, what I did was definitely worse than what you did."

I was being sarcastic, but Summer nodded as if satisfied.

"Enough," Ruthie snapped. "We all do what we think is best at the time."

Luther's gaze met mine, his no longer hazel but

deep brown. I knew Ruthie was thinking of the things she'd done, things that had hurt me and others. I understood her so much better now. I even felt an annoying camaraderie with Summer. The things we do for love.

Though I sympathized with the fairy, I couldn't help but point out, "I can confine the new demon. You're always gonna owe Satan a favor."

Summer's eyes widened.

Luther sighed, shook his head, and cast me a disappointed glance. "Lizbeth."

"Well, it's true. Isn't it?"

"Suspect so."

"Except you're gonna need someone who loves you to confine it, and Jimmy's gone." Summer didn't stick out her tongue but I could tell she wanted to.

I stilled. "What was that?"

Summer appeared to have swallowed a rotten egg. "Nothing," she said, but her voice was strangled.

"I thought the *plenus luna malum* spell was a *sex* spell."

"No, child. It's all about love."

"Did Jimmy know it was a love spell?"

Summer's lips tightened. She wasn't going to tell me.

"Of course," Ruthie said.

I thought of that night, of the candles and the incense, how strange it had been for Jimmy to use them.

"Pink candles."

Summer scowled; Luther's eyebrows shot up.

"Conjures memories," Ruthie said.

Jimmy had been trying to bring back our memories of love. Had he been unsure of my feelings or his?

"Love is stronger than hate," Ruthie continued, something she believed utterly, but about which I still had many doubts. "And sex with love is the most powerful kind of magic."

I swallowed against the sudden tightness in my throat. Jimmy still loved me. No wonder Summer wanted me dead.

On the heels of that thought came another. Summer and Jimmy had done that spell. I guess he loved her, too.

I couldn't be too angry. The only reason any of us was alive right now was because I'd loved—

"Sawyer."

"He isn't going to be much use for a love spell," Summer observed. "Considering he tried to kill you." She tilted her head as an exaggerated expression of deep thought spread over her face. "But did he ever love you? Or did you just love him?"

I'd never been certain about that myself. Right now, though, I had a more important question. "Where is he?"

"Turned into a wolf and—" Luther's huge hands flipped upward in a very Ruthie-like gesture. "Disappeared into the mountains."

"Frick." We were never going to find him there.

"I tried to warn you," Ruthie said.

"Consequences." I took a deep breath. "He isn't the same."

"He's exactly what he's always been."

I glanced up sharply. "You saw him. He's—"

"He's a skinwalker, child. He's always walked the line. The only thing that kept him from the dark side was you."

"Now he's crossed over?"

Luther's long finger slid slickly down the side of my neck then appeared in front of my face covered in blood. "What do you think?"

"Just because he's annoyed with me doesn't mean he's gone to the dark side."

"I'd say tearing out your throat and leaving you for dead goes beyond annoyance."

I'd have to agree.

"You get any word from above about this?" I asked.

Ruthie's wise old eyes narrowed in Luther's bright young face. "Why you think I whispered 'skinwalker' to the boy? Sawyer's more Nephilim than human now."

"Nice job, Ace," Summer muttered.

"Can I kick her?"

No one answered. It had been rhetorical anyway.

Luther's head swung toward the front window just as headlights flashed. He breathed in deeply, let the air stream out slowly. "No evil vibes." His lips tightened. "But I still don't like it."

Neither did I. It was late. We were in the middle of nowhere.

Stones crunched beneath tires. First the lights died, then the motor.

"I'll go." Luther had returned.

"Like hell." I reached for him, and his lion rumbled.

"We go together or not at all," he said.

"Fine."

I followed him into the hall, Summer at my back, only to discover the front door had been blown off its hinges. Sawyer. He always did like to make an exit.

I stood between them, shoulder-to-shoulder on the porch, as two men climbed out of a pickup truck. They were white, not Navajo.

Stranger and stranger. We were deep in Navajo country and as I'd said, it was late.

"Evening." The nearest one to me pushed back the brim of his hat. He was about thirty. Nothing special, unless you counted his total forgettableness. He was dark; the other was blond and just as forgettable.

The blond looked between me and Summer then settled on me. "You Liz Phoenix?"

"Who wants to know?"

"We're just delivery boys."

"It takes two?"

"We heard you might be…" The blond's voice trailed off.

"Unhappy," the dark man finished.

I liked this less and less by the minute.

"Who sent you?"

"Don't know. Instructions and package came US mail."

"And you just do what you're told?"

The blond appeared confused. "That's what we *do.*"

I found no point in continuing this. They'd said they were delivery boys. Add to that the lack of a demon "buzz" on both mine and Luther's part, as well as Ruthie's dearth of info, and I found myself believing them.

"Better hand it over," I said.

The blond came forward with a brown-paper-wrapped box. When he reached the bottom of the steps, Luther moved in front of me. The guy took one glance at the kid's face and tossed it the rest of the way. I hoped whatever rested inside wasn't breakable.

By the time I bent and retrieved the package, the two men had climbed in the truck.

"They were human." Luther watched them leave. "One hundred percent."

"That way we don't feel them coming."

"But they were only delivering" —he waved his hand in my direction— "whatever that is."

"If they'd been Nephilim, we'd have killed them."

"You think—" His gaze turned to the taillights of the pickup. "You think they sent people after Faith this time, too?"

"Maybe," I said.

Probably, I thought. The Nephilim were getting wise. They knew we'd have a hard time killing people in cold blood. Unlike them.

The three of us trailed into the living room, and I set the box on the coffee table. I didn't want to open it. At least the container was too small for a head, unless it was a very small head.

A strange noise escaped me—half sob, half battle cry—and I yanked off the top. Faith's binkie lay inside.

I snatched it up, pressing the pink flannel to my face—baby powder, baby sweat, baby tears, and—

"Faith."

"There's a note." Luther's voice sounded the same as mine—choked with both fury and fear.

Summer picked up the paper, glanced at it, then handed the page to me.

"You for her," I read.

Exactly like my dream, except for one thing.

"Bring Daddy along, too."

Epilogue

Let's recap…

Faith's been kidnapped.

Jimmy's missing.

I've got another demon inside me.

Luther's Ruthie. Again.

Summer still owes the devil her soul.

And I need Sawyer to save Faith, but he appears to have embraced his own darkness.

Does that about cover it? Chaos anyone?

At least I know what I have to do. Same thing I always do. Whatever it takes. I'm getting Faith back, Jimmy too, and while I'm at it I'll deal with Sawyer.

I made a bad choice, a stupid decision based on love and a dream. I'm not the first woman to do that, and I definitely won't be the last. In my case, there's one important difference.

When I get where I'm going, there'll be demons at the gates.

THE END

If you enjoyed *Chaos Bites,* I would be honored if you would tell others by writing a review on the retailer's website where you purchased this title.

Thank you!
Lori Handeland

Read on for an excerpt of
IN THE AIR TONIGHT,
the first novel in Lori's
Sisters of the Craft witches trilogy

IN THE AIR TONIGHT

NEW YORK TIMES BESTSELLING AUTHOR

LORI HANDELAND

Three sisters lost to time... Can one find what she desires most?

IN THE AIR TONIGHT

SISTERS OF THE CRAFT

Prologue

Scotland, four hundred years ago

Three men with large, hard, dirty hands lifted three infant girls from their cradles.

"No!" Prudence Taggart cried, and a crockery bowl fell off the table, shattering against the floor.

Roland McHugh, the king's chief witch hunter, flicked a finger in her direction, and two other dark clad men dragged her out the door of the cottage. Several more yanked her husband, Henry, along behind. Those not occupied hauling the five Taggarts from their home built a pyre. From the speed at which they completed their task, they'd done so before.

"More than one soul in a womb is Satan's work." McHugh's lip curled as he contemplated the sleeping children. "How many lives did you sacrifice so your Devil's spawn might be born?"

Both Henry and Prudence remained silent. There was nothing they could say that would save them, and they knew it.

Since King James had nearly been killed, along with his Danish queen, in a great storm he believed had been brought about by witchcraft, his majesty had become slightly obsessed on the subject of witches.

However, as he didn't want to seem backward

and superstitious to his English subjects, who had very little regard for the Scots in the first place, he had been forced to commission a secret society, the *Venatores Mali,* or Hunters of Evil, to do his bidding. In McHugh the King had found a leader who hated witches as much as he did.

Their captors lashed Henry and Prudence back-to-back against the stake then formed a circle around them. McHugh snapped his fingers, and two lackeys appeared with torches.

The witch hunter removed a ring from his finger and a pincher from his wool doublet then held the circlet within the flame until it glowed. He pressed the red hot metal to Henry's neck. The scent of burning flesh rose, along with a nasty hiss, and the livid image of a snarling wolf emerged from Henry's flesh.

"Are you mad?" Henry managed.

"Sometimes the brand brings forth a confession."

"Shocking how pain and torture makes people say anything."

"It did not make you." McHugh shoved his ring back into the flames, and his gaze slid to Prudence.

"I did it," Henry blurted. "I sold to Satan the lives of your wife and child to bring forth our own."

"Of course you did," McHugh agreed.

He was convinced magic, sorcery, witchcraft had been involved in the deaths of his loved ones. Nothing would change his mind. Not even the truth.

Some things could not be healed. McHugh's wife had been one of them. By the time he had fetched Prudence, the woman had lost far too much blood, and the child was already dead.

McHugh pressed his ring to Pru's neck. She stiffened until the stake creaked. Lightning flashed, and somewhere deep in the woods a tree toppled over. Wolves began to howl in the distance—a lot of them—and the circle of hunters shifted uneasily.

"I confessed, you swine."

"You thought that would save her?" McHugh tut-tutted, then he snatched the blazing torches and tossed them onto the pyre. The dry, ancient wood flared.

Henry reached for his wife's hands. They were just close enough to touch palm-to-palm. "Imagine a safe place where no one believes in witches anymore."

The forest shimmered. Clouds skittered over the moon. Flames shot so high they seemed to touch the sky. When they died with a whoosh, nothing remained but ashes and smoke.

And the men who had held the three infant girls held nothing but empty blankets.

Chapter 1

I understand that my dream of being normal is merely that.

For one thing, I'm adopted and everyone knows it. In a town like New Bergin, Wisconsin adoptions are rare. Strapping Scandinavian farm folk produce blond-haired, blue-eyed children quick as bunnies. Which means my blue-black hair and so-brown-they'll-never-be-blue eyes make me stand out like the single ugly duckling in a lake full of swans. Even before factoring in that I'm an only child.

The *only* only child in New Bergin. Which doesn't necessarily make me abnormal, but it doesn't mean I fit in either.

No, what makes me abnormal are the ghosts. As the freaky little kid in the movie said: *They're everywhere.*

At first my parents thought my speaking to empty corners and laughing for no reason was cute. As time went on, and people started talking...not so cute anymore.

"Should we take her to a psychiatrist?" my mother asked softly.

Ella Larsen always spoke softly. That night she whispered, yet still I heard. Or maybe one of the ghosts told me. I'd been four at the time. My recollection is muzzy.

"Take her to a psychiatrist?" my father repeated. "I was thinking of taking her back."

Perhaps that was the beginning of my feelings of inadequacy in New Bergin, or at the least, the birth of my incessant need to please. If I wasn't "right" I could be returned like a broken chair or a moldy loaf of bread.

I stopped mentioning the ghosts the next day. I never did see that psychiatrist, although sometimes I think that I should. I'm still living in New Bergin. My name's still Raye Larsen.

Once I stopped chattering to nothing my father and I came to an unspoken understanding. He coached my softball team and took me fishing. I pretended to be Daddy's girl. I had to. I didn't want to go "back."

According to my records, I'd been abandoned on Interstate 94, halfway between Madison and Eau Claire. Whoever had left me behind had not liked me very much. They'd dumped me in a ditch on the side of the road—naked without even a blanket.

Assholes.

Lucky for me it was a balmy July day, and I was found before I had succumbed to even a tinge of sunburn. I'm just glad it wasn't November.

My mother died when I was twenty. Cancer. Haven't seen her since. The one ghost I wouldn't have minded turning up a few times and not a word. I don't understand it.

As I hurried down the sidewalk my best friend,

Jenn Anderson, appeared at my side. "You wanna slow down?"

"Not really," I said, thought I did just a little.

We weren't late for a change, probably because I hadn't waited for Jenn. We worked for the New Bergin School District, Jenn as the attendance secretary, me as a kindergarten teacher and walked to school together each morning.

In choosing my occupation, I'd tried to get as far away from the dead as possible, figuring I'd be safe from ghosts in a kindergarten classroom.

Boy, had I been wrong. As previously mentioned: Ghosts are everywhere.

While I might have come to teaching for a reason that wasn't, I'd discovered quickly why I should stay. Good teachers could be made, but the best ones were born, and I was one of them.

Who knew I'd be great with kids? Not me. That they were honest and happy and full of energy, and being around them made me feel better than anything else was an unexpected bonus.

I'd even started to consider that I might want a few of my own. Perhaps if I created a family from scratch, rather than joining one already in progress, I'd feel like I belonged somewhere, to someone, and that constant emptiness inside might go away.

Of course finding a man in New Bergin wasn't easy. They were the same ones that had been here all along, and I wasn't impressed.

They hadn't been either. Though I tried to be

like everyone else, the fact remained that I wasn't. In truth, the only people who had ever accepted me as I was, and loved me for me no matter what, were my mother and Jenn. Which was no doubt why I loved them the same way.

Jenn and I had met on the first day of preschool and become BFFs. No idea why. We were so different it was scary and yet...we worked.

Even without the long, perfect mane of golden hair and equally gorgeous face, complete with a pert little nose—although *this* Jenn's nose was actually her nose, plastic surgery being a no-no in New Bergin—Jennifer Anderson was too close to Jennifer Aniston for high school kids to resist. When she'd begun dating the only Brad in town, she'd just been asking for it. As a result, one did not mention *Friends*, or Brad for that matter, ever. Do not get her started on Ross.

Jenn, who was several inches shorter than me, had to take three steps to my one. The flurry of her tiny feet, combined with the spiky ponytail atop her head, made her resemble a coked up Pomeranian.

"Where's the fire?" she asked.

A breeze kicked up, making her silly hairstyle waggle. For an instant, I could have sworn I smelled smoke; I even heard the crackle of flames.

But if there were a fire, the local volunteer fire department would have been wailing down First Street by now. Which meant...

I turned my head, and I saw him. Nothing new.

I'd been seeing this one for as long as I could remember.

Clad in black, he reminded me of the pictures in the Thanksgiving stories I read to my kids. Puritan. Pilgrim. One or the other. Although why the Ghost of Thanksgiving Past had turned up in Wisconsin I had no idea. According to the stories all those persecuted Puritans had lived, and died, on the East Coast.

Maybe he was Amish.

Neither case explained the sleek black wolf that was often at his side. The creature's bright green eyes were as unnatural as the creature itself.

Every time I approached, they melted into the woods, an alley, the ether. Unlike all of the other specters that just had to talk to me, neither my Puritan, nor his wolf, ever did.

Jenn snatched my elbow. Considering our daily walk, you'd think she'd be in better shape.

I slowed, and as soon as I did the man in black—no wolf today—went poof. Now you see him—or at least I did—now you don't.

He'd be back. Most of the ghosts went on, eventually—wherever it was that they went—but not that guy. Some day I'd have to find out why.

"Sheesh," Jenn muttered. I'd started speed walking again. She stopped, leaning over and setting her palms on her knees as she tried to catch her breath.

I kept going; the sense of urgency that had

plagued me as soon as my Keds touched First Street that morning had returned.

"You—" Deep breath. "Suck!" Jenn shouted.

I squashed the temptation to comment on her shoes, which were too high for walking and too open toed for a northern Wisconsin October. But then, as Jenn always pointed out, she didn't have to chase children. Ever.

The days of a school nurse had gone the way of the Dodo. If a child became sick, they were sent to the office—Jenn's office—then sent home.

Certainly they puked, or sneezed, but usually not on her. Her fashionable clothes discouraged it—today's body-hugging, red sweater dress appeared fresh from the drycleaners—her attitude ensured it. The instant a student walked into her office, she jabbed a pointy, painted nail at the bank of chairs against the far wall. If they puked or sneezed, they did it over there.

Jenn always told me my comfortable jeans, complemented by soft tees and sweatshirts, often of the Packer, Brewer, Badger variety, invited disaster. Maybe so. But at least I matched everyone else in New Bergin.

Except Jenn. Funny how *she* was the one who fit in.

I reached the cross avenue B—those New Bergin founding fathers had been hell on wheels in the street naming department—and stopped so fast I nearly put my toes through the front of my shoes.

Gawkers milled about, blocking the sidewalk and spilling into the road, but since the police had roped off the avenue they weren't in danger of becoming people suey.

Brad Hunstadt—yeah, that Brad, Jenn's Brad, make that ex-Brad—stood on the inside of the rope, arms crossed, face stoic. He'd only recently joined the force following the relocation of another officer to Kentucky so he could be nearer to his grandchildren.

Before that, Brad had been kind of a loser. He might be pretty—like the famous Brad—but he'd never been a candidate for rocket science school. He'd graduated from high school, gone to tech school. I'm not sure for what because he'd never worked for anyone but his father, the local butcher, until now. Jenn and I figured his daddy had paid someone off to get Brad out of his business and into another.

As I approached, my gaze was drawn to the woman standing at the edge of the crowd, staring at the dead body propped against the wall of *Breck's Candy Emporium*—home of twenty-five different types of caramel apples. The staring itself was not remarkable. Who wasn't? What was remarkable was that this woman could be the twin of the one she stared at.

She was a stranger—believe me I knew everyone—in a place where strangers stuck out, even when they weren't covered in blood and lying dead on the sidewalk.

I'd seen hundreds of ghosts, but each one still made my heart race. They were *dead.* I could see them. It was hard to get used to, and really, I probably shouldn't.

"Huh." Jenn had caught up. "I can't remember the last time we had a murder."

"Murder?"

She cast me an irritated glance. "Look at her."

My gaze went to the standing woman, but contrary to most movies about them, ghosts don't walk around with the wound that killed them evident on their spectral bodies. No gaping brains. No holes in their heads, their chests, or anywhere else there shouldn't be. Even the massive amounts of blood on the reclining figure was nowhere in evidence upon the spectral one.

Jenn snapped her fingers in front of my face. "Not there." She pointed slightly to the left of the ghost. "There." She transferred her pointy nail south until it indicated the dead woman.

One of her arms was missing—that wasn't easy to do—and her body, from the chest down, was blackened. The scent of charred flesh reached us on a frigid breeze. Weird. When I'd left my apartment, I could have sworn it was Indian summer.

Jenn clapped a palm over her nose and fled, her itty-bitty Barbie feet and short legs moving so fast they appeared to blur. Jenn could move when she wanted to.

Chief Johnson stood next to the body, wringing

his hands. He'd been the police chief since the last chief—his father, Chief Johnson—had keeled over in his lutefisk.

I had to agree with him. I'd rather die than eat it too.

However, as long as the present Chief Johnson had been in charge, there hadn't been a murder in New Bergin. Had there ever been?

The funeral director was our medical examiner. The extent of our CSI was probably to put up yellow tape and hope for the best. It appeared that Chief Johnson had managed the first and was hip deep in the second.

Though I wanted to stay, I needed to get to school. If I weren't in class when the bell rang it wouldn't be pretty. You think kindergartners are delightful? They are. But I learned not to turn my back on them. Or leave them alone long enough to trash the place.

I planned to cut through the alley between B and C—my shoes would get indescribable gunk on them, but I didn't have the time to care—and the ghost poured from the air, filling the space right in front of me. Her eyes were solid black. No whites left at all. I'd never seen anything like it before. I never wanted to again.

She had a burn, make that a brand, of a snarling wolf on her neck. I glanced at the body. Sure enough, there was the brand, though it was impossible to tell from here if it was a wolf. I probably wouldn't have seen it at all, beneath so much blood, unless I'd known where to look.

That I knew confused me. The wounds on the living did not transfer to the dead. Why had that one?

She grabbed my arm. I bit my lip to keep from screaming. Her fingers were fire and ice. Smoke poured from her mouth. In the center of her too-black eyes, a flame flickered. "He will burn us all."

Then she was gone. If it hadn't been for the trailing whiff of brimstone, and the blue-black imprint of her fingers just above my wrist, I'd have thought I imagined her.

"What the fuck?" I muttered, earning a glare from Mrs. Knudson, who stood in the doorway of her yarn shop, *Knit Wits*, contemplating the most excitement to hit New Bergin in a lifetime.

"I certainly hope you don't speak like that in front of the children."

"Children!" I resisted the urge to use the F-word again and ran, skidding through Lord knows what in the alley, then bursting out the other side, trailing the mystery muck behind me.

* * * * * *

Book List

Sisters of the Craft Trilogy

IN THE AIR TONIGHT
HEAT OF THE MOMENT
SMOKE ON THE WATER

The Phoenix Chronicles

ANY GIVEN DOOMSDAY
DOOMSDAY CAN WAIT
APOCALYPSE HAPPENS
CHAOS BITES
IN THE BEGINNING (e-short story)
DANCES WITH DEMONS (novella)

Short story set in the Phoenix Chronicle World
HEX APPEAL (anthology) – "There Will Be
Demons"

Nightcreature Novels

BLUE MOON
HUNTER'S MOON
DARK MOON
CRESCENT MOON
MIDNIGHT MOON
RISING MOON
HIDDEN MOON
THUNDER MOON

MARKED BY THE MOON
MOON CURSED
CRAVE THE MOON
SHADOW OF THE MOON (e-short story)
FIFTY WAYS TO KILL YOUR LARRY (e-collection) – "Blame It On the Moon"

Short stories and novellas set in the Nightcreature World

STROKE OF MIDNIGHT (anthology) – "Red Moon Rising"
MY BIG, FAT SUPERNATURAL WEDDING (anthology) – "Charmed by the Moon"
NO REST FOR THE WITCHES (anthology) – "Voodoo Moon"

Shakespeare Undead Series

SHAKESPEARE UNDEAD
ZOMBIE ISLAND: A SHAKESPEARE UNDEAD NOVEL

Paranormal novellas

WHEN MIDNIGHT COMES
DATES FROM HELL (anthology) – "Dead Man Dating"
MOON FEVER (anthology) – "Cobwebs over the Moon"

Contemporary paranormal novel

D.J.'S ANGEL

Historical paranormal novels

FULL MOON DREAMS
DREAMS OF AN EAGLE

The Luchetti Brothers Series
Contemporary Romance

THE DADDY QUEST
THE BROTHER QUEST
THE HUSBAND QUEST
A SOLDIER'S QUEST
THE MOMMY QUEST

Contemporary Romance

OUT OF HER LEAGUE
FRIENDS TO LOVERS
LEAVE IT TO MAX
A SHERIFF IN TENNESSEE
THE FARMER'S WIFE
WHEN YOU WISH
MOTHERS OF THE YEAR (anthology) – "Mommy
for Rent"

The Rock Creek Six
Western Historical Romance

REESE – by Lori Handeland
SULLIVAN – by Linda Devlin
RICO – by Lori Handeland
JED – by Linda Devlin
NATE – by Lori Handeland
CASH – by Linda Devlin

Historical Romance Novels

SECOND CHANCE
CHARLIE AND THE ANGEL (sequel to SECOND CHANCE)
JUST AFTER MIDNIGHT
LOVING A LEGEND

Romantic Suspense Novel

SHADOW LOVER

Western Historical Romance w/a Lori Austin
The Once Upon a Time in the West Trilogy:

BEAUTY AND THE BOUNTY HUNTER
AN OUTLAW IN WONDERLAND
THE LONE WARRIOR

Stand-alone westerns w/a Lori Austin

WHEN MORNING COMES (Novella)
BY ANY OTHER NAME
AN OUTLAW FOR CHRISTMAS

About the Author

Lori Handeland sold her first novel in 1993. Since then she has written many novels, novellas and short stories in several genres—historical, contemporary, series, paranormal romance, urban fantasy and historical fantasy—for such publishers as Dorchester, Kensington, Harlequin, St. Martin's, HarperCollins, Simon and Schuster and Penguin.

She has been nominated five times for the RITA Award from Romance Writers of America, winning twice, for Best Paranormal and Best Long Series Contemporary. She is a Waldenbooks, Bookscan, *USA Today* and *New York Times* best-selling author.

As well as writing Sisters of the Craft, The Nightcreature Novels, The Phoenix Chronicles, The Shakespeare Undead series, The Luchetti Brothers, The Rock Creek Six and several stand alone novels, Lori also writes gritty, sensual western historical romance under the name Lori Austin.

Lori lives in Southern Wisconsin with her husband enjoying occasional visits from her grown sons.

She can be reached through her website at:
www.lorihandeland.com or
www.loriaustin.net

CPSIA information can be obtained
at www.ICGtesting.com
Printed in the USA
FSOW04n2045041016
25760FS

9 780986 392139